"*Amber Wolf* is enjoyable as a narrative, edifying as history, and inspirational as a story of struggle, survival, and ethnic pride—the David of Lithuania is caught between the twin Goliaths of Russia and Germany. What can a young girl do? You'd be surprised."
—Steve O'Connor, author of *The Witch at Rivermouth* and *The Spy in the City of Books*

"Captivating. *Amber Wolf* is a compelling story of bold resistance in the face of insurmountable odds. Wong skillfully paints a portrait of the hidden and mostly forgotten people who struggled to survive behind the front lines of the cataclysm of World War II."
—Guntis Goncarovs, author of *Telmenu Saimnieks – The Lord of Telmeni* and *Convergence of Valor*

"*Amber Wolf* is a compelling story that captures the brutal truth along with fictitious elements of Lithuania in World War II. Before my parents passed, I listened to countless hours of stories just like this and the reasons why they fled their beloved homeland. Bravo to Ludmelia for never giving up!"
—Daina Irwin, daughter of Lithuanian survivors

"In *Amber Wolf*, Ursula Wong turns an unflinching yet sympathetic eye on a brutal slice of history. Compelling and engrossing, and almost impossible to put down."
—Leigh Perry, author of the *Family Skeleton Series*

"Ursula Wong takes on a heavy subject: the grass roots of World War II—not of large-scale mass destruction, but of hand-to-hand combat, villager against soldier, deep in the forests of Lithuania. Ludmelia Kudirka is a girl who must quickly grow up if she wants to survive and ultimately fight for her people, her land, and her freedom. In *Amber Wolf*, Wong gives us a story complexly woven, yet easy to follow, and impossible to forget."
—Stacey Longo, Pushcart Prize-nominated author of *Ordinary Boy*

"*Amber Wolf* is a trek into territory that, seventy years after the dramatic events enacted there, still remains largely unexplored. Ursula Wong, using new source material and careful research, has crafted a harrowing, heroic, and at times poetic, tale of people caught up in the cataclysms of war."
—David Daniel, author of *The Skelly Man* and *The Marble Kite*

Amber Wolf

Ursula Wong

10/14/17

Ursula Wong

Genretarium Publishing ~ Chelmsford, MA

Copyright © 2016 Genretarium Publishing

Cover Design by Ana Lucia Cortez

ISBN: 0692733868
ISBN-13: 978-0692733868

For more information about the author and her works, go to:

http://ursulawong.wordpress.com

Second printing, March, 2017
3 5 7 9 10 8 6 4 2

Other works by Ursula Wong

Purple Trees

The Baby Who Fell From the Sky

With other Authors

Insanity Tales

Insanity Tales II: The Sense of Fear

Ursula is available for speaking events and lectures on writing and publishing. For more information, contact her at urslwng@gmail.com or through her popular Reaching Readers website at http://ursulawong.wordpress.com.

Looking for something great to read? Get Ursula's FREE award-winning mini-tales, guaranteed to shiver, shake, and make you laugh. All you have to do is tell her where to send them. You'll get one to start, and a new one every month. Sign up at http://ursulawong.wordpress.com/mini-tales.

DEDICATION

To Steph, for this is part of your legacy.

Better to die on one's feet than to live on one's knees.
—*Jean-Paul Sartre*

ACKNOWLEDGMENTS

In the years it took to research, write, and publish *Amber Wolf,* many people helped in different ways. I wish to thank my editorial reviewers Dale T. Phillips, Vlad Vaslyn, Stacey Longo, and Rob Smales. Diana Irwin, daughter of survivors of the Soviet occupation in Lithuania, provided language advice, and valuable insights. Maria Givelber, Susan Radak, and Jacquelyn Malone provided review comments, as did Guntis Goncarovs, who provided a special perspective about the geography. I'd like to thank Rolandas Kačinskas, Deputy Chief of Mission Embassy of the Republic of Lithuania, and Thorsteinn Gislason, Honorable Consul General of Lithuania for information and contact lists.

A special thanks to Masheri Chappelle for her unique observations.

I'd like to thank Genretarium Publishing for their help, advice, and for keeping me on track. In particular, I'd like to thank Dale T. Phillips for his friendship, and constantly demanding more of my writing. I'd like to thank Melinda Phillips for her ongoing support.

I'd like to thank all members of my Reaching Readers email list for their help during the months I vetted various aspects of the novel. I continue to learn from you.

My husband Steve suffered through many evenings where *Amber Wolf* was the center of one-sided conversations. A loving listener with thoughtful insights made a tremendous difference.

Finally, I'd like to thank you, my readers, for letting me try to capture your imagination. Without you, I'd be nothing.

Ursula Sinkewicz Wong
July 2016
Chelmsford, Massachusetts

PREFACE

The inspiration for *Amber Wolf* came from a manuscript I found among my uncle's possessions after he died. It was an early draft of *Tarp Dviejų Gyvenimu* by Vytautas Alantas, published in the 1960s. The story focused on the summer of 1944 when Lithuania was at a crossroads. The Nazis were gone. The Soviets had returned for the second time since the beginning of the war. Lithuanians were deciding whether to stay and oppose Stalinism, wait for the West to push the Russians out, or leave their country.

Mr. Alantas' passion for his country drew me in, and I began researching Lithuania's WW II history. I read the stories of people who survived under horrific conditions, such as *The Bielski Brothers* by Peter Duffy, *Leave your Tears in Moscow* by Barbara Armonas, and others. Timothy Snyder's *Bloodlands: Europe Between Hitler and Stalin* and other historical accounts gave insights into the magnitude of the suffering. I broadened my historical understanding by reading Albertas Gerutis' book and other references. A reading list is in the back of *Amber Wolf*.

I determined to expand Mr. Alantas' idea into an indelible picture showing the vacuum left in families affected by the deportations in 1941, the political indecision during the summer of 1944, the passion of the partisan movement, the sense of a people in turmoil, and in particular, the suffering women endured during the occupations.

The major historical events in the novel are true. The Bolsheviks invaded Lithuania in 1919. Soviets invaded Lithuania in 1940. The Nazis drove them out in 1941. The Soviets returned three years later to occupy the country again, and stay until 1990. Some members of the Soviet Militia were called "destroyers." The partisan movement in Lithuania opposed the Soviet occupation. Pamphlets were circulated advocating Lithuanian independence. The battle of Stalingrad was true. On June 23, 1941, Lithuanians wrested control of the Kaunas broadcast station from the Soviets, and read a declaration of independence over the airwaves.

Kaunas and Vilnius are real cities. The village of Vilkija in *Amber Wolf* is purely fictitious, chosen because loosely translated, it means 'town of the wolf.' Paunksmis Lake and its geography are also fictitious.

Lithuanian words are in italics, although *chastushki* are Russian songs. Most legends are relevant to Lithuanian folklore.

I included some of what I knew about the old traditions, particularly the food that was part of my childhood. My cousin Vera taught me about mushrooming (the Lithuanian word for mushroom is *grybi*). Aunt Anne taught me the delicious combination of onions, *grybi*, and bacon. Try it. It's wonderful. My mother taught me how to prepare *kugelis*, a baked potato dish, cabbage (*kopusta*), and the sweet raisin bread, *pyragas*.

The characters and circumstances beyond the basic historical elements are fictitious. Any resemblance to real people is purely accidental. While Ludmelia Kudirka wasn't real, I believe her spirit lived in the hearts of those who struggled for freedom and the right of self-determination.

Finally, to those brave souls who fought and died in the forests of Lithuania, never feeling the thrill when Vytautas Landsbergis took his oath in 1990 to lead a free Lithuania, God bless you. We remember you still.

CHAPTER 1

Soviet-Occupied Lithuania, August 1944

Ludmelia Kudirka lay folded into an awkward shape on the floor of the cramped attic, her long legs aching. There was barely enough room for a child, let alone an athletic young woman. She strained to hear Mama in the kitchen below, in her skirt, blouse, and the kerchief covering her hair, probably looking at the floor, as she often did. She had always said if you hide your face, people might forget who you are.

Ludmelia heard a door slamming against the wall, and the clomp of heavy steps. She held her breath, and peered into the darkness.

"Where's your husband?" a mellow voice asked in perfect Russian. The tone was seductive but commanding, ranging from high to low in melodious timbre. Ludmelia knew the language, even though it wasn't her native tongue. Despite the threat of soldiers in the cottage, she couldn't help but admire the voice's beauty.

"Dead," said Mama. Her voice betrayed no fear. Ludmelia choked back a sob. *Did Mama really think Papa was dead?*

"Who else lives here?"

"No one."

"Don't lie to me, woman. Where's your daughter?"

"In the city, visiting relatives."

"When did she leave?"

"A few days ago."

"When will she be back?"

"A few days."

A glass crashed to the floor. The steps grew louder.

"There's no one here," said the mellow voice. "You two stay and finish it. We'll come back later for the girl."

Ludmelia flinched. She wondered what they could possibly want with her.

"Yes, sir," said a low and deep voice.

A door slammed. There were footsteps, and the scrape of chair legs against the floor. Soon, the sound of an engine faded in the distance.

"Get us something to eat, woman," said a raspy voice that sounded like a sleigh scraping over gravel.

Ludmelia closed her eyes, praying that food was all the soldiers wanted. After they left, she and Mama would run away. They would cross Paunksmis Lake and hide in the vast, old forest with its spruce trees, and giant oaks. They knew places where they would never be found.

Plates banged against the tabletop. Mama's footsteps clacked along the floor. After a pause, spoons rattled. Ludmelia smelled the stew. Her stomach growled as she listened to the soldiers eat what should have been *her* supper.

"And something to drink," said the raspy voice.

Heavy glass scraped against the table. In the winter, a little drink of the homemade vodka would warm them quickly.

"Leave the bottle on the table, woman," said the man with the deep voice.

The space where Ludmelia hid was small, and she couldn't stand or sit, so she lay on her stomach. She stared at the dark floor, picturing the soldiers sitting at the kitchen table, and Mama standing near the stove, with her hands on her hips. Ludmelia prayed that they would finish their food and go.

"Get on the bed, woman," said the deep voice.

"You go first, Uri," said the raspy one.

"No, Denis. You go."

She noted their names, and dreaded what was to come. Ludmelia heard the squeak of the bedsprings from the corner of the kitchen, and dug her fingernails into the palms of her hands. Mama cried out. The squeak became rhythmic, growing faster and faster. *She had to save Mama. If she gave herself up, they'd leave Mama alone.* But Mama had told her to survive, so Ludmelia didn't move. Ludmelia thought she was going to be sick. *Leave Mama alone!*

The creaking stopped, and a soldier grunted. *Please God, let it be over.* There was quiet followed by the thud of glass against wood.

"More stew," said the deep voice.

"That house today burned like tinder," laughed the raspy voice.

"I never expected that boy to charge at us with a shovel. Idiot. He's better off dead. His mother, too."

"It was no great loss."

The soldiers laughed, and Ludmelia cursed them under her breath. As they talked, she focused on their voices, memorizing every nuance and intonation. She silently repeated the names Denis and Uri to brand them in her memory. The first voice, the beautiful one with no name, was another she couldn't forget, for it had commanded the others to *'finish it.'* Ludmelia couldn't bear to think about what that meant.

"Your turn, Uri," said the raspy voice.

Please God, no more. The bed squeaked in painful rhythm as the bottle of vodka thumped against the table. Ludmelia dug her nails into the wood as she strained to hear anything from Mama, but no sounds came.

If only she had a gun. When she was little, Papa had taught her how to shoot. If she had a gun, she could kill the soldiers. But the pistol was buried in the garden. She pictured herself leaping down, grabbing a soldier's gun, and firing. Their blood would wash the floor. She could almost smell it. She pointed a finger at the floor. Papa's voice rang in her ears: *breathe, aim, squeeze.*

The room below grew quiet, and Ludmelia had to pee. She pictured the liquid falling from the cracks in the ceiling onto the heads of the soldiers and into their vodka, surprising them. They would shout up to her, "Come down, Ludmelia." They would shoot her for peeing on them. She couldn't relieve herself, so she pumped the muscles in her pelvis until the urge went away.

Ludmelia closed her eyes and prayed for Mama to wake her and say the soldiers had been only a dream.

"Get up," said the raspy voice.

Ludmelia started. They had taken Papa away years ago. She pictured his bushy moustache and round red cheeks, and felt her heart wrench. *Please God, don't let them take Mama, too.* She heard steps and the squeak of the door.

A gunshot exploded in the kitchen.

Ludmelia bit the back of her hand to stifle a scream and tasted blood. She held her breath at the rumble of an engine. When the sound faded, she cracked open the door in the ceiling and peered down. On the bed, Mama moaned under the patchwork quilt. No one else was there. Ludmelia lowered herself so she was hanging by her fingers. She dropped to the floor like a cat, the lamplight playing with her shadow against the wall.

She looked outside through the window. She could barely make out the road through the trees and darkness. She couldn't see any trucks. She ran to the bed. "Mama!"

Ludmelia drew back the quilt, and cried out at the bloom of red on Mama's naked breasts. She put her hand on the wound, pressing down, trying to stop the bleeding. She willed her strength to pass from her hands into Mama, but the older woman sighed, and something changed. Her lips parted, the deep wrinkles in her forehead softened, and her entire body sagged. An unnatural stillness settled over Mama's features. Ludmelia pulled her hands back, suddenly frightened of Mama, whose face had become the symbol of death.

CHAPTER 2

Amber light brightened the entrance of Bablia's grog house as Comrade Commander Roman Zabrev climbed the worn steps, the raid on the Kudirka cottage still fresh in his mind. It infuriated him that Ludmelia hadn't been home. He touched the shirt pocket containing her photograph that he had taken from the bedroom. No one escaped him, especially not the daughter of that subversive intellectual, Victor Kudirka. He would find her and peel away her resistance until she begged him to take her. He would have her before shipping her off to Siberia.

Zabrev hesitated at a door that held only the memory of brown paint. Were it not for the war, he might be singing at the opera tonight, entertaining hundreds of people with his beautiful voice. He took a moment to admire his strong jaw and high forehead reflecting in the small pane of glass set into the wood. He would have made a fine Rodolfo or Don Jose, but that dream was for a different time and a different place. His role was Soviet officer: demanding, ruthless, and willing to do anything to accomplish his goals, especially if it got him out of this godforsaken country.

Zabrev pushed the door open and immediately smelled the stench of burning tobacco. Against a backdrop of dull walls, the smoke mingled with the dark clothing of the patrons in an indeterminate haze. It took his eyes a moment to adjust to the gloom.

Soldiers in faded brown uniforms stood next to local Party members at the bar. A tarnished spittoon with gobs of saliva clinging to the side lay near the wall. Four Communists dressed in dusty black suits dozed over their glasses at a table in the corner. Other Party members hunkered over plates of food, while a few just stared listlessly into the smoke.

Zabrev stepped over the threshold onto a floor permanently stained from its nightly additions of vomit. Faces turned to him and voices cheered. Hands holding glasses rose into the air, and lips touched the sharp-tasting liquid cherished for its ability to dull the senses and weaken the mind.

As the newly assigned chief of the Security Militia in the NKVD, Soviet Russia's feared police organization, Zabrev had been in Vilkija for just over a week. The celebration at Bablia's was in his honor, arranged by local Communists to welcome him to their town.

It was the least they could do. After all, we Russians liberated these peasants from the Nazi oppression.

He squared his shoulders and strode into the room.

Bablia, a fat man with a bald head, appeared behind the bar as if he had popped out of the woodwork. He took a clean glass from the shelf, filled it with vodka, and waddled over to a table occupied by two young soldiers. Bablia kicked the chair under one of them, and nodded his head toward Zabrev. The man looked up with watery eyes, and punched his companion in the arm. They jumped to attention and saluted, their gazes fixed on Zabrev. They mumbled words of welcome, and went to the bar, where they squeezed in between other patrons.

Bablia bowed. "Good evening, Comrade Commander. People have been asking for you. Will you want anything to eat tonight?" Bablia set the glass down, pulled out a chair, and swatted the seat with his bar towel.

As if that filthy cloth would make a difference, thought Zabrev.

"What do you have?"

"Kopusta and sausage.*"*

Zabrev grimaced at the prospect of the sour-tasting cabbage, but here he ate what everyone ate, for there was nothing else. How he missed Moscow, and the delicacies he had washed down with vodka so cold that it warmed the soul.

Zabrev nodded, and the fat man went off in the direction of the kitchen, past the door to a storeroom full of provisions taken from raids. Since the local currency, the ostmark, was worthless after the Nazis left, and few rubles were in circulation, most people paid their

6

tabs by bartering with Bablia. A small sack of potatoes was worth a glass of vodka. A pig was worth a keg of vodka. The value of a butchered cow was negotiable. Bablia's wife used the bartered goods to make food for the patrons, who paid for their meals and drinks with more plunder.

As Zabrev settled his long body into the chair, noises emerged from inside a closed door behind the bar. The room hushed. Soon, the rhythm of a creaking bed resonated through the saloon. The sound became louder and faster, reaching a crescendo as the patrons stood with their backs straight and necks extended. At a shuddering moan, they burst into cheers.

A short time later, the door opened and a young, red-faced Communist emerged, buckling his belt and trying to suppress a grin. The cheering stopped when a lean woman appeared behind him, her dark hair disheveled, her skirt on sideways. She stopped at the bar, took the glass from a startled soldier, and drank its contents in one gulp. She crossed the room slowly, all gazes on her swaying hips. She came to Zabrev's table, where she stopped. Even through the smoke, he could smell a heady scent of musk on her. She walked her fingers across the surface and said, "Welcome to Vilkija, Comrade Commander. Maybe I'll see you later." She winked and walked to another man waiting in the doorway. He followed her outside, letting the door slam behind them.

Cheering erupted again. Men slapped the back of the grinning Communist as he took his place at the bar.

The men dozing at the corner table awoke, and made their way to Zabrev. One stammered an introduction and held out his hand, visibly relieved when Zabrev took it. Another gestured to Bablia for more vodka. They drank a toast and returned to their seats.

A little man in a threadbare suit that drooped from his body left the bar and strode to Zabrev's table. It was his new informant, Petra Sukas.

"Good evening, Comrade Commander," said Petra. Deep wrinkles lined his face, and his ferret-like eyes darted from side to side in an expression undamaged by intelligence. His oversized suit jacket showed stains of grease. Thin red Communist Party ribbons pinned to his lapel danced like kite strings. He wore a farmhand's shoes, dusty and creased from working in the fields.

"Your information was lacking. The Kudirka girl wasn't home," said Zabrev.

"You found the mother?"

"The mother is no longer a problem. I want the girl."

"Ludmelia seldom goes anywhere except the Ravas farmstead. Occasionally, she and her mother go to the forest to pick mushrooms, or to the lake to fish, but they never spend the night away from home."

"Search those fields behind the cottage."

"But, Comrade Commander, it's almost three kilometers from there to Paunksmis Lake, and there are woods. How can I possibly search that entire area?"

"Just find her."

"Of course, Comrade Commander," squeaked Petra.

"I don't care if you have to search the old forest, the bog, and the lake. Search everywhere, but bring her to me!"

"Yes, Comrade Commander."

"Listen to me, you worm. If you don't find her, you'd better hide, because I will come looking for you next."

"Yes, Comrade Commander." Petra scuttled to the bar, where he squeezed in between the wall and the spittoon.

Zabrev looked around. He had power, knew important people, and most of all, he was from Moscow. *These people had better be scared.*

Bablia returned from the kitchen, carrying a bowl of cabbage and sausage, and a plate of crusty brown bread. He set everything down before Zabrev and stood by the table.

"Who's that man?" Zabrev gestured toward a stranger in a worn coat watching him from the corner of the bar. He was among those who had not yet paid their respects.

"His name is Jonai Gabe. He just joined the Party. He has a small farm on the outskirts of town, and lives there with his young son," said Bablia.

"Where did he get that hair?" laughed Zabrev.

"Yes, it's red like strawberries. People tease him, but it's the way God made him. His son has the same curse."

A spatter of fat flew up as Zabrev cut into the sausage. He nodded, and Bablia went back to the bar.

Jonai Gabe swallowed his drink and made his way to Zabrev's table.

"I'm at your service, Comrade Commander." Jonai extended a hand with chipped fingernails, and dirt marking the crevices in his skin.

Zabrev ignored it. "Joining the Party is just a first step. Find out where the bandits are hiding, and maybe you'll earn my respect."

"Bandits?"

"The partisans, fool!" *How can these people be so ignorant?*

"Yes, Comrade Commander."

Zabrev returned to his food. Jonai Gabe stood there awkwardly for a moment, and went back to the bar.

After Zabrev had finished eating, an elderly man limped in, leading a young woman by the hand. She wore a black skirt and a red blouse. The room hushed as all faces turned to her. Zabrev pushed his plate away and watched her move. She walked with the grace of a dancer. Her face was beautiful, with pale features and sparkling eyes. She looked to be about eighteen years old, but her hair was almost white. Zabrev suspected it was her natural color, although if luck were with him, he would find out for certain later in the evening.

The elderly man took off his hat and held it. The woman leaned back as the man pulled her to Zabrev's table.

"Welcome to Vilkija, Lieutenant Zabrev. I'm Mikas Lankus." The man spoke softly, reverently addressing a superior. "I hope you are well."

"I'm very well, thank you."

"I'd like to introduce you to my daughter, Eda."

Zabrev didn't stand or offer his hand. He examined the young woman. As his gaze lingered on her breasts, she crossed an arm over her chest. She pulled at her father's hand. He didn't let go.

"Eda is a fine girl, Comrade Commander, as you can see. May I sit?"

Zabrev gestured toward a chair. Mikas let go of Eda's hand, hooked his hat on the back of the chair, and sat down. He reached into his pocket, pulled out a packet of cigarettes, and offered one to Zabrev. Eda stood behind her father, staring at the door.

"I know the Comrade Commander is a powerful man." Mikas gestured to Bablia for a bottle and held up three fingers. "I have long supported the Communist Party, but in a place such as Vilkija, it has been difficult to find a position where I can truly be of service."

Mikas struck a match and held it out to Zabrev, who lit the cigarette, puffed, and blew out smoke. Mikas suppressed a cough. Zabrev smiled at Eda. Bablia put a bottle and three glasses on the table. Mikas filled Zabrev's glass.

"Now that the Comrade Commander is here, and the Party is looking for people to fill positions in the organization, perhaps there is a place for me, provided there is someone who would put in a good word."

Zabrev drained his glass. Mikas filled it again, and poured some vodka into the other two glasses. He glanced at his daughter and gestured toward a chair. She pulled it out and sat on the edge of the seat. Mikas put a glass in front of her.

"To your health," said Mikas. He raised his glass to Zabrev, drained it, and set it down.

Mikas glanced at his daughter. "Drink."

Eda shook her head. She looked down at the table and folded her hands together on her lap.

"Drink it!" Mikas hissed.

Eda pressed her lips together. Mikas picked up her glass and handed it to her, but she pushed it away. Vodka splashed onto the table. His face reddened. He seized a handful of hair on the back of her head, and pulled. She yelped. He brought the glass to her mouth and forced her lips apart, pouring vodka in. Eda swallowed and coughed, spraying the table. She wiped her mouth with the back of her hand. Mikas filled the glass and handed it to her again. This time she took it in a shaking hand and sipped, making a face as she swallowed. She put the glass down.

"Excuse my daughter's rudeness, Comrade Commander," said Mikas. "Of course, if someone were to recommend me for a job, I wouldn't expect such a favor to go unrewarded." Mikas glanced at his daughter. "Is there something Eda or I can do in exchange for a few words of recommendation? Provided of course, the Comrade Commander thinks it appropriate?"

Zabrev stubbed out the cigarette, stood, went to Eda, and held out his hand.

"Please, Papa, no." Eda gripped her father's arm and choked back a sob.

"Go!" Mikas pulled his arm free.

Eda wiped her eyes. Her chair made a high-pitched scraping as she pushed away from the table and stood.

As Zabrev led Eda past the bar, the men hastily turned back to their drinking. Jonai Gabe stood with his shoulders hunched, staring down at his drink. After Zabrev and Eda were inside the back room, he slammed the door shut.

Petra stroked the red ribbons pinned to his lapel as he gazed at Mikas sitting alone at the table in the middle of the room. Soon the old man looked up as if he had just awoken from a trance. He carried his bottle to the bar, where he shook hands with a soldier and gestured to Bablia for another glass.

CHAPTER 3

Ludmelia sank to her knees beside the rumpled bed where Mama lay. Tears fell to her cheeks as her hands came together in prayer. *God, please take care of Mama.*

The smell of blood overcame the raw shock of Mama's death. Ludmelia had to take care of the body. She had to protect Mama from the soldiers. When they returned, they would expect Mama to be on the bed, but the prospect of leaving her at their mercy was unbearable. They might toss her outside like garbage, leaving her for the wolves. It would take hours to dig a proper grave, and there was no time. Ludmelia had to do something to show respect for Mama and to protect her. It was the least she could do.

Ludmelia pulled off the quilt and gaped at Mama's nakedness. She spread the quilt on the floor and tried to roll her mother onto it gently, but Mama fell to the floor with a thud.

"I'm sorry, Mama," she sobbed.

Holding the edges of the quilt, Ludmelia dragged her mother out into the moonlight. She considered leaving Mama in the chicken coop, but the door was fragile. With a start, she noticed that the hens were gone. *Had the Russians taken them, too?*

Tucked into a little hill behind the cottage, the cold cellar was a better place for Mama. The food they carefully preserved for the winter was stored there, and it had a stronger door to keep out scavengers. She hoped that the soldiers hadn't found it.

The thought of animals gnawing at Mama's body turned Ludmelia's stomach. She forced back the urge to vomit, and took a shuddering breath. She put all her strength into dragging, because she had to take care of Mama before the soldiers returned.

Ludmelia sweated as she dragged Mama past the garden and up the small rise to the cellar. The body was heavier than seemed possible. As she opened the door, cool air washed over her. She backed into the dark room, protecting Mama's head as she pulled, the body thumping down a step to the dirt floor. Shelves stacked with jars of fruit and vegetables lined the room, the dim moonlight glinting off the glass. Everything seemed to be intact. She felt for the edges of the quilt and wrapped them around the body. *"Bless you, Mama."*

As Ludmelia fell to her knees and crossed herself, she had never felt so alone.

She thought back three years ago to 1940, when it had all started. The Soviets came to Lithuania in a frenzy of pillaging and murder that had left the country gasping for breath. It felt like they were living in a vise. The Soviets took their food, their valuables, and their animals, leaving little behind for families to survive. Papa had protested the invasion by writing pamphlets that he typed, mimeographed, and distributed.

Then the Soviets began deporting the smartest, wisest, and most influential among them. One night, Papa didn't come home from work at the Vytautas Magnus University in Kaunas, where he was a history professor. Mama waited for him in the kitchen, crazy with worry. When Matas ran to Papa's office on campus to try to find him, she said that the soldiers would capture Matas and force him to join the Red Army. Matas didn't come back until nightfall. Mama threw her arms around him when he came in through the door.

"I thought you were gone, too," Mama said.

"The Soviets took most of the professors to the train station in trucks and loaded them onto cattle cars. I went there, but people were everywhere. I couldn't find Papa." Matas sat down to catch his breath.

"It was those pamphlets. I told him to stop writing those damned pamphlets. I told him it would get us all into trouble," Mama cried. She ran to the cupboard and lifted out a loaf of bread. As she reached into the back and pulled out a stack of pamphlets, an envelope fell to the floor. She opened it and unfolded several sheets of paper. Ludmelia glanced over Mama's shoulder. One was a letter from Papa. Before Ludmelia could read anything more, Mama stuffed the papers back into the envelope and slipped it into the pocket of her skirt.

"We've got to leave. They might come for us, too," Mama said, bustling to the stove. She opened the lid and shoved the pamphlets inside. They crackled in the

heat. One sheet drifted to the floor. Mama snatched it up and crushed it before throwing it into the flames. "I told him these stupid things would destroy us, and he didn't believe me. He said he wrote what people were thinking, that we must defeat the Russians, so how could that be bad?" *Mama choked down a sob.* "Now he's gone."

Mama turned to her children. "Go pack a suitcase. We've got to go."

"No, Mama," *said Matas.* "We can't leave, not right away. What if he comes back?"

"What if the Russians come for us?"

"We didn't do anything."

"They'll come for us anyway."

"The Germans are near. If they drive the Soviets out, we won't have to leave. Wait a few days. Just a few days. Give Papa a chance."

So they stayed. Soon, the Germans were bombing the Kaunas airport. Looking out the kitchen window, Ludmelia noticed a strange glow in the sky from the distant explosions.

"The Germans are going to defeat the Soviets," *Matas said.* "I know it."

"You think that's going to make a difference?" *Mama asked.*

"We'll be free again."

"No one is free under the Gestapo."

"There's no reason for them to stay. When the Russians are gone, they'll leave too, once they see how desperately we want to be free."

"We're a little country. Why does everyone want to control us?"

"I want to fight the Russians, Mama. Anything is better than Communism. If we work with the Germans, we can rid ourselves of Stalin's grasp once and for all."

"You want to fight with the Germans?"

"I want the Soviets out."

"None of this makes any sense."

"Our leaders are scrambling to make a government. If the Germans defeat the Soviets and we have a government, the Germans won't have a legal reason to stay. The Germans will have to leave if we show them we're organized as a nation."

"What makes you think having a government will make them leave? Let someone else do the fighting."

"There is no one else, Mama."

Days after they took Papa away, in the quiet of morning, they listened to the wireless, where a man's voice cracked. They didn't understand what he was saying at first, but soon realized it was a declaration of independence. Mrs. Dagys from next door ran down the street yelling and waving her arms. "We're free!"

Ludmelia watched from the window. "Are we really free, Matas?"

Her brother wiped his eyes with his handkerchief.

Later, Mr. and Mrs. Dagys, Matas, Mama, and Ludmelia huddled around the radio in the Kudirka kitchen, listening to the man read the declaration over and over.

"Can we trust them when they say we are free?" cried Mama.

During the day, the sound of gunfire came closer. Mama locked the doors and rushed everyone into the cellar. Matas dashed upstairs for the wireless, while Mama screamed at him to come back down. They hid in the cellar, sitting on crates while listening to the radio that was propped against the small window.

Airplanes droned overhead, and bombs exploded in the distance. At night, tracers of light flew across the sky.

Matas announced he was going to join the fight. Mr. Dagys said he would fight, too.

"I want to fight too, Mama," said Ludmelia.

"You can't."

"Why not?"

"Because you're too young; because you're a girl; because this isn't our war!"

"Whose war is it?" Ludmelia sulked in a corner and cursed God for making her a girl.

At midnight, the sound of bells rang over the airwaves.

"They're freedom bells," said Mrs. Dagys as she dried her eyes.

Ludmelia fell asleep on an empty crate. When Matas draped his coat over her, she snuggled into it.

"I don't want you to go off to fight the Russians, Matas."

"I must."

"Why?"

"For you, to give you a chance to be free. For a hundred years the Russians have been trying to make us forget who we are, and we can't give in now. We have our own language, our own flag, and our own ways. Giving up our culture is like telling a mother not to love her child. We must fight to save the essence of who we are. I must fight to save Papa."

"But he's already gone," Ludmelia choked.

"I believe he's alive, and that we'll see him again one day." Matas touched her cheek. "Never, ever forget how deeply you are loved, little one."

16

Surrounded by jars of beets and pears, and with Mama lying dead at her feet, Ludmelia knew she had to run. She would need food. She reached for a sack hanging on a hook, and groped with her hands along the shelves. She picked up jars of pears and put them in the sack. She reached into loose straw for carrots and packed them, too. She leaned over Mama's body and snatched jars of canned pickles. She dragged the sack outside and closed the door. *Nothing can harm you now, Mama. Good-bye.*

Ludmelia pressed her hand against the cellar door, reluctant to leave Mama, but knowing she must. She laid branches and bushes in front of the door to hide it from the soldiers. She hoped it would be enough to keep Mama safe. She lugged the sack of food to the back door of the house and left it there while she went inside.

Ludmelia found the axe leaning against the wall, and placed it outside next to the sack. She went back inside, to the bedroom. Clothes and bedding lay on the floor. Stuffing bubbled out of the mattress. Pieces of a broken vase lay near the wall. Ludmelia picked up a blanket and flung it over the ruin of a bed. On top of it, she threw a pair of trousers, a shirt, and a coat. She added a pot, a fork, and a spoon from the kitchen. She tied the edges of the blanket together to form a bundle. As she slung it over her shoulder, she caught a glimpse of her face in the cracked mirror. Her amber hair was wild and unkempt, and her skin flushed. Already she looked older. She didn't know if the woman in the mirror had the nerve to flee into the unknown. The lines of strain deepened around her mouth, but Papa's clear gray eyes looked back and gave her strength.

The photograph of her that Mama kept tucked in the mirror's frame was gone. The soldiers had taken it, so they knew what she looked like. Ludmelia's heart chilled.

She took Papa's knapsack and canteen from behind the door. She went to the cabinet in the kitchen, squatted down, and reached under it to a small box pressed up against the wall. She pulled it out, opened it, and retrieved the hunting knife Papa had given her years ago for winning a shooting match. Ludmelia attached the sheath to her belt. She pulled a chair up to the cabinet and stood on it, reaching for the wedge of cheese and loaf of bread lying out of sight on the top shelf. She put both into the knapsack.

Ludmelia laid the bundle of clothes and utensils next to the bag of food outside. She took the spade and ran to the far corner of the garden, with the knapsack bouncing against her back. She dug. Soon, she found the sack buried in the dirt. Ludmelia sank to her knees and pulled it out. When she opened it and took out Papa's boots tied together by the laces, an envelope wrapped in string fell to the ground. She untied it and saw sheets of paper covered with writing. One looked like a letter from Papa. It was too dark to read, and she had no time anyway, but she knew they were important, because they had been buried. As Ludmelia stuffed them back into the envelope, some crumbled from moisture and age. She snatched up the pieces and put them inside the knapsack. She reached inside one boot and pulled out a pistol and bullets. She put the bullets into her pocket and slipped the gun under her belt. Already she felt stronger.

The sun was barely up when Ludmelia heard Matas digging in the garden. Soon, he came inside with a canvas sack that he put it on the table next to the bread and butter Mama had laid out for breakfast. When Matas opened it, a bit of dirt fell on the butter. Mama didn't say a word as Matas pulled out Papa's rifle and began cleaning it. Ludmelia watched as if her brother was doing the most important job in the world. When he was done, Matas hugged Ludmelia and Mama. They all went out to the street, where Mr. Dagys was waiting with his wife. The women waved their handkerchiefs as the men walked away together with rifles in their hands, and wearing white armbands. To Ludmelia, they looked like warriors.

That day, the chatter of submachine gun fire grew louder than it had ever been. Planes buzzed overhead. Bomb blasts came closer in a confusion of sounds. A sense of commotion seeped into the house as Ludmelia and her mother huddled together in the cellar.

Ludmelia thought that everything would be fine, that Matas would return, and the gunfire would avoid their house. She even thought Papa would come home, and kept watching the door, hoping he would walk in. When Mama told her to be ready to leave as soon as Matas came back, Ludmelia knew that things would never be the same again.

Late that night there was a knock on the door. Three strange men crowded past Mama, carrying a body wrapped in a blanket. They put it on the kitchen table.

"Mama, is it Matas?" asked Ludmelia.

Mama prayed to the Virgin Mother as she gently moved a corner of the blanket away from the face. Mama cried with relief. She hugged Ludmelia, who cried, too.

Mama took Ludmelia by the hand, and they went into the street. The houses looked dark and still, like sentinels. Mama's face was solemn as she knocked on Mrs. Dagys' door.

"The soldiers brought your husband to my house by mistake," whispered Mama.

"My God. Is he hurt?" asked Mrs. Dagys.

Mama shook her head and put her arm around Mrs. Dagys' shoulders.

They washed Mr. Dagys on the table where the men had placed him. They dressed him in a clean white shirt to meet God. Another neighbor helped them put Mr. Dagys into a small wooden cart, and they wheeled him toward the cemetery near the church. Mr. Dagys' arms kept slipping onto the ground and dragging in the dirt. The gunfire was louder than it had been all day. They dug the grave quickly, until it was just deep enough. They laid Mr. Dagys in the hole, using a cross from Mama's closet to mark the spot. Mama said a few hurried words over the grave, for the priest was off fighting, too.

They rushed home.

Other men carried Matas into the house later that night, also covered in a blanket.

This time, Mama didn't cry. "They get no more from me," she said.

The men stayed to help. They carried Matas to the cemetery, where they dug a second grave. They covered Matas with the blanket, laid him in the hole, and put dirt over him.

Mama marked the spot with a rock draped in her rosary beads, for she had no more crosses.

Ludmelia and Mama hurried home, and put food into a sack. Mama ran outside with a spade and dug another hole in the garden. She pulled out a cloth sack containing Papa's spare boots and a pistol with bullets. She handed the gun to Ludmelia.

"Papa said you were the best shot he had ever seen."

Ludmelia tucked the gun under her belt. It felt heavy next to her waist. Despite it being warm outside, Ludmelia took Matas' jacket from the peg near the door and put it on to hide the pistol.

Mama wanted to leave Papa's boots behind, because they were old and creased. Ludmelia said they were strong boots that she could wear, but she just wanted to keep something that belonged to Papa.

Ludmelia followed Mama down the steps and onto the street. Mama carried a suitcase and a sack of food. Ludmelia took Matas' compass, the knife she had won for shooting at the Ravas farmstead, Papa's boots which she hung by their laces over her shoulder, his knapsack, and another suitcase filled with clothing.

They went to Mrs. Dagys' door and knocked. Mrs. Dagys moved them inside. Her eyes were red. "Matas, too?"

Mama nodded.

"Where are you going?"

"North. And you?"

"I don't want to leave my husband."

"You can't stay. Soon, the Russians will be everywhere. They already occupy the countries around us. There'll be no place to go. Come with us."

"I was thinking about Germany."

"You'd be jumping from boiling water into hot oil."

"Bless you both."

Mrs. Dagys kissed Mama on her cheek, mingling their tears, and softly closed the door.

"Where are we going, Mama?" asked Ludmelia.

"Vilkija, to the summer cottage. The Russians will never find us there."

CHAPTER 4

With Papa's pistol under her belt, and his boots and knapsack dangling from her shoulders, Ludmelia glanced back at the cellar where Mama lay. She was fleeing like she had from Kaunas, but this time, Ludmelia was on her own.

She left the garden and placed the knapsack next to the provisions outside the cottage's back door. Going into the bedroom, she found three pairs of socks, and put them on. She pulled on Papa's boots. As she laced them, it felt like he was with her. She remembered his pipe that Mama kept on the nightstand, but it was gone. She didn't have time to look for it. Maybe the soldiers had taken that, too.

On her way out the kitchen door, Ludmelia paused and looked back at the memories. The bloodstained bed and the dirty plates told of the horrors, but in a corner of the cabinet sat a doll. Dressed in a colorful skirt, embroidered apron, and peasant blouse, it beckoned to Ludmelia. *Take me with you.* Ludmelia took it down, hugged it to her breast, and gently put it back in its place. She wouldn't need a doll in the woods.

Outside, Ludmelia paused at her pile of provisions. It was a lot to carry, but she had no choice. It had to last her for a long time.

On the night Matas died, they began their trek to Vilkija. They left Mrs. Dagys' house and quickly walked along streets crowded with buildings. Each time heavy steps approached, they hid in a doorway and held their breath. Rockets exploded with thunderous sounds and ghostly light. Shots rang out, and they fled down a garden path behind a house where shadows danced on the walls. They passed a man leaning out of a window, calling for a woman named Aldona. That was Mama's name, too, but he wasn't shouting for her. Mortar rounds whistled through the air as mother and daughter made their way along a dirt path near a church. The rectory next to it lay in ruins, crushed from roof to cellar. Stone dust hung in the air. Flames leaped up as if escaping from hell.

They ran past the rubble into a cemetery. Shattered grave markers lay on the dark ground. An old woman sobbed near one, her swollen knuckles entwined in rosary beads. Mama put her arms around Ludmelia's shoulders and they hurried past without even offering a word of comfort. They squeezed through a gap in a fence onto the road that led north, and stumbled along in the sallow light of the moon.

Eventually, the gunfire dimmed, but military vehicles with soldiers crammed in the back sped down the road toward the city. Every time an engine grumbled, Mama and Ludmelia hid behind trees or in the tall grass and waited until the sounds faded.

With her head down while trudging through mud, Ludmelia bumped into something. She froze, thinking it must be a soldier. She and Mama would be dead in an instant. She looked up and touched the arms of a cross attached to a column that was as tall as she was. She caressed the nail in Jesus' hand, almost giggling in relief. Mama didn't even notice.

Just before dawn, they peed in a field, and wiped themselves with grass. Before the sun came up, they hid under bushes and shivered as dew covered them. They ate what Mama had packed, and just enough to keep going, for the food had to last. They hid all day long, under bushes that scratched them as they tried to sleep. At midday, the heat stifled them. Toward evening, mosquitoes feasted on their flesh. Ludmelia didn't even swat at the bugs, for Mama had told her to stay perfectly still.

At night, they crawled out from their hiding place and walked until dawn. They nibbled bits of food and sipped water.

After days of drudgery, they arrived at the outskirts of Vilkija. They bypassed the town, skirted the Ravas farmstead, and headed for the cottage tucked in behind a cluster of trees.

Years ago, the little place had been the perfect jumping-off place for their many excursions into the woods. It was about to become a refuge where they would wait out the war.

Approaching the cottage, they saw that the door was open. They hid behind the trees and waited. No one came or went. After a time, they went to the door. Mama knocked as Ludmelia held the pistol ready. No one answered. They went inside. The kitchen chairs had been knocked over. The mattress hung over the edge of the narrow bed along the wall. The quilt was crumpled on the floor.

Outside, the chicken coop behind the house was intact, but the chickens were gone. Near it lay a pile of dry wood. Dug into the side of a small rise was the cellar, to store vegetables and canned food. They went inside it, looking for something to eat. Most of the shelves were empty, but far in the back of the bottom one, Ludmelia found jars of canned beets. Mama said that luck was on their side. Ludmelia didn't think they were lucky at all.

The first night, they slept in the cellar. Mama worried that someone might come by, so she tied one end of a rope to the door handle and the other end to a shelf, so no one could open it from the outside. They lay on the handmade quilt from the house. The room was dark, and the air felt damp. Ludmelia wondered if the devil, Velnias, was hiding in a corner waiting to murder them in their sleep. She snuggled closer to Mama, even though at seventeen, she was too old for that sort of thing.

The next morning, they ate beets for breakfast. After hiding their few possessions under leaves, Ludmelia followed Mama to Paunksmis Lake.

Ludmelia stank of sweat and dirt. She took off her shoes and socks and ran into the water with her clothes on.

"Hey, crazy girl," said Mama, smiling.

After bathing, Ludmelia lay in the sun to dry off while Mama looked for mushrooms. That night, she fried them up in a pan they found on the floor behind the stove.

Mama collected pears from trees next to the cottage. They weren't ripe, but Ludmelia ate until her stomach hurt. The next day, Mama went into the overgrown garden and gently pulled the weeds away from the large leaves of potato plants that would be ready in the fall. She smiled for the rest of the day.

"When are we going to visit Gerta Ravas?" asked Ludmelia.

"We're not, unless we have to."

"She's our friend."

"I don't want anyone to know we're here. That way the Russians won't find us."

No one visited or even walked past the little cottage for a week. They moved from the cellar into the house. They cleaned and put everything in order. Mama placed Papa's pipe on the nightstand by the bed.

"Where did you get that?" asked Ludmelia.

"I took it when we left the house."

"Why did you put it by the bed?"

"For when he comes back."

"Did he know this was going to happen?"

"No one knew. He just wanted to protect us."

Eventually, the need for food forced them to venture beyond the cottage. Wearing clean skirts and blouses, and kerchiefs on their heads, Mama and Ludmelia set off for the Ravas farmstead.

"If we meet someone, don't look them in the eyes," said Mama. "Keep your head down. Don't talk to anyone."

"Why?"

"Do as I say!"

Soon, they entered a yard with a house on one side, a barn on the other, and a water pump in the center.

They climbed the steps to the house and knocked on the door. Ludmelia noticed something move in the window. When she turned her head to look, it was gone. A moment later, a woman opened the door a crack.

"Hello, Gerta," said Mama.

The woman's face glowed in recognition. She opened the door and threw her arms around Mama. She turned to Ludmelia and kissed her on the cheek. "Come in, come in."

Gerta led them into the kitchen where she made tea. She put a loaf of brown bread on the table, a block of cheese, and a piece of sausage. "Help yourself."

Ludmelia put a piece of sausage in her mouth and barely chewed before swallowing, she was so hungry. The simple fare tasted better than the richest feast, for they had fed on pears and beets for days, until even those ran out.

As she reached for a second slice of bread, Mama put her hand on Ludmelia's arm and shook her head.

"Eat," said Gerta. "No one goes hungry in my house, as long as we have food to share."

"Thank you," said Mama. She wiped her eyes and nodded to Ludmelia, who snatched up another slice of bread and bit off a large chunk.

Mama told Gerta about Papa and Matas, but she didn't say they had walked for days to get to Vilkija, cowering in fear with every step.

Mama asked who had been living in the cottage.

"A young family wanted to stay there for a while. I couldn't say no to them. The girl was pregnant. She visited me occasionally, and we drank tea while she knitted for the baby. They left a few months ago, and I haven't seen them since."

When Mama and Ludmelia left the Ravas farmstead that day, they carried two hens. Soon, Mama was cooking and doing chores for Gerta in exchange for food.

CHAPTER 5

Even in the moonlight, Ludmelia could see footprints in the dirt, and the marks from dragging Mama's body to the cellar. For a moment, she wondered what to do. She rubbed them out with her feet.

She put part of the load of provisions over her shoulders, and carried the rest in her arms. She walked past the chicken coop and into the field. Cutting across the grass, Ludmelia felt exposed, so she walked faster. Soon, she began to pant. Her arms ached, and the sack of jars began to slip. She tightened her muscles and kept up the pace. She stared at the bushes at the end of the field and told herself it wasn't far.

When she had crossed the field, Ludmelia set everything down and stood up straight, immediately feeling relief. When her breath calmed, she listened for the sounds of trucks, but heard nothing. She glanced back. The cottage was out of sight, but dark tracks marked her path across. She cursed herself for being so stupid. The soldiers would be able to follow her, even at night.

Ludmelia picked everything up again, and went around the edge of the next field to avoid making more tracks. With each step, she prayed for more time. She imagined soldiers nipping at her heels like angry dogs, and went faster.

Ludmelia crossed a meadow of short grass, grateful that here she didn't have to worry about leaving tracks. Her back felt sore from the load she was carrying. She entered a field of potato plants, stepping carefully so the soldiers wouldn't see broken stems and know she had been there. From the corner of her eye, she saw something move. Ludmelia fell to the ground, crushing the plants beneath her. *Soldiers were already waiting.* She pulled out the gun and lifted her head. Plant leaves moved, and soon a hare appeared at the edge of the field. It paused for a second before dashing under a bush. Ludmelia wanted to laugh, but didn't dare make a sound. She stood, picked up her things, stepped over the broken plants, and continued.

Ludmelia entered a wood, where branches and thorny bushes plucked at her clothes. Roots tried to trip her. She went past bramble bushes and climbed over rotting logs, fighting exhaustion with every step. Views of Paunksmis Lake appeared through the vegetation and energized her. The large lake was the last obstacle between her and the old forest, where Mama had told her to hide. Old folks claimed the lake hid evil nymphs waiting to attack those who crossed at night. A chill ran up Ludmelia's spine, even though she didn't believe in such things.

At the shore, Ludmelia put the provisions down and observed her surroundings. Moonlight reflected across the water, as if showing her the way to the little beach on the opposite side. It was one of the few areas not choked by vegetation, and easily approachable by boat. Heavy growths of reeds and bulrushes obstructed the rest of the shoreline around the massive horseshoe-shaped lake. Here and there, the dark shapes of willows reached out over the reeds, near clusters of birch and oak. On the far right side of the lake, hidden around a bend forming a little cove, lay a makeshift dock stretching over the duckweed and water lilies. There, Russian soldiers protected their lone patrol boat, and made rounds on the lake, guarding their territory. Ludmelia remembered the night she watched the Russians speed out to a man in a skiff in the middle of the lake. The Russians shot him. As they left, the empty craft and lone fishing pole bobbed like a cork in the waves.

The locals avoided the cove, and Ludmelia would avoid it too, for she knew if the soldiers captured her, they would do to her what they had done to Mama.

On the left side of the lake, a bog stretched around the old forest. The bog was accessible by foot through the woods where Ludmelia stood, or by boat from the lake. The bog was a dangerous place of rotting trees, deep mud, and stinking decay, impossible to cross in a rowboat. Even on foot, one misstep and the mud pulled victims down into a grimy hell. However, there was a trail through the bog, fortified with rock and dirt hidden under the water and plants. Ludmelia knew it was there, and so did Papa and a few others. Their ancestors had forged it to transform the desolate swamp into a refuge. Long ago, they had hidden there from invading armies, sometimes luring the enemy in and killing them before letting their bodies sink into mud deep enough to swallow a horse.

In the isolation provided by the lake, the bog, and the sheer size of its woods, the old forest was the safest place possible.

Ludmelia couldn't go directly across the lake, as the patrol boat might make its rounds at any time. If they saw her, they would shoot. Her only choice was to row around the edge of the lake, but the old forest was too far away to reach by sunup. She didn't want to be on the water in broad daylight. Even if she hugged the reeds along the shoreline, the soldiers might spot her.

Ludmelia couldn't go to the old forest by foot, for she had too much to carry. She decided to row to the bog as her first destination. She would hide there for the day, and get back on the water after dark.

She found her boat in its usual spot, floating among the vegetation, a thin line tying it to a jutting tree. She remembered drifting aimlessly on the lake just days ago, dreaming of a life without war. She would have pretty clothes, go out, and have fun. She would finish her studies at university, and find a job. Maybe she'd even get married one day.

Envying the languid boredom of those dream-filled hours, Ludmelia took off her socks and Papa's boots, rolled up her trousers, and stepped into the cool water. Her feet sank into the soft bottom, and drifting plants tickled her legs. She guided the boat from the reeds back to the spot where she had left her provisions. She loaded them in and climbed inside.

Ludmelia took to the oars and rowed with all her strength, going as fast as she could, in a race against the dawn. She rimmed the tall grasses, fighting them with her oars, rowing even though her shoulders ached.

Light behind the trees grew brighter. The black water turned blue with the dawn. Every muscle in Ludmelia's body ached. She kept glancing in the direction of the dock. She cut into the reeds as the sun shone in her eyes, hoping for some protection. She pulled through the plants, and rowed for her life.

The sun had been up for twenty minutes by the time she backed into the bog. Her relief in reaching the safety of this place was so great that she sat in the boat with her head in her hands and sobbed.

Soon, Ludmelia recovered to the desolate view surrounding her. Tufts of grass encircled the pools of water, muddy earth, and rotting trees that refused to fall down and die.

Ludmelia maneuvered the boat behind a mound where two dead trees had fallen against each other, looking like a cross lying on its side in the mud. This mound, along with others displaying their shaggy green heads, lay along the path that her ancestors had built.

Ludmelia stepped onto the island of tall grass and tied up the boat. She found the cheese in the knapsack and took a bite. The stink of the bog made her sick, but she swallowed anyway, for there was no food to waste. Her body sagged from fatigue. Her arms felt like they were still pulling against the water, even though they rested on her lap. She was even too tired to swat at the mosquitoes that buzzed in her ears.

She lay back with her head resting on Papa's knapsack, and thought of Mama and the words they had spoken before the soldiers had come to the cottage just hours ago.

Ludmelia had been pacing the floor while darning a sock in the light of the kerosene lamp, her fingers tender from pinpricks, and her mind ready to explode from boredom.

"I'm stuck here, while I should be studying at university," Ludmelia said.

"There is no university. The Germans closed them," Mama said, as she stirred the stew. "Besides, I teach you everything you need to know. You should be glad."

"I could have stayed. One of the professors would have tutored me."

"They were all sent away with Papa." Mama swallowed a sob.

"Why aren't we looking for him?"

"What, do you expect me to walk all the way to Siberia?"

"He might be in Kaunas."

"No, he'd come to Vilkija. It's what we had planned."

"Why don't we join the partisans and fight the Russians? Papa would have wanted it. He said we need to do our part."

"They took Papa away. They shot Matas. I've already lost enough."

"I want to do something."

"The Russians will kill us if they find us, don't you understand?"

"I wish I had never been born."

The women froze at the rumble of trucks. No one ever visited them. Mama's face twisted in fear. "He's here."

"Who?"

"The Devil." Mama sprang to her feet and put a chair under the door to the attic. "Climb up quickly." Mama pushed Ludmelia up and through the opening in the ceiling.

"You too, Mama." Ludmelia stretched her hand down and wiggled her fingers.

"Pack some provisions and go into the old forest. Never come back." Mama looked at Ludmelia with eyes that demanded obedience. "Survive for me, Ludie."

Then Mama shut the door.

CHAPTER 6

Lieutenant Roman Zabrev put his elbow out the window of the truck and slapped the door. The Studebaker had been provided by the United States on a lend-lease program to Soviet Russia, along with crates of Thompson submachine guns. Already the Studer felt like an old friend. And Zabrev didn't have many friends, but he didn't need them. He had survived the Great Purge, when anyone suspected of anti-Soviet activity had been killed. He had survived Stalingrad. His superior, Colonel Karmachov, thought of him like a son. Once Zabrev succeeded in this assignment, there was no telling how far he would go.

A mild hangover interfered with the relaxed pleasure he still felt in his loins from the young woman at Bablia's last night, Eda Lankus. If his luck held, there'd be many such nights before he went home to Moscow.

The Studer rolled past farmhands in the field working behind a horse-pulled reaper. Another horse nibbled grass nearby. In the distance, the roofs of the Ravas farmstead peeked through the trees in a storybook picture.

As chief of the Security Militia in the Soviet NKVD, Zabrev had a hundred men under his command. About half were with the Public Militia under the Ministry of Internal Affairs, or MVD. Public Militia was composed of people from many nationalities, as well as locals who supported the Red cause. The rest were People's Defenders, also called the People's Militia. It was composed mostly of Russian colonists who had settled here during the reign of the tsar. Locals called them "destroyers" because they took payment for their work by pillaging. One of their jobs was taking property from the wealthy and redistributing it according to the Communist Party's policies. That the destroyers redistributed wealth to themselves was merely a consequence of the time. Most had never lived so well before. Sometimes the destroyers went too far, like the thugs Uri and Denis Mastev, who took pleasure in raping women, but Zabrev needed men like that to keep order.

As far as Zabrev was concerned, they were all just soldiers with varying degrees of experience, there to obey him or suffer the consequences.

"I think that man is trying to get your attention, sir," said Anton Tadnik, Zabrev's driver and aide. Tadnik pointed at a shriveled man in a suit, waving at them.

"Pull over," said Zabrev.

Tadnik moved the Studer to the side of the road and stopped. The truck behind them, with Uri and Denis Mastev and other soldiers inside, also came to a halt.

The shriveled man ran to Zabrev like a dog to his master.

"Good morning, Comrade Commander," said Petra Sukas as he tried to catch his breath.

"Any news since last night?" snapped Zabrev.

"Not yet. I'm on the way to the woods to search for Ludmelia Kudirka, Comrade Commander." Petra clicked his heels and hooked dirty fingers over the side of the door. Zabrev looked down, and Petra snatched his hands away.

Petra smiled, baring teeth that were brown with rot. "I see that you're about to pay a visit to the Ravas family."

"If Dana Ravas is a partisan, as you say he is, he'll provide us with valuable intelligence."

"Yes, Comrade Commander. I assure you he is a member of the Brothers of the Forest." Petra stroked the red ribbons pinned to his suit

"Good. Now go find the Kudirka girl. I have some business to settle with her." Zabrev nodded to Tadnik, and the truck sped off. The tires kicked up a cloud of dust that made Petra invisible as he headed into the woods around Paunksmis Lake.

Zabrev knew little about this corner of the world, but before he'd left Moscow, he'd been given a quick course in history. He and Sasha, his lover, were in a teahouse on Myasnitskaya Street. Waitresses in dull white aprons reached over the tables, while balancing glasses containing steaming tea. Sasha's mother, Mrs. Garin, arrived unexpectedly. Zabrev suspected that Sasha had orchestrated the meeting, to make something more of their liaisons than the casual fun that he preferred. He would deal with that later. The old woman sat down and slurped from Sasha's glass before even saying hello. It amazed Zabrev that the beautiful Sasha had come from this unsightly woman cloaked in black.

"I heard you're going to Lithuania, Commander Zabrev," said Mrs. Garin. Her soft voice belonged in a bedroom. Zabrev watched her lips in disbelief, wondering how the alluring tones could come from such an ugly creature.

"I was born there, you know," continued Mrs. Garin. "I'll tell you something. Don't try to understand those people. You'll never understand them, so don't even try."

Zabrev's gaze settled on the blushing Sasha. "You told me you were Russian."

"My daughter is Russian. I married a Russian. I'm Lithuanian." Mrs. Garin slurped Sasha's tea. "Whatever you do, you must never underestimate them."

"Mother Russia is sending her very best to guide the peasants into the Soviet way of life," said Zabrev. "Of course, with my military background, I'm an obvious choice to lead the effort. Just the other day, I was reviewing the situation with Colonel Karmachov."

Mrs. Garin waved a finger at him as if she were casting a spell. "Listen, I'll tell you the story of Pilenai, an ancient fortress in old Lithuania, attacked by the Teutonic Knights. Inside the fortress, Duke Margiris and his soldiers knew they couldn't win. So what did they do? They killed their families. They set fire to the buildings and killed themselves. The last man died in the flames. They destroyed everything they owned to avoid giving even a crumb of bread to the enemy. These are the people you are dealing with."

Zabrev scoffed. There were no longer any fortresses, just farmers, workers, and old women who could have been Mrs. Garin's sisters. Even if they had guns, Zabrev was relatively sure that none of the peasants knew how to use them.

The Studers screeched to a halt in a yard rimmed by a farmhouse and a barn. A water-well with a pump rod and several wooden buckets stood in the center. At the commotion, a rooster squawked angrily and fluttered his wings. He rose into the air, set back down, and strutted toward the house.

Zabrev took his time getting out of the lead truck, while Denis and Uri Mastev jumped down, carrying their Thompson submachine guns. They were followed by the other destroyers.

A woman came out of the house and stood on the steps, as a man with a cane emerged from the barn. He limped to Zabrev. "You must be Comrade Commander Zabrev. I'm Bronai Ravas. What can I do for you this morning?" He extended his hand. Zabrev ignored it.

"I'm looking for Dana Ravas."

"Dana is in the fields, but perhaps I can help you. I have some cheese that you and your men might like. We farmers don't know much, but we know how to make good cheese. This is my wife, Gerta. Mama, go and get the cheese for the Comrade Commander."

"Stay where you are," said Zabrev.

Gerta didn't move. Her husband smiled. "You can see Dana over there by the reaper. We're always busy. There's so much work to do on a farm, there's no time for anything else. I can go and get him."

"We'll summon him." Zabrev nodded to Denis and Uri Mastev, who walked toward the barn. Denis put a cigarette in his mouth, lit it, and let the flaming matchstick drop to the ground. A piece of hay flared into a flame and died. Uri opened the door and both men went inside.

"Please don't smoke in the barn. It's full of hay," called Bronai. "Comrade Commander, there's no need for your men to search the barn. Dana's out there, next to the reaper. You can see him from here." He pointed to the field with his cane.

Uri and Denis returned as the scent of burning hay wafted into the yard.

"My God, what have you done? We need the hay to feed the animals this winter."

Gerta came down the steps and stood next to her husband. She turned her face into his shoulder as plumes of smoke drifted into the sky.

"You don't need to worry about your animals," said Zabrev. He glanced at the soldiers, who had their guns trained on the couple. Gerta leaned against her husband. His arms cradled her as he gazed at the flames.

A horse and rider galloped into the yard. The man was tall, fair, and glistening with sweat. He dismounted.

"You're Dana Ravas?" asked Zabrev.

The man ignored him. He ran to the well and frantically worked the pump, filling the buckets with water.

The fire crackled. The horse whinnied and pawed the dirt with his hoof.

"Come here," called Zabrev.

Dana kept pumping water. He gave an angry glance at the intruders. "What have you bastards done?"

"Dana, be quiet," said his father.

Denis and Uri Mastev stepped up behind Zabrev, grins on their faces, their submachine guns pointed at Dana. Zabrev put his hand on the barrel of one of the guns and shook his head. He stepped into the middle of the yard, and unclasped the whip clipped to his belt. The leather uncoiled as it fell to the ground.

Zabrev flicked the whip into the sky, and grinned at the looks of horror on the faces of the farmers.

Dana didn't seem to notice. He picked up a bucket in each hand and ran toward the flames already leaping out of the barn windows. White smoke billowed into the sky.

"Stop!" Zabrev commanded.

Dana kept running, water sloshing over the sides of the pails. Zabrev cracked the whip, and it slashed into Dana's back. Dana stopped. His shoulders straightened as a line of red appeared on the back of his shirt.

The horse gave a whinnying scream and bolted, almost knocking Zabrev down.

"My wife has a piece of amber jewelry hidden under the bureau upstairs. Take it. Just stop this," said Bronai.

Dana continued to move toward the barn.

Zabrev flicked the whip again, and slashed Dana between the shoulder blades. Dana's back arched and he stopped.

"Dana, don't be a fool!" shouted Bronai.

Zabrev smiled.

Bronai glanced at his son, and then turned back to Zabrev. "Take me. I'll tell you everything I know."

"Tell me now."

Bronai hesitated.

"I thought so." Zabrev lashed the whip again. Dana fell forward. Water splashed out of the pails. More blood seeped through his shirt.

Dana moaned and lifted his head. Zabrev went to Dana's side and kicked him. *Observe the face of your conqueror,* he thought, kicking Dana again.

The old woman fell to her knees, sobbing. "My son, my son."

"Throw him into the truck," said Zabrev. "He's the one we want. You heard what they have in the house. Save the amber jewelry for me." Lithuanian women treasured amber, a golden fossil made from pine resin. It was a symbol of the country itself. Sasha might enjoy a souvenir.

Denis and Uri Mastev lifted Dana into the back of the second truck, and went into the house, while the remaining guards kept their guns trained on Bronai and Gerta.

Zabrev forced himself to display a sense of calm as he returned to the truck. His mind burned, even though he had won. He had overcome the farmers, although it had taken men with guns, and a good thrashing. With his handkerchief, Zabrev wiped the blood off the whip. As he rewound it, he imagined the satisfaction he would feel when Dana Ravas spilled his secrets in the interrogation room. Perhaps he would use Dana's parents as leverage. Maybe he would trade information for their lives. Dana didn't have to know they would already be dead. Zabrev smiled as he clipped the whip to his belt.

"Finish this," he said to the guards as he climbed into the Studer.

Tadnik started the engine, and drove the vehicle away from the stench of smoke.

"Take me to the Kudirka cottage," said Zabrev, lighting a cigarette.

They passed the field where the horse still stood in front of the reaper. The one who had carried Dana into the farmyard had already returned, and was nibbling grass. As they drove, gunshots cracked behind them.

The sight of the horses brought Zabrev back to the summers of his youth, when the sun was hot and the air was cool, and his horse, Kirill, followed him around like a dog.

He remembered the trips he took with his father to a peasant's farm in the countryside where they boarded Kirill. Zabrev would clutch Kirill's mane and feel the animal's raw strength under his legs as they raced across the fields. Kirill ran so fast that Zabrev had to close his eyes to the wind and dust. Back then, he believed they could run to the very edge of the earth.

Those blissful afternoons ended with the drought of 1921. The last time Zabrev had ridden on Kirill, the peasants were working in the fields, but they moved so slowly, it seemed they were in a daze.

"What's wrong with them, Father?" Zabrev asked. The gangly young man gazed into his father's face.

"They're hungry."

"Why don't we give them some food?"

"We have none to spare."

A few days later, Zabrev's father told him that Kirill was gone.

"Where did he go?" asked Zabrev.

"He's dead. The peasants killed him. For food."

"Why don't they eat their own food? They didn't need to eat poor Kirill!"

His father shrugged.

"They have to pay, Father. They have to pay for killing Kirill."

CHAPTER 7

Across the road from the burning barn, three men stepped out from behind the bushes as the last Studer sped away, carrying chickens, pigs, food, a piece of amber, and Dana Ravas. One of the men was just forty-four years old, but the eye patch and gaunt cheeks made him look like he had escaped from hell. Even though he limped, Simas Vargas moved cautiously, as if a trap awaited him at every corner.

Two brothers, Jurgis and Vadi, followed him. Standing beside each other, the brothers looked like a sapling next to an oak. Jurgis, small and agile, could wiggle into cramped spaces and climb a tree as fast as a squirrel. Perched on his head was a blue beret his friend had sent him from Paris before the war. Vadi, the older of the two, was so big he practically shook the ground when he walked, and exuded strength from every pore. Despite his size, Vadi had the grace of a ballet dancer.

All three men lived and worked on the Ravas farmstead.

The brothers moved to the water pump, but Simas put his hand up to stop them. Even from where he stood, he felt the heat from the flames. Plumes of smoke escaped from the decaying structure. No one could save the barn now.

As Simas went to the two bodies lying in the dirt in front of the house, the rooster flew down from the porch roof, flapping his wings near Simas' head, as if the one-eyed man had been the cause of this devastation.

Simas already knew that Bronai and Gerta were dead. He had seen that profound stillness before, when he was in the Lithuanian Army fighting the Bolsheviks. Still, he knelt by Bronai's body and put an ear to the chest, hoping that by some miracle the old man would open his eyes and know Simas was there to take care of him, even if it was the end.

After hearing nothing, Simas shifted his weight to take pressure off his bad leg. As ash from the fire drifted over him, he relived the scene from minutes ago. The Mastev brothers had come out of the house, their arms loaded with bread, cheese, sausage, and bottles of vodka. Uri placed his load in the truck and went back inside, returning with the amber brooch. He showed it to Denis before slipping it into his pocket. As Gerta stood trembling next to her husband, Uri shot them both. From their spot in the bushes, Vadi sprang to his feet, but Simas took hold of his arm and forced him back down. They had no weapons. Revealing themselves would only bring their deaths. As Bronai and Gerta collapsed to the ground, Vadi pounded the dirt with his fists in frustration, and Simas helplessly watched.

As the fire raged, the brothers carried the bodies to the garden behind the house. In the potato patch near the pear trees, they began to dig with the shovels that Gerta kept near the back door. Simas watched them work, his anger tempered by the rhythmic scrape of the shovels against the dirt. The sweet smell of earth mingled with the scent of the blood in a bitter perfume. He craved a drink so badly, his stomach twitched.

Memories came back to Simas in a flood. He remembered buying a little cottage from Bronai Ravas decades ago, and bringing his young bride, Klara, there. He was so proud that this beautiful woman was his. He remembered her unpacking the chest containing the samovar with wooden handles, the glass cups, and two little silver spoons. The last thing she took out was a doll dressed in a colorful skirt, an embroidered apron, and a peasant blouse, its face darkened from a thousand kisses. As she placed it in a corner of the cabinet, she said she couldn't bear giving up this last vestige of her girlhood.

The cottage smelled of violets.

Klara cried the first time they made love, and Simas held her until she was quiet. When they made love again, she didn't cry anymore.

In the weeks that followed, Klara treated him with a kindness that felt almost fragile, and Simas thought himself a lucky man. He couldn't imagine being happier, until hearing that the Bolsheviks had killed the tsar. Nicholas was dead. The Russian empire had fallen. They were free. Simas pulled Klara to her feet and spun her around the kitchen, knocking into the table and spilling the soup. Klara squirmed away while grumbling about their ruined supper. When she began sopping up the mess with her apron, Simas pulled her into the bedroom.

Their joy was short-lived, for the Bolsheviks kept marching westward. When they invaded Simas' country, he told Klara he had to join the army and drive them out, so their children would be free. "It's the honorable thing to do," he had said before leaving.

By the time the Lithuanians defeated the Bolsheviks, Simas was blind in one eye, and his leg was shattered from a grenade blast. He made his way back to the little cottage, imagining Klara running into his arms, making him feel that his life mattered, and that he had saved the future for his unborn children.

Simas' brother, Adomas, was feeding wood into the stove as Simas entered.

"What are you doing here?" asked Simas, leaning against his cane. The room was the same as before, with the table and chairs, the dish cabinet with the doll staring down at him, and the narrow bed against the wall. But the scent of violets was gone.

"Klara left," said Adomas.

Simas wanted to run into the bedroom, but all he could manage was a painful limp. The doors to the armoire hung open, the inside empty, except for Simas' suit. The drawers in the tiny bureau were open, with nothing inside. Klara's hairbrush lay half-hidden on the rumpled bed. Simas threw it at the mirror hanging on the wall above the bureau, and it hit a corner, leaving a crack.

"She didn't think you were coming home. None of us did." Adomas lingered in the doorway.

"Where did she go?"

Adomas handed him a letter. "We tried to take care of her, but when she didn't hear from you, she went crazy."

Dear Simas:

They say the Bolsheviks are close, and there's no one here to protect me, for you are off fighting. Why did you have to leave? Aren't I important to you? My heart breaks knowing that you didn't love me enough to stay.

Adomas says I'll be safe, but I don't believe him. If the Russians find me, they'll do horrible things.

I'm going to my cousin in Poland. If by some miracle you survive, know that I won't come back to Vilkija. I won't live with the Russians.

Klara

"I'm going after her," said Simas.

"You can't."

"Why not?"

Adomas hesitated. "She's dead."

Simas collapsed to the floor. Adomas pulled him up, and helped him over to sit on the bed. It creaked under his weight and his sorrow.

"It was typhus," said Adomas. "We got word from Klara's cousin. She wants to know what to do with Klara's things."

His pride broken from defending his country for the woman who left him, Simas spoke. "Burn them."

That day, Simas' hatred for the Russians became an obsession. If it weren't for them, he would be happy. If it weren't for them, Klara would be alive and living with him in the cottage. If it weren't for them, he'd have a future.

For a month, Simas drank vodka every day until he was in a stupor. At night, he held shouting matches with the dark.

Almost blind with hurt and anger, Simas didn't recognize Bronai Ravas the day he came to visit. Simas lay on the narrow bed in the kitchen. A bottle of vodka sat on the floor beside him. Bronai moved some rumpled clothes from a chair and pulled it over to the bed. He sat with his cap in his hand.

"I was beginning to think Gerta and I were getting too old to have children. She's going to be forty in a few years, but she's pregnant. Can you believe it, Simas?"

Simas reached down and handed him the bottle, but it was already empty.

"Isaac Sukas helps me in the barn and the fields. He's not the smartest man I've ever met, and his heart is not the strongest, but he manages to do a decent day's work. His wife was wonderful though, nursing Gerta when she was sick, helping in the house and taking care of the gardens for so many years. After she died, I felt sorry for Isaac and their son, Petra. Now, Gerta has no help in the kitchen, and she's watching the boy during the day while his father works. If you could stay with us until the baby comes and do some light chores, it would help a great deal."

His voice sounded far away.

"We even cleaned out the storeroom off the kitchen, hoping you'd come. It's not big, but there's a bed, a chair, and a place for your clothes. Please, Simas. You'd be doing me a favor."

Bronai went in the bedroom and packed some clothing. After helping Simas on with his coat, they left the cottage and all its memories behind.

The next morning, Simas woke to the smells of steeping tea and warm bread. At first he thought Klara was making him breakfast. When he realized where he was, the craving for a drink hit him hard. He got up and rummaged through the shelves for a bottle, but found none. He wondered how he was going to manage.

"Is that you, Simas?" called a voice.

He dressed, and went into the kitchen where Gerta was taking out thick slices of toasted bread from the oven. A little boy, Petra Sukas, sat on a chair swinging his legs.

Isaac Sukas followed Bronai inside.

"*Labas, Teti,*" said Petra.

"Good morning," said Isaac, taking the chair next to his son.

They all ate together. Afterwards, Simas brought in wood for the stove, pumped water for the dishes, and sat at the table, figuring out how to fix the clock from the sitting room.

Every day there was work to do. Simas collected the eggs from the chickens, and fed the pigs. He repaired a shelf in the kitchen, and replaced the handle on a hoe. He even went outside to fix a broken fence.

Gerta often sat with him when his work kept him in the house. She told him how happy she was that he was there, and how much they needed his help. Once, she put his hand on her stomach, and he felt the baby move. She even made special tea from herbs in the forest to help heal his wounds.

After a few months, Simas was helping in the barn, too. When he nursed a sick cow back to health, Bronai called him Mr. Marvelous, saying he could fix anything and do anything.

The evening Gerta cried out in pain, Simas hitched up the horse and whipped the poor animal to a gallop in his rush to fetch the midwife. The wagon flew over the ruts in the road, rattling Simas until he thought his teeth would fall out. Later, he sat in the kitchen with Bronai, Isaac, and little Petra, while the women were upstairs. Bronai stared out the window with a look of worry on his face, glancing up at the ceiling each time his wife cried out.

"She'll be fine," Simas said, as he put a piece of wood in the stove.

"God will take care of her. Even if she goes up to heaven, God will watch over her like he does my mother. People in heaven don't feel pain, and they're never sick. That's what *Teti* told me," Petra said, smiling at his father.

Isaac Sukas may have filled his son's head with foolishness about heaven, but God hadn't taken care of me, thought Simas. Still, he nodded at the boy.

When the midwife came downstairs, carrying the plump, red-faced baby, Bronai hugged Simas before holding his own son.

Bronai and Gerta named the baby Dana.

Later that night in his room, Simas cried. His hopes for a child of his own were dead, just like his wife. No decent woman would marry a one-eyed man with a limp. He got up and walked all the way to Bablia's, where he bought two bottles of vodka. When he returned to his room, he was too weary to drink and too tired to sleep, so he lay in his bed wondering why God had put him on this earth.

Simas tried to stay busy, and tried not to think of what might have been. Eventually, he was strong enough to go into the fields, and that was a blessing, for it gave him even more to do.

At night, he struggled to stay away from the bottle. His salvation was the letters from his friend, Dr. Vera Alexas, who had treated his injuries during the war. She had spent more time with Simas than any other patient. At one point, he wondered if she felt something for him. He thought about how sad she had looked the day he left the hospital, but he had been so anxious to get back to Klara that nothing else mattered.

Vera wrote about moving to Vilnius and working in the hospital there. She told him about going into the woods to help a peasant family. She wrote about saving a man who had been attacked by wolves. He read the letters to avoid the overwhelming urge to drink. Sometimes it worked. Sometimes he got so angry with Vera for keeping him alive that he turned to the bottle for comfort.

Three years later, Dana's brother Tomas was born. Four years after that, Dana, Petra, and Tomas went to Paunksmis Lake with

Isaac Sukas for an excursion. Instead of swimming with the boys, Isaac sat on the shore and took a nap. Tomas went under. As Dana tried to save his brother, Isaac jumped into the water, but he was too poor a swimmer and too late to help. Tomas died that day, and Bronai sent Isaac and Petra off to live in the woods, in a run-down hut that was on the property when Bronai had bought it. A poor family had lived there long ago, but now it was where Bronai kept the spare plow.

After learning about Tomas' death, Simas stayed with Bronai in the sitting room, watching him cry. When he couldn't stand it anymore, Simas got on the horse and rode into Vilkija. He came back drunk, and with several bottles of vodka that he hid in the storeroom.

The next morning, despite Simas' hangover, Bronai made him foreman.

At first, Simas thought Isaac should have been banished from the farmstead. Instead, he had a place to stay and still had his job. Simas didn't know how Bronai could even stand looking at Isaac every day, let alone working with him. But Petra was little, and Bronai didn't wish to punish the child anymore for the sake of the father.

Dana was plagued with nightmares after Tomas died, and soon stopped talking altogether. Simas suspected that Dana felt anger and guilt for not saving his brother. Simas tried to help by teaching Dana about farming. Simas kept the boy with him constantly, and showed him how to raise chickens, pigs, and cows, grow crops, and fix the reaper. After two weeks of Simas' instruction, Dana blurted out, "I know all there is to know about farming. Just leave me alone."

Bronai taught Dana how to shoot, but Dana never did well on their hunting trips. He always had an excuse: he missed the deer by inches; his father distracted him; the animal was too small. Simas thought Dana might have been a good marksman if he had practiced. Eventually, Dana announced that he wasn't going into the woods anymore, because he would be a lawyer one day.

Simas and Bronai were digging potatoes on a crisp fall afternoon when the old man leaned against the spade and spoke. "If anything happens to me, I want you to take care of Dana."

Simas nodded and went back to digging.

"Did you hear me, Simas?"

"Sure."

Bronai dropped the spade and clasped Simas' shoulders. "Promise me. When I'm gone, he'll need someone to teach him how to be a man."

"You'll outlive us all."

Bronai's eyes grew wide. His hands gripped harder and he shook Simas.

"Alright," said Simas.

When Bronai wouldn't let go, Simas had the strange feeling that the old man knew that their future held a deep darkness.

"I promise," said Simas.

"Promise what?"

"I'll take care of Dana. I'll keep him with me."

Bronai picked up the spade and went back to digging.

The next summer, a man with red cheeks found Simas working in the rye field. He introduced himself as Victor Kudirka. He was visiting Vilkija with his wife, Aldona, and their two children, Matas and Ludmelia. Victor wanted to know who owned the abandoned cottage tucked behind a cluster of trees just down the road. Since Simas no longer lived there, he agreed to rent out his cottage for the summer.

Victor and Simas came to know each other while relaxing with Bronai Ravas on the bench behind the farmhouse after supper. Ludmelia, Matas, and Dana played in the fields as the men watched. Although the youngest of the three, Ludmelia out-ran and out-threw both boys. Dana always had an excuse for losing at their games, but Matas seemed genuinely proud of his sister.

From the beginning, Simas felt a connection to Victor. They both shared the belief that war was normal, peace elusive, and that precautions were necessary in order to survive the next time the world slipped into bloodshed. Both worried that Ludmelia, Matas, and Dana would come of age in a world that burned with war.

They discussed the pamphlets Victor would write, and the words he would use to call the people to unite in protecting their freedom. Simas began stockpiling supplies of canned food, sheets of canvas, spare shovels, rifles, bullets, and even some warm clothing. Bronai joined them in their discussions of how to resist an invasion from the Germans, or worse, from the Soviets. They expanded their sphere to include Vadi and Jurgis, friends who Bronai had hired on as farmhands. The men were careful to discuss their plans in private.

The Kudirka family returned to the cottage the next summer, and the summer after that. Each year, Victor and his children spent more time in the woods. Simas went with them on occasion, as Petra was working on the farm by then, and Simas could afford time away.

Each year, the stockpile got a little bigger, the maps more refined, the plans a little clearer, and Victor's pamphlets more decidedly anti-Soviet. With Vadi and Jurgis, Simas even scouted out places for a partisan camp.

The summer before Dana left for university, Victor bought the cottage from Simas. To celebrate, Gerta arranged a picnic in the orchard. Vadi and Jurgis brought out the kitchen chairs and set them around a table covered with a red cloth. Kazys Espertus, a pig farmer who had a place near the lake, came with his son. They contributed a tray stacked with delectable smoked sausage. Victor kept the beer flowing as the friends laughed and talked under the sparkling sky.

The event of the day was a shooting match, and the prize was a new hunting knife that Victor had bought in Kaunas. Simas nailed the target to a tree. Everyone did well, hitting the inner circles. Dana made a good shot for a change, using Simas' beautiful hunting rifle. Dana grinned when his father slapped him on the back in congratulations.

Ludmelia stepped up to take her turn. Papa handed her the pistol, but she refused it. Instead, she held her hand out to Dana. He looked at her with a perplexed expression, and after a moment, handed her Simas' rifle. She ran her hand along the smooth barrel, glanced at Papa, and smiled. She toed the line, aimed, took a quick breath, and fired four shots dead center.

Later, Dana watched resentfully as Victor handed Ludmelia the prize.

The day Dana left for university, he said good-bye to his parents and Simas, and told them his life was about to begin.

Bronai spoke of Dana's scholastic achievements with inflated pride, but soon the war started and the Soviets invaded the little country. The Russians began combing the universities for fresh recruits for the Red Army, so Dana fled school and returned home. Before long, Dana was barking orders at Simas and the others. They all suffered Dana's anger at having to give up his dream of becoming a lawyer, for a future as a farmer.

While Simas didn't like Dana's attitude, he didn't mind letting Dana run the farm. The homestead was Dana's legacy, not his. It was the way things should be.

In 1941, a devastating wave of deportations targeted the intellectual elite of the country. Thousands of people were sent into the bowels of Russia on cattle trains. In the summer of that year, the German Army invaded, and fighting broke out against the weaker Russian force.

Ludmelia and Aldona Kudirka escaped to the cottage. When they told Simas that Victor Kudirka had been sent to Siberia and that Matas was dead, Simas raged with fresh hatred for the Russians.

Under the Germans, things were barely better for some, and worse for many. But few wanted to fight the Germans, as it might help the Russians win the war and bring a future of brutal and permanent Soviet rule. Simas, Vadi, Jurgis and a few men from Vilkija selected a place for a campsite in the old forest, across the lake, where they hid armaments they had stolen from the fleeing Russians. They began building a bunker as a more permanent structure in case the Russians ever came back, and they had to go into hiding. The brothers even hollowed out areas under rotting tree trunks so they could conceal themselves at various places in the forest, should a hasty escape become necessary.

Then came the day in 1944 when Eda Lankus, daughter of a recently deceased childhood friend of Gerta, arrived for a visit. Eda and her father had given up their house in Vilnius for the peace of Vilkija and a place within walking distance of the local saloon.

Sitting in the farmstead kitchen, Eda was like a slice of cake in a room full of brown bread. For a moment, Simas forgot about his eye, his leg, his dead bride, and even his hatred for the Russians and Nazis. He dreamed about Eda that night. From that day on, whenever Eda visited Gerta, he found a reason to go into the house. Her smiles encouraged Simas to spend even more time with her.

One afternoon, Simas and Eda escaped into the rye field near the woods, with a picnic basket. They lay on a blanket and sipped honey-flavored Krupnika liquor.

"There's something I want to ask," said Eda.

While Simas chewed a piece of cheese, he smiled at her softness. She was as pure as cream, as white as snow, as innocent as a butterfly.

"Do you wear your eye patch when you sleep?"

"Maybe one day you'll find out what I wear to bed."

Eda blushed.

"Why do you love me?" Simas tilted his head back and watched her.

"Because I know you'll take care of me."

Simas raised an eyebrow. "Is that all?"

Eda gazed into the trees. "To me, it's the most important thing."

"You have a father who takes care of you."

Eda's lips quivered.

"Is something wrong?"

Eda shook her head. "Since Mama died, it's been hard living with Papa."

"Families can be like that."

"You never told me about yours."

"My parents are gone. I have no family."

"You have a brother."

"How do you know?"

"People talk."

"Adomas is dead."

"I'm sorry. I didn't know. When did he die?"

"When I found out he was working for the Gestapo."

She looked shocked. "That can't be true."

"Many unbelievable things are true these days. Before the war, Adomas was with the Lithuanian Police. Mother and Father were proud of him. When the Germans came, he thought they were going to win the war, so he joined them. He wanted success, and it didn't matter how many people he put in their graves."

The mere thought of his brother conjured up a sour mixture in Simas' stomach. Besides hating Adomas' work with the Gestapo, Simas lived with the thought that somehow Adomas could have prevented Klara from leaving.

Adomas wrote to his brother, but Simas destroyed the letters without reading them, and without saving the address. Not knowing where Adomas was living kept Simas' hatred under control. It kept Simas from punishing his brother for everything.

"What happened to your parents?"

"My father got sick just after the Germans drove the Soviets out. My mother died three months after he passed. She couldn't go on without him."

"That's sweet."

Simas looked at her, shocked. "That they died?"

"That she loved him so much."

As Simas gazed at this snowy beauty, he told himself not to lean too close, not to nuzzle Eda's neck, or feel the smoothness of her buttery skin. He was old enough to be her father. He wouldn't survive if she ever left him. But his body wouldn't listen to his head. When their lips touched, he knew she was the warmth in his life.

He imagined them taking their vows in a church in front of God, and cutting the *sakotis*, a traditional Lithuanian tree cake. He imagined a happy future with Eda, their children, grandchildren, and an old age that faded into a smile.

When a butterfly landed on the rim of his glass, Simas asked her to marry him. Eda said, "Yes." They stayed together on the blanket until the sun went down.

The next morning, with the smell of toast in the air and the sound of eggs sizzling on the stove, he told Gerta that he and Eda were getting married. Gerta smiled and kissed him on both cheeks.

"It's a good match, Simas."

Just a few months later, the Russians were at the farmstead murdering the two people Simas loved as much as his own parents.

Toiling behind the farmhouse under the hot sun, Vadi and Jurgis managed to dig one grave for Bronai and Gerta. There was no time for more. Vadi slid the old ones down into the hole, and covered them with the red cloth from the kitchen table. He and Jurgis shoveled in the dirt.

Jurgis placed a rock at their heads to mark the grave. The men took off their hats, and Simas said a prayer. When he was done, they shook hands. Simas told them to go into the woods behind the Kudirka cottage and watch for Russian soldiers.

"We'll need to get our guns first," said Jurgis. He and Vadi picked up the shovels and headed toward the pigpen and the underground bin where they kept their weapons.

Simas hobbled in the opposite direction, already thinking about helping Dana escape, and taking Eda into the forest. No one was safe anymore.

CHAPTER 8

Tadnik turned off the engine and rolled the truck to a stop, just down the road from the Kudirka cottage. If Petra hadn't told them exactly where the place was, they might have missed it entirely. The road ambled along without any indication that a building was there at all. There were no tracks leading to the house, and there was no place to park a truck or horse and wagon, other than in the ditch, or in the road itself. The cottage stood behind a cluster of trees. Beyond the cottage, a row of bushes marked an expanse of rolling fields. On the other side of the fields loomed more dark woods, and farther on, the massive Paunksmis Lake that protected the oldest and largest part of the forest.

Zabrev pulled out a packet of cigarettes and offered them to his driver. Tadnik took one, struck a match, and held it out for Zabrev. Tadnik's gaunt cheeks caved inward as he held the match to the cigarette dangling from his lips, and puffed.

"Father Stalin has the vision. *Upon the brink of a wild stream, he stood and dreamt a mighty dream.*' Do you know who said that, Tadnik?"

"Pushkin."

"Yes, that's right." Zabrev was astonished that the dullard would know this. "Well, these people are stubborn, and must be forced to believe what we believe. Wild animals must be beaten into submission."

"Yes, Comrade Commander."

"In Russia, men like me have the intellect to form a new societal plan. When Lenin said that the average man wasn't capable of making his own decisions, and that government must do it for him, I think he had these people in mind." Zabrev laughed.

"Yes, Comrade Commander."

"In a fortnight, I'll have these people singing *chastushki*."

The driver said nothing.

"You lived here in the forest for some time, didn't you? You must know something of the natives."

"My years in the forest were the longest of my life."

"How long were you here?"

"It started in 1941 with the German invasion. I was injured during our retreat. Whether my comrades didn't realize I was hurt, or whether they were just fleeing for their lives, they left me behind. I managed to crawl to a church, and a priest hid me." Tadnik took a puff and held the smoke in. He slowly let it out. "The priest said that as a man of God, he was obligated to help, but others didn't feel that way. When I recovered, I fled to the woods near Vilnius. That's where I learned how to survive among the wolves."

"These people aren't like wolves. Wolves are strong. They're more like wild dogs."

"Each day was a struggle. In the summer, I fought the bugs, and in the winter the cold. I was constantly hungry. Once, I went for a week without food. I stole vegetables from gardens. I broke into houses and took whatever I could: food, blankets, and clothing. I snuck into barns in the middle of the night and took milk from cows. Sometimes I slept with the animals."

"Yes, well, many have had it hard. My time in Stalingrad was particularly difficult."

"I thought there might be other soldiers from the Soviet Army hiding in the area, having been left behind like me. I walked along the roads at night from forest to forest searching for them. Once, I heard people speaking Russian. I called out to them, and they shot at me. My own countrymen shot at me."

"At Stalingrad, the snipers found us, no matter where we hid. I saw the Germans shoot a man while he was taking a piss."

"Eventually, I found a family of Russian colonists, and they took care of me for a good while, but the neighbors became suspicious, and I had to leave. I wandered, trying to avoid both Germans and locals. I was hiding in the woods when a group of armed men captured me. They beat me and said they were going to kill me. But the priest had taught me a few words of Lithuanian, so they let me go."

Zabrev chuckled. "In Stalingrad, soldiers ran away to avoid the snipers, but they were cowards and had to be executed for deserting. If soldiers don't obey their orders and fight, what should we do, give them a medal? Officers are soldiers, too. We have our orders. We have to obey them. I had to shoot some of my own men. A Party member, a commissar, was observing the action, and I had no choice. Every night, he wrote a report for his superiors. If I had let even one man get away, I'd have been executed."

Tadnik went on. "One night I came out of the woods and happened upon a dead German lying in a ditch on the side of the road. I took his gun, and walked along, hungry and alone, until I couldn't go any farther. All I could see ahead of me was another year of drudgery. I sat in the road and waited, trying to think of a reason to go on living. I even put the gun into my mouth and was about to squeeze the trigger when a vehicle came along. I jumped up and began firing. I had had enough. If I couldn't end this by my own hand, their return fire would kill me, and I would be at peace. It was a single car, and by sheer luck, I killed the Germans inside. One body had a chest covered in metals, so I took them as souvenirs. Within a week, the Russians were back. Colonel Karmachov promoted me for assassinating a high-ranking Wehrmacht officer. It was the happiest day of my life."

"So now you're my aide."

"Yes, Comrade Commander."

"Where are you from originally?"

"I was born and raised in Saratov, so I am from Ukraine."

"Ah, so am I. I was raised in Lviv. Do you think of home often?"

"All the time, Comrade Commander."

"Follow orders and we'll get along just fine. You might even get home someday."

"Thank you, Comrade Commander."

As Zabrev observed the wisp of a cottage through the leaves and branches, he imagined Ludmelia Kudirka appearing along the road. She would be sobbing and looking for someone to comfort her as she mourned the death of her dear mother, for he was certain his men had killed the old woman. Ludmelia's soft flesh would feel good in his arms. He glanced at Tadnik.

"Are you married?" asked Zabrev.

"No, sir."

"Are you one of those who believe there is only one woman for you?"

"I like to think so."

"One must taste many apples before making a pie."

"Of course, Comrade Commander."

"I hear you're efficient, Tadnik. It's a good thing, for a dreamer has no place on my staff. Do you understand?"

"Yes, sir." Tadnik sat up straighter.

Zabrev flicked the cigarette out the window, and thought of the little man who had told him where the Kudirkas were living. Petra had acted as though he held a grudge against the family, but it didn't matter. The NKVD had their own intelligence. Zabrev knew that Victor Kudirka had been deported for running an underground newspaper that spewed drivel about a free Lithuania. That was reason enough to seek out the rest of the Kudirka family. He knew Victor's son, Matas, was dead. He knew that Ludmelia and Aldona, the wife, had left Kaunas and had disappeared. Petra's contribution had been telling him where to find Ludmelia and her mother.

Zabrev motioned to Tadnik. They quietly opened the truck doors and left them ajar, so there wouldn't be any noise. Tadnik trotted down the road to the cottage, clutching his rifle. A minute later, he waved Zabrev in.

Zabrev passed the cluster of trees and went into the cottage. He studied the large stain on the bed in the kitchen. He guessed what the men had done to Aldona Kudirka before shooting her. The quilt was gone, and the body. He was certain the Mastev brothers hadn't moved it, for they had the manners of wild pigs. It was possible that a neighbor had buried her.

Zabrev went into the bedroom. He kicked away the mattress stuffing on the floor near the cracked mirror, and reached into his breast pocket for Ludmelia's photograph. Her smile gripped him. Her look was innocent, yet somehow seductive. It spoke to his lust. Her unadorned beauty enticed him. Yes, he would find her. It was only a question of time. She probably had gone to stay with friends or relatives in town. It didn't matter. All he had to do was ask questions. Someone would talk. He could always make them talk.

Shards of pottery crunched under his boots as he went to the armoire. He used his foot to untangle an old skirt and two blouses on the floor. *Nothing but rags.* Zabrev put Ludmelia Kudirka's photograph back in his pocket and left the room.

He went outside, and Tadnik followed. Poorly concealed footprints behind the house led to a garden, and a chicken coop that held nothing but feathers. A small pile of dirt lay next to a hole in a corner of the garden, but it was barely big enough to bury a dog, let alone a grown woman. It was clear someone had been digging there, though.

Zabrev bent over the hole and picked up a scrap of paper partially hidden under an overturned potato plant. He could see a name under the smudges of dirt. Maybe it was significant. Maybe it was part of a longer list. Victor Kudirka's wife may have buried other papers here that contained even more secrets.

"Dig." Zabrev put the piece of paper in his breast pocket, next to the photograph.

Tadnik returned with a shovel, digging where Zabrev directed, destroying plants and leaving holes in the patch of earth. They found nothing but potatoes.

Zabrev walked past some pear trees, toward a pile of bushes in front of a mound of dirt built into the rise. Tadnik pulled the bushes aside to reveal a rough-hewn door with a wooden latch. Gun at the ready, Tadnik opened the door to a small, dark room with a dirt floor and walls lined with shelves. A figure wrapped in a quilt lay on the ground.

"Put your hands up," shouted Tadnik. He kicked the figure. It didn't move. Tadnik drew the quilt aside with the tip of his gun.

Mrs. Kudirka lay there, her eyes closed in eternal rest.

"Someone put her here," said Zabrev. He curled his lips as he gazed down at the body. Ludmelia could have been hiding in here during the raid last night. The Mastev brothers should have done a thorough search, instead of spending their time inside the house with Mrs. Kudirka.

"When we get back to headquarters, get a party of men together and search the woods back there." Zabrev pointed toward the lake. "You lead them."

"Do you want us to go across the lake and into the old forest?"

"I don't think she'll go that far. After all, she's just a girl. Focus on this side for now. Find her, and any partisans who are hiding with her. Take them alive and bring them to me. We need their information."

"Certainly, Comrade Commander."

"And do a thorough job."

They left the door to the cellar open when they left. As Zabrev glanced back, a breeze lifted a corner of Mrs. Kudirka's quilt. It looked like she was waving good-bye.

They climbed into the truck and drove past more fields and trees, and the occasional farmer walking alongside the road. Zabrev's thoughts drifted back to the night his superior and mentor, Colonel Karmachov, had told him of this new assignment. They were sipping vodka in the Colonel's spacious office. The Colonel sat behind his desk. His cheeks moved when he breathed. "You're like a son to me."

Zabrev smiled. He was sure his new assignment would catapult him through the ranks. Nothing was more important to Lieutenant Roman Zabrev than his rank.

"Your new assignment will be hard, but if you succeed, I think it will be good for your career."

Zabrev's gaze darted to the picture of Stalin hanging on the wall. Zabrev had barely survived Stalingrad. He didn't want to go to the front and face the Germans again. No one did. He took a deep breath and held it. "Yes, sir. What is it?"

"I want you to go to Lithuania, to a place called Vilkija. The native population is mounting a resistance. The partisans call themselves Brothers of the Forest. We call them bandits. They're farmers who roam the woods, like the wolves they boast about in their legends. They emerge from their camps to sabotage the railroads, cut telephone lines, and blow up bridges. They melt into households and milk cows for a while, then go back into the woods and plan another attack. They need to be stopped." The Colonel gulped down his vodka and refilled his glass. "I want no partisans in the area of Vilkija when you're through, and I want the job done quickly."

"Why don't we just burn them out?"

"Destroying the forests is an option, but there are many, and some are vast. We don't know where the partisans are hiding. Besides, it rains a good deal this time of year."

"Are they doing much damage?"

"The resistance is small, but growing and gaining strength every day." Colonel Karmachov leaned forward. "The Lithuanians have been part of Russia for over a century, yet they still practice their own customs, and speak that damn language of theirs, when they should be learning Russian. They're stubborn. Watch out for them."

"They're farmers armed with pitchforks."

"They have far more than pitchforks. We left behind armaments in 1941, and recently, so did the Germans. I guarantee that the locals took whatever weapons they could find, and are using them against us.

"You'll only have a hundred men to begin with. Most will be local Russian colonists. If things get tough, some may run, so be prepared. The young ones in particular won't have much experience, or stomach for a real fight. Very few are battle hardened. Make do with these soldiers for now. I'll get you more men soon. Russia always has more men, but it will take time to get them here. Besides, our best troops are fighting their way to Berlin."

"I should be able to manage with a hundred men, Colonel."

"Trust no one. Locals might say they're pro-Soviet, but just be careful they don't stick a knife in you." Karmachov drained his glass and put it down. "Their talk of independence is ridiculous. They wouldn't know what to do with freedom, even if they had it."

"I would be happy to remind them of their heritage, Colonel."

"Do more than that, Zabrev. Get rid of those partisans. I don't care how you do it, but first, you'll have to find them."

"Don't worry, Colonel." Zabrev held up his glass. "Death to the bandits."

CHAPTER 9

Petra slogged through the fields behind the Kudirka cottage, the red ribbons on his lapel swaying from side to side. If he found Ludmelia Kudirka and reported her location, Lieutenant Zabrev might get him a job that could lead to greatness. If Petra didn't find her, he might end up with a bullet in his head.

Even from almost three kilometers away, he could smell the fresh scent of the water. It made the warm air seem cooler. Petra took the wrinkled handkerchief from his pocket and wiped his forehead.

With a little luck, things should go well, and he would get what he desired. For a start, Petra wanted Zabrev to appoint him to the Executive Committee in the Party organization for the county. The four Committee positions had been vacated during the German occupation. The leader of the Executive Committee was the Secretary, who had the most coveted position. He and the three men below him wielded the local authority of the Communist Party. Candidates for Executive Committee appointments needed to have a good reputation, and it helped to be a Communist. A person here and there who wasn't a Communist made the Executive Committee seem less threatening. Eventually, everyone would have to join the Party, though.

Petra had already joined, so he was ahead of most people. Besides, he had a fine reputation. Sure, he went to Bablia's, but the Party couldn't be interested in that. After all, a man had to relax occasionally. Once he was a member of the Executive Committee, he could work up to the top position. There, he would offer important opinions, determine who lived and died, and be loved as a great leader. It was much better to give orders than to receive them.

Maybe women wouldn't shun him anymore. All he needed was a little luck.

The best part of being a member of the Executive Committee was that it would get him a share of whatever the destroyers found during their raids: amber, vodka, pigs, cheeses, linen, furniture, and strings of homemade sausage. His stomach growled. He wouldn't abuse his position, merely take what he felt was adequate compensation. The rest would go to the needs of the Party, of course.

He didn't want to be a destroyer, though, because they worked too hard. Besides, he was small in stature, although a gun made any man big.

First, he had to find Ludie Kudirka, and that worried him. If she suspected he was behind the raid on the cottage, she might actually hurt him.

The last time he saw Ludmelia, she was swimming in the lake. He sat on a rock, mesmerized by the graceful movement of her body through the water. He waited until she got out, and stole toward the grove of trees where she was drying herself. She was naked. Her divine breasts quivered.

"Excuse me," he said as Ludmelia slipped a dress over her head. She quickly pulled it down, picked up her bathing suit, and rushed past him. He caught her arm.

"What's your hurry?" he asked.

"Mama's waiting for me at home."

He shoved her against a tree and pushed his tongue into her mouth. She bit down, and slammed her knee into his groin.

When he doubled over, Ludmelia pushed him so that he fell onto his backside. She snatched up a thick branch and hovered over him. "You disgust me. If you ever touch me again, I will kill you. If you ever talk to me again, I will kill you. Do you understand?"

"You can't talk to me like that. I'm a member of the Communist Party!" cried Petra.

Ludmelia smacked him in the legs.

"I will shoot you, beat you, and kick you, you stinking pile of filth." By the time she finished, Ludmelia's face was inches from his, and Petra was scurrying backwards like a crab.

He rolled and managed to scramble to his feet. Ludmelia swiped at him again. He ran, and she followed, swinging harder each time.

"Get away from me, you crazy bitch." Petra put his head down, stumbled forward, and ran away.

Petra made his way past downed logs and sinewy branches to the cluster of birch trees where he had seen Ludmelia's naked breasts. She wasn't there. He peered under bushes and into the decayed cavity of a tree. He kicked a pile of leaves and hit his foot on a rock.

He hopped in pain, picturing Ludmelia's face in his hands as he squeezed out her defiance. Now he was Zabrev's man, or almost. Soon, Petra's power as a member of the Executive Committee would change her attitude towards him.

He imagined her sinking to her knees. "How could I have treated you so badly, Petra Sukas?"

Petra would straighten his back and say nothing.

Ludmelia would continue. "I thought perhaps you didn't want me. My heart beats so fast when I'm near you that it frightens me. Forgive me, Petra." She would throw her arms around his legs.

Petra would smile and help her to her feet. "I forgive you, Ludie," he would say as he kissed and caressed her.

The daydream pleased him as he stepped closer to the water's edge, peering out. Mud seeped through the cracks in his shoes. He stepped up on a branch reaching out over the water. Ludmelia wasn't on the lake. No one was.

The forest was too big to search inside every cave and under every rock. If she had taken her boat, she could be anywhere. Finding Ludmelia was an impossible task. He was meant for better things. Zabrev had no right to order him about like a lackey.

Besides, it would be dark soon. He remembered his childhood fear of *baubas*, the ghosts who feasted on people wandering the woods at night. The thought of such creatures still made him uneasy. He didn't like being out in the forest alone at night. Even being near the lake after dark made him anxious, because it was where Tomas Ravas had died.

Petra climbed down from the branch, and headed for the road, where he got a ride on a cart driven by an old farmer. The clop of the horse's hooves, the slow creak of the wheels, and the sweet, comforting smell of dry hay lulled him. The pace was agonizingly slow, but at least it was better than walking.

The cart inched past wooden crosses on tall columns, some with tiny roofs protecting carvings of Jesus. The tops of some crosses had been broken off, and pictures of Stalin or Lenin had been nailed to the posts. Occasionally, Stalin's picture lay in the road under hoof prints, or in the manure, his moustache always prominent, no matter how bad the damage.

Petra considered the places he might hide from Zabrev if he didn't find Ludmelia. Hiding would be hard, for he would have to be constantly alert to soldiers, and he would have to move often. He couldn't leave the country, for there was nowhere to go. Russians occupied almost all of the territory around them, and German troops marched in the west. He could make his way north and try to get to Stockholm, but getting there would be a problem, because Russians were everywhere. And all he knew was farming, yet he couldn't bear the thought of milking another cow, or harvesting another blade of grass.

He had to stay and make the best of his situation. There were opportunities in the Party. All he had to do was find one young woman, and he'd be on his way to success.

When the cart reached the area near his hut, Petra jumped off, waved his thanks to the old farmer for giving him a ride, and headed home.

As Ludmelia lay on the tuft of grass in the bog, she dreamed of soldiers chasing her through the forest, and reaching for her with blackened hands. Branches scraped her skin. She ran faster. The soldiers were so close, she could hear them panting. A hand gripped her neck and squeezed. She startled herself awake, and was relieved to be in the bug-infested bog. The sun had already moved across the sky.

She cursed herself for not saving Mama. She could have jumped down from the attic. She might have snatched a gun from the soldiers before they realized what was happening. She could have forced them to their knees and made them apologize to Mama, before shooting them. She would have felt good about that. Instead, she had cowered like a child, inches away from Mama's torture, holding her hands over her ears so she couldn't hear the bed creak.

Ludmelia didn't want to eat, but knew that she had to keep up her strength. She nibbled cheese as tears streamed down her face. If only she had saved Mama. If only the soldiers had stayed away. If only she had been a better daughter. If only . . .

Simas hitched a ride on a truck going to the dairy processing plant in Vilkija. Although he knew the driver, he crossed his arms over his chest and pretended to sleep. After burying the old folks, the last thing he wanted to do was talk.

The driver let him off down the road from Eda's house. As Simas approached the dwelling, he hoped that she was home and her father wasn't. Simas wanted to bring Eda to a safe place, but Mikas Lankus had joined the Party, and Simas didn't want to do anything to help the man, even if he was Eda's father.

The house where Mikas Lankus lived with his daughter had a small backyard with a kitchen garden surrounded by a low fence. Simas went to the side of the house and threw a pebble against Eda's bedroom window. She didn't appear, so he threw another pebble. When nothing happened, he went to the back and squinted through the kitchen window. Eda was sitting at the table with her hands folded on her lap. She looked solemn. He was about to tap on the glass when Mikas came into view. Simas ducked. When he looked again, Mikas had passed out of sight. When Simas and Eda locked gazes, she burst into tears.

The window was open a crack and Simas could hear what they were saying.

"It's your duty to help your family," said Mikas. "This is wartime. We're an occupied country. All we have are the looks God gave you, you silly girl. Do what I tell you and stop talking about moving away. This is your home; your country."

"We had a home when Mama was alive," said Eda.

Mikas raised his hand as if he was going to slap her, but instead, he slumped into a chair. "What will you have me do? Beg in the street for food? Zabrev will take care of us if you treat him well. That means food, shelter, and clothing. It means survival. He's our only chance."

"I hate him," said Eda.

"You'll hate him more when he sends you away. And what of me? The Germans shipped us to Stutthof, and the Russians ship us to

Siberia. How long do you think I could last there? Is that what you want?"

"They're Communists. How can you stand them?" Eda covered her face with her hands.

"They're already here, and we have to learn to live with them. We have to adapt."

"We could go to Germany. Some families in town are fleeing to Germany."

"And live with the Nazis? Never!"

"Simas could help us. If we got to the Baltic, we could buy passage to Sweden."

"With what? You have money hidden away somewhere? How do you propose we get to the coast? Flap our arms and fly? My legs can barely carry me into town. Besides, do you think they'll let us go where we want just because we ask them nicely?"

"We could sell Mama's jewelry."

"Those few pieces? It wouldn't be enough. Even if we could get out, we'd be refugees. We'd be homeless. We'd have nothing. We'd have to live off the trash left by others and the pittance of charity."

Tears streamed down Eda's cheeks. "What of me? You've made me into a whore. I can't stay here with the neighbors talking about me behind my back."

Simas couldn't believe what he was hearing. Eda was his. She was going to be his bride. The sensation that his future was slipping away again hit him like a bullet.

"We have no choice but to stay, and you must learn to do what I tell you. If Mother were alive, she would know what to do with you. I thank God she's dead, so she doesn't see how you talk back to your father."

Mikas looked out the window. Simas crouched down.

"This is about survival, Eda. I don't care if you have to lay with Zabrev a hundred times. He's our best chance. Tell Simas not to come here anymore, and stop this nonsense about marrying him. I don't want Zabrev thinking you're interested in someone else."

Simas clenched his jaw. It took all his fortitude to remain silent and hidden.

A door slammed. Simas glanced around the corner as Mikas limped down the street toward Bablia's. If what Simas had heard was true, Eda's father deserved punishment, but death wasn't good enough. It would merely release the old bull from his constant struggle for food and money. Mikas deserved a beating, at least, but he would just recover and continue using Eda to get what he wanted. The only blow Simas could deliver was removing what Mikas valued the most, and yet treasured the least.

Eda held a handkerchief as she opened the back door. "I can't see you anymore."

Simas led her to a chair, and sat next to her. "Did something happen?" He couldn't look at her face.

"I can't tell you. It's awful."

He waited.

"Father whored me to Zabrev for a job." A sob escaped Eda's throat and she covered her face with her hands.

Simas thought it would have been kinder to find Eda with a bullet in her head. *Zabrev would pay for what he had done.*

"I know you can't love me anymore." Eda wiped her eyes. "My father said this is the only way we can survive. I just don't want you to hate me."

"What?"

"I don't want you to hate me."

Simas took her hand and led her up the stairs. The first door opened to a girl's room. A doll rested on a narrow bed, and the picture of a pony hung on the wall. The next door opened to a wide bed covered in a red blanket.

Maybe there was still hope. Maybe he could reclaim what was his. Maybe making love to Eda would erase Zabrev's stink from her skin. He wondered if Eda had resisted. Had she kicked him and scratched at his eyes? No. If she had, she would be dead.

He led her to the bed, and they both sat down. Simas moved to kiss her lips, but at the last second, turned his head away. He stared at her neck as he unbuttoned her blouse. It wasn't in her nature to fight. Simas moved his hands over her shoulders, easing the blouse away. Had Zabrev caressed her? Simas pulled his jacket off and lowered her to the bed.

"You still love me," said Eda, nuzzling his neck.

If they died today, Zabrev wouldn't be the last man Eda knew. Simas pulled down his pants and lifted her skirt. He put his hand on her belly, picturing Zabrev standing in the Ravas farmyard, the bloody whip in his hand, Dana bleeding from his back. He pictured the expression of terror on Gerta's face, and the anger on Bronai's face when they died. He pictured Eda in bed with Zabrev. Did she stroke Zabrev's back the way she was stroking his? Did she willingly wait with her thighs spread apart, just as she was waiting now? He pictured Zabrev sneering as he took her.

Simas thrust into Eda. *She belonged to him!*

She cried out in pain.

He thrust again, but the images didn't waver. Zabrev joined them, the delight on the Russian's face sharpening with each plunge. Simas ground his hips against Eda, and Zabrev laughed. Simas closed his eyes and thrust into her with all his weight. Someone was crying. At the next stab, Simas reached a climax that racked his spine, and even shivered his scarred leg. He rolled off Eda. She lay back like a rag doll.

"I don't blame you for being angry, but I didn't have a choice." Her breathing was uneven, her cheeks wet with tears.

"Pack a few things and let's go."

"Where?"

"The old woods across the lake."

"I'll have to tell Papa."

"You can't. There's no time."

Eda gazed at Simas, her expression full of pain. "Alright." She wiped her nose with the back of her hand as she stiffly got up. "I'll only be a minute."

CHAPTER 10

As they drove along the dusty road toward headquarters and Vilkija, Zabrev couldn't stop thinking about Ludmelia. It was silly, for he had only seen her photograph, but her silken beauty excited him, and the fact that she had eluded him thus far interested him. He pictured her long, white thighs. He swelled at the thought of her touch. He lit a cigarette and took a deep puff. When he found her, he would put her in prison, and enjoy her company for a time. Afterward, she would probably go to a labor camp in Novosibirsk, or somewhere else in Siberia, and he would find another apple to taste.

Perhaps she knew about the scrap of paper he had found in the garden. It had to be significant. If he could find the rest of the papers, information on them might get him out of this country and back to civilization.

Zabrev gazed out the window at women walking along the road, wearing long skirts and vests like their grandmothers and great-grandmothers. Next to them walked old men in dark pants, shirts, and jackets. Many slumped, as if carrying burdens on their shoulders. Only the young women were spry. Their light hair and pale coloring were like the flesh of golden apples. No young men were about, no doubt hiding to avoid conscription.

They passed cottages with steep roofs, rolling fields dotted by trees, and farmers busy with the harvesting. Tall grasses led to streams in a terrain that seemed timeless, as if it had been this way for centuries, and would be this way for centuries to come.

Occasionally, they drove by the charred carcasses of burned homes serving as stark reminders of the occupation. Chimneys crumbled around black timbers. Next to the ruined buildings, abandoned animals roamed in neglected fields, through grass so tall it hid their bellies. Soon, soldiers would find and butcher them, or families would claim them for their own.

They drove past the rocky remains of a fortress on top of a ragged hill, and Zabrev remembered Mrs. Garin, as she had slurped her second glass of tea that afternoon in Moscow. Sasha was rubbing her foot against Zabrev's leg and beaming at him, apparently pleased that her mother was talking so freely. The earthy scent of black tea filled the room.

"You're going to Vilkija?" Mrs. Garin asked. "I know that place. It's a nice town with a sugar plant, but the Germans blew it up. They have a prison."

"My headquarters will be in that prison, and I'll be running things. I was selected to go there and put things in order. I have a reputation for completing jobs that others think impossible." Zabrev smiled and sipped some tea.

"I'll tell you another story. This one is about a fortress like the one near Vilkija," Mrs. Garin said, as she filled her spoon with tea. "It's gone now, and the hill where it stood is a place for picnics. A long time ago, a Duke lived there with his three sons and their wives. One day, when the brothers were out hunting, Russians came and surrounded the fortress, putting it under siege.

"When the brothers returned, they realized their wives and families were trapped inside. They went to the people in the village and asked for help. Together, they attacked the Russians. One of the sons fought with such courage that the townspeople called him *Liubartas* for Lion, but they couldn't drive the Russians away."

"Of course. They were Russians." Zabrev smiled.

"One night, the Russians found the brothers hiding in their camp in the forest and attacked, but two of the brothers got away. The Russians captured Liubartas though, and took him back to the fortress. They put him in chains and demanded surrender, or Liubartas would die. Liubartas' wife, Egle, begged the Duke not to give in, for she said the Russians would never release her husband. The old man agreed. When the Russians heard that their demands would not be met, they tied each of Liubartas' legs to a different horse and made them run. Liubartas was ripped apart. The people got angry, and attacked so fiercely that the Russians fled. The people hounded the Russians, who found no food and no place to rest. Most of them died.

"Egle spent the rest of her life visiting places she had been with Liubartas. One night, overcome by sadness, she drowned in the lake where they used to picnic. People say even now, Egle appears under a full moon, sitting on branches hanging over the water, braiding her hair and singing to her dead husband."

Zabrev chuckled at the ridiculous idea that these people once defeated Russians. Mrs. Garin must have her facts wrong. Besides, he had access to an army that was many times bigger than any resistance the native population could possibly muster.

Zabrev snapped out of his daydream as they sped past a dairy, where two older men loaded milk cans into the back of a truck. The passed a grammar school built in the decades after the Great War. They drove past an old white church with a portrait of Jesus Christ in the stained glass window above the door. A rickety bell steeple leaned toward the back. Nearby lay a cemetery, surrounded by a decaying wall, where two old women with kerchiefs on their heads prayed over a grave.

They followed along a rock fence lined with overgrown burdocks, and passed through a wooden gate into the prison compound and headquarters. The center of the courtyard held a fountain surrounded by weeds. A wing of jail cells lay to the right, and another building containing offices and barracks commanded the left. The prison tower with its spotlight overshadowed the gate.

Guards snapped to attention as the truck ground to a halt over pebbles and cigarette butts. Zabrev suspected that some guards sat on the fountain smoking while he was away. He even suspected that some drank while on duty. A few soldiers would drink vodka for breakfast if they could. The young ones drank because they were away from their mothers for the first time in their lives. Others drank to show how tough they were. Some found it a way to cope with the war. Whatever the reason, it was a sign of bad discipline. Zabrev had punished the guards already with beatings and extra work, but there still appeared to be a problem. He would deal with that later.

He got out of the truck and went into the long, low building that housed his office, eager to get to Dana Ravas' interrogation.

When it came to the forest, Jurgis and Vadi knew it as well as their room behind Gerta's kitchen. They had found hiding places in caves and upturned roots of trees. They had created a few cramped bunkers, and had camouflaged them with moss and ferns. In the forest, the brothers could disappear like gusts of air.

It was already afternoon as they trudged through a cluster of saplings in the woods behind the Kudirka cottage. Simas had told them to watch for Russian soldiers. They also wanted to reach the Zelberg family hiding in a remote corner of the woods not far from the bog, and tell them that the Germans were gone and the Russians had returned.

The Zelbergs, a husband and wife, had lived in the ghetto in Kaunas. Their friends were dead, because they were Jews, and it was a miracle the couple had survived this long. He was a tailor and she was a cook, so the Germans had put them to work. When a violent storm hit Kaunas, the Zelbergs decided to escape. They knew they were doomed if they stayed. It was only a matter of time. As the wind blew and the rain pounded down, they squirmed through a cellar window and cut through a barbed wire fence. They walked for days, until they finally got to the rolling fields around Vilkija.

This was about the time when Gerta had sent Vadi out to the raspberry bushes near the rye field to collect berries for jam. All the fruit in one section of bushes was gone, as if someone had feasted. That evening, Vadi and Jurgis hid, waiting for the thief. Soon, the Zelbergs crept out of the bushes, and began stuffing raspberries into their mouths. The couple were filthy, and looked more wild than human. When Vadi spoke, the Zelbergs froze. Vadi tried to convince them they weren't Nazis, but the couple ran away. The next night, the brothers returned to the field and left a jar of beets from Gerta's kitchen. In the morning, it was gone. Each night for a week, the brothers left something: a blanket, a shirt, a wedge of cheese. Finally, the Zelbergs dared to stay and talk to them.

Vadi showed them a remote spot where they could live and probably not be disturbed. Once there, the couple survived on berries, roots, fish from the lake, and small animals they could ensnare. The brothers occasionally brought them a few scraps of food. Jurgis gave them a pistol he had stolen from a German foot soldier. The Zelbergs even dug a bunker to protect themselves from the elements, and hide from humanity. They told Vadi how frightened they were that strangers would tell the Nazis about them, so they hid from everyone except the brothers.

Vadi and Jurgis hadn't seen the Zelbergs since the Nazis left, and suspected that they hadn't heard the news that the Germans were gone, as it had only been a few weeks. While most families hated the Russians, the Zelbergs feared the Nazis more, and for good reason. They would think that the Russian invasion was a positive development, removing the prospect of a certain death if they were found. The brothers wanted to tell the Zelbergs that the Russians were raiding farms in the area, and were likely to sweep the forest. If the Russians found them, they would probably think they were partisans, and shoot them.

As a jaybird complained in a bush, the peace of the day disappeared into the sound of men clumsily moving through the forest. Jurgis and Vadi sank to the ground.

Tadnik emerged in the middle of a line of soldiers, each standing about five paces apart. With guns poised, they trampled ground covered with bushes, ferns, saplings, and the rotting carcasses of fallen branches. To the left, a grove of oak trees stood over scraggly firs reaching up to the sun. Far to the right lay Paunksmis Lake.

With each step, the half-crouched and frightened-looking troops straightened a fraction, looking slightly more confident that they might live a little longer.

After following the soldiers for a time, Jurgis and Vadi slipped into a foxhole they had dug under a group of bushes. The spot was big enough to accommodate even Vadi's substantial body. The soldiers were heading in the direction of the Zelbergs' bunker.

"I'd give anything if Zabrev were here right now, so I could pay him back for what he did at the farmstead, but Tadnik will have to do," Vadi whispered, raising his weapon.

"It won't bring Bronai and Gerta back. Besides, there are too many of them. Simas wants us to watch and report back. That's all," said Jurgis.

Vadi brushed his cheek with the back of his hand. "They didn't deserve to die like that."

"No one does."

"What are we going to do about the Zelbergs?"

"Pray. There's nothing else we can do, now."

Moments later came the sound of a single gunshot, and the day erupted with gunfire. Some soldiers dove for cover. Others ran. Shouts and gunshots tore through the still of the forest. The brothers pressed themselves into the earth, the gun blasts so close they couldn't help but think they were the targets.

It was over quickly. Tadnik called to his men, and they answered back. The brothers looked out from their hiding place as Tadnik made his way to a soldier sitting on the ground, blood dripping from his hand.

Another soldier crouched next to him, taking a dressing out of a backpack. After a moment, Tadnik walked to a group of soldiers standing around two bodies. He picked up a pistol off the ground and tucked it under his belt. He stared at a nearby pile of branches for a minute, and pointed at it. Two soldiers moved the pile aside and descended into a hole. Both came back a moment later, coughing. They returned to Tadnik and spoke. One soldier shook his head.

"Reform the line," said Tadnik.

The soldiers went back to their places, and resumed the sweep. Soviet boots crushed everything beneath them as they moved away.

When they were out of sight, Jurgis and Vadi left their hiding place.

Jurgis knelt beside Mrs. Zelberg, whose dark, curly hair lay across the leaves. Her chest was covered in blood. He closed her eyes. Her husband lay beside her, his long gray beard awash in blood, his lifeless arm reaching toward his wife. Vadi pointed a finger at the bunker. Putting them inside would be like burying them. Since the brothers had been too late to warn them, it was the least they could do, but they would have to wait until the Russians left the forest.

The brothers went back to their job of following the soldiers. At the bog, the soldiers turned and took another path back through the forest.

When the Russians had driven off in their trucks, Vadi and Jurgis went back to the Zelberg's bunker. It was almost indistinguishable from the forest floor, except for the opening disguised by the branches that Tadnik's soldiers had moved aside. Jurgis and Vadi climbed down a crude ladder. They crawled through an opening into a tiny room, too small for even Jurgis to stand up straight. The stench of earth and sweat hit them both. It took a moment for their eyes to adjust to the darkness. The room had shelves on opposite walls. Two were covered in blankets. The roof and walls were fortified with wood cut from narrow trees. A small pile of potatoes lay on another shelf, neatly stacked in a sort of shrine, away from the leaves and dirt that covered everything else. A stove cobbled together from spare parts and a chimney made of tin cans stood in the corner. A pile of kindling lay in another corner.

Jurgis moved a square piece of wood leaning against one wall and recoiled at the stink of shit. He put a handkerchief to his nose. The family had released their bowels inside the hole where they ate and slept, so pursuers couldn't find their waste.

The men left the filthy hovel and gulped fresh air. Jurgis took off his cap and slapped it against his leg, as if dispelling the horrible scent.

Vadi carried the bodies one at a time down the ladder. Jurgis pulled them into the hovel and lay them on the shelves. Inside, the brothers knelt and crossed themselves, for it was all they knew to do. They put the potatoes in their pockets and climbed out, leaving the Zelbergs in the hole that was their home in life, as it had become their home in death.

CHAPTER 11

Dana tried moving his arms, but they were tied to a wooden chair. He sat across from a large desk that looked like it belonged in an accountant's office. Light from a single bulb shone overhead. He smelled blood, probably his own, and a stink that he realized was stale piss.

He still couldn't believe this was happening to *him*. His heart thudded in expectation of the unknown tortures he was about to receive. His head pounded, and his back stung from the whipping.

Zabrev sat behind the desk as one of the guards asked the questions: *What is your name? Where do you live? What do you do for a living? Where did you go to school? What do you partisans call yourselves? Are you one of them?*

Two more guards stood behind Dana as he mumbled his answers. He told them what he knew, which was nothing. Still, they hit him. Blood dripped from Dana's mouth and nose. His forehead was wet with sweat. His head fell to his chest. *He had to convince them he didn't know anything.*

Zabrev held up a sheet of paper and read off a name.

"Of course, I know him. He lives in town." *Maybe he should make up a story.*

A guard hit him in the mouth. Dana wiggled the loose tooth with his tongue.

Zabrev pulled out a decayed scrap of paper from his shirt pocket. "Do you know anyone with the name of Vargas?"

"No." Dana shook his head at the mention of his one-eyed farmhand. *Vargas was a common name. It couldn't be Simas.* Dana

75

remembered the times when Simas, his father, and Victor Kudirka had huddled in secrecy over the kitchen table. He couldn't imagine they were discussing anything important. Now, he wasn't sure.

Zabrev put the paper away. "Where were you on June 23, 1941?"

"It was summer, so I must have been out in the fields." Dana thought of Vadi and Jurgis working together and talking quietly, only to stop entirely when Dana came within earshot. Dana had assumed they were talking about *him*.

A guard hit him in the mouth.

"I was at university in Vilnius, but left in 1941. I wanted to be a lawyer, but my father needed help on the farm," said Dana.

"I don't believe you. I think you left the city to avoid conscription into the Red Army. You hid among your cows so we wouldn't find you."

"My father was getting old. His foreman was getting old. I had to go home." He remembered the times Simas had come to breakfast, looking tired and disheveled, and with mud on his shoes, as if he had been up all night walking around in the woods.

"We were taking all the young men, and you fled to the country. You avoided the army like the rest of your stinking brethren. You people are such cowards."

"Why should we fight for you? You're invaders, just like the Nazis." Dana regretted the words as soon as he had spoken them.

Zabrev nodded to the guard who delivered more blows. Dana groaned.

Zabrev stood in front of Dana, and bent down so their faces were inches apart, in odd familiarity.

"So you'll join the Red Army now?"

Dana hesitated.

"I know you're with the Freedom Fighters."

"Who?" The secrecy, and the long nights away from the farm all fit, but Dana wasn't sure. Besides, his father wouldn't keep such a secret from him. They all had to be innocent. They weren't partisans. They were just farmhands, so there would be no harm in telling. It might stop the beating.

"The partisans, Freedom Fighters, Brothers of the Forest. They're all just criminals." Zabrev returned to his chair behind the desk, and nodded to the guard, who pulled out a pistol and showed it to Dana.

Zabrev leaned back and smiled as if he was about to enjoy a theatre performance. "By the way, your parents will be in here next."

Dana's eyes opened wide. *They're alive.*

Zabrev shrugged his shoulders. "If you talk, maybe I'll let them go."

"If you let them go, I'll talk."

The guard hit Dana in the mouth.

"You don't make demands," said Zabrev.

"Let me see them."

Zabrev nodded to the guard.

Dana gripped the arm of the chair and braced himself for the impact of the bullet. "Why are you doing this?"

"Because I can."

"If you're going to shoot me, make it quick."

Instead of firing, the guard gripped Dana's right arm. Dana strained against the rope, twisting his wrist and fluttering his fingers. As they struggled, the chair scraped against the floor. The guard, pressing down on Dana's forearm and steadying it, slammed the butt of the gun down on Dana's hand. Dana moaned at the crunch of his bones. The room went quiet as he passed out.

"Maybe in the morning, you'll talk about something other than your damn cows," said Zabrev. He motioned the guard to drag Dana to a cell.

Eda was wearing three skirts, two blouses, a vest, an extra pair of stockings, and several undergarments. She wore the clothes to avoid carrying a suitcase, for she didn't want to raise suspicions from onlookers, who might ask where she was going.

Simas walked next to her, holding the handle of a picnic basket. They had already reached the outskirts of Vilkija.

"Stop looking over your shoulder," he said.

Eda's gaze went to the ground. "Why are we going to the old forest?"

"It's someplace safe."

They walked in silence until the driver of a wagon pulled by a donkey came to a stop beside them and offered them a ride. Simas moved a crate of chickens to the side, climbed in, and sat down. Eda climbed in and sat beside him.

Simas didn't speak, or even look at her. Eda wondered how long he would stay angry. Her stomach churned and she put her hand over it. She felt drained. After what had just happened in her father's bed, she wasn't sure whether Simas still wanted her or not. She glanced at his expressionless face and imagined how terrible her life would be without him. As her body swayed to the motion of the wagon over the rough road, she tried to pretend that her encounter with Zabrev had been a bad dream.

They got off the wagon near Kazys Espertus' pig farm, and walked down a short dirt road past a hillock, to a yard surrounded by a small house, a barn, a rickety smokehouse, and a large pigpen with a shed next to it. An old truck was parked next to the barn. A broken hoe, slats from a barrel, and bits of straw littered the yard. Weeds grew along the side of the pen, and near the house. The air smelled of a sour and repulsive stench from the pigs. Eda breathed through her mouth to avoid gagging.

Long-time neighbors to the Ravas family, Kazys and his son lived as bachelors ever since Kazys' wife had died a few years ago. Everyone in Vilkija said that Kazys was a genius at raising pigs, and lived like one.

Simas went up to the back door of the house and knocked. Sows grunted in the nearby pen, and their piglets squealed. He knocked again, and after a minute entered the house. Eda stayed on the doorstep.

He soon emerged, crossed the yard, and went into the barn.

"No one's home," he said, returning to Eda.

Eda picked up the picnic basket and followed him as he went back toward the barn. "Maybe he went to Kaunas. I heard his son was there recovering from breaking his leg when he fell off the roof."

"Kazys would never leave his pigs."

"Why do you want to see him?"

"I need to talk to him. We'll wait here until dark. If he doesn't come home, we'll borrow his boat and cross the lake."

"Why don't we go now?"

"The patrol boat can see us in daylight. It's safer at night, after the boat comes in from its rounds." Simas opened the barn door and waited for Eda to pass through. He took an uneasy last look around before going inside and closing it.

Impatient to get to her destination, Ludmelia had her oars in the water as soon as it was dark. As she pulled, the breeze on her face relieved the stifling heat of the bog. She had only managed a restless nap during the day, her mind still churning with the events of the last twenty-four hours.

Ludmelia's body fluidly contracted and relaxed as the boat glided forward. Her gaze constantly moved between the faraway area of the cove where the patrol boat was docked, and the old forest where she was going.

She felt a knot in her stomach, wondering if the Russians had come to the cottage because of Papa's pamphlets, or for some other reason. She couldn't imagine what it might be. Ludmelia forced the thoughts away. Papa would have told her not to worry about things she couldn't control. He would have wanted her to focus on the important task of crossing the lake.

Ludmelia thought about the old forest, where she would be safe. There were caves, clearings, streams, and wonderful old trees that made day seem like dusk, and dusk seem like night. She and Mama knew it well, for they went there to collect *grybi*, the mushrooms they loved to eat. They had many picnics of bread and sausage under the fir trees. By rowing directly across, they could spend most of the day there, and be back before nightfall. But that was before the patrol boat went after anyone on the lake.

When the moon appeared, Ludmelia said a prayer for good health. As fatigue set in, the painful memory of Mama's cries and that awful gunshot echoed in her mind. She had been an ungrateful daughter, telling Mama she wished she had never been born. She wished she had told Mama how much she loved her. Ludmelia wanted to slip into the water and disappear. No one would notice she was gone. It would be easy to swim until she couldn't swim anymore. Finally she would be with Mama and her big brother Matas.

She longed for Papa's comforting advice, and could almost hear him. *Stay near the reeds where they can't see you.* She was so scared she could barely breathe. *Be calm.* She was all alone in the world. *I'll always be with you. All you have to do is think of me.*

Papa had been gone for three years, and Ludmelia didn't know whether to hope he was alive, and risk a shattering sadness in learning of his death, or to mourn him and lose faith in his survival.

Ludmelia scanned the nearby shoreline for soldiers, but couldn't see any distinct shapes against the dark of the trees. She jumped when a fish snatched a bug on the surface of the lake.

Far away, an engine growled, and a cone of light shone across the water. Ludmelia froze. The light came closer. If she kept rowing, they might see her. *You know what you need to do,* came Papa's voice. Ludmelia backed the rowboat into some bushes near the shore. Twigs scratched her skin and yanked her hair. The light came right toward her. She forced the little craft farther into the undergrowth, pulling until she couldn't pull anymore. The light flashed across the reeds where she had just been. She had no place else to go, except into the water, where they would look until they found her. She took out the pistol and aimed at soldiers she couldn't see. *At least she wouldn't be the only one to die tonight.* As if hearing her thoughts, the light turned away, and the boat went in another direction.

It seemed that hours had passed before the engine went silent, and the searchlight went dark. Ludmelia pushed off into the open water. The tiny splash of her oars made it sound as if the lake were whispering to her, encouraging her on.

Her body ached, but she rowed with all the energy she had, trying to reach the old forest by daybreak, one grueling stroke at a time.

CHAPTER 12

As Zabrev smoked, the setting sun tinted everything inside his office with an odd pink light. The horn of the old gramophone on top of the bookcase glowed. The light fell across the bound volume of Pushkin's poetry. It brightened a wrinkled score of Donizetti's *L'elisir d'amore* on the top shelf, the single remaining memory of his one youthful operatic performance. He had a wonderful voice. Some had called it magnificent. But Russia needed men like him, so he had followed his father's footsteps into the army. Sometimes he played a record, sang along, and languished in imagined applause.

Across from the file cabinet stood a table covered with useless maps, none of them containing the detail he needed of the forests. *He couldn't even get good maps here.* Through the window, Zabrev could see the fountain, the barracks, and the low building containing the jail cells, the interrogation room, and his prisoners.

He looked up at a knock on his door. "Come."

Tadnik entered, and stood at attention as he always did, sporting a look of seasoned strength.

"Yes?"

Tadnik stared straight ahead. "Good news, Comrade Commander. We found two partisans, a man and a woman."

Zabrev grunted. *Finally, some progress. He wondered if Tadnik was more of a soldier than he thought.* "Where are they?"

Tadnik paused. "We left them in the forest. They're dead."

"I told you to take any partisans alive."

"They were waiting in ambush, and fired on us. We didn't know how many there were, and the men fired back before I could stop them. One man was slightly wounded. Here is the pistol I recovered." Tadnik lay the weapon on Zabrev's desk.

Zabrev picked up the gun, a Luger, admiring the feel of it in his hand. He aimed it at the window and slowly swept it across the room. Tadnik didn't even flinch. Zabrev grunted again and put the gun down. *Two dead partisans was progress.* "You were supposed to find Ludmelia Kudirka."

"She wasn't there."

Zabrev took a long puff of the cigarette and let the smoke out slowly. "Tell me about the pig farmer who owns the place near the Ravas farmstead."

"Kazys Espertus. The interrogation went well. When Espertus heard we had brought his son here from Kaunas and had locked him up, he was eager to talk. He said the partisans came by regularly for food."

"Did he mention any of them by name?"

"He said he doesn't know who they are. Only two come at a time. They should be by for some food in another day or so."

"Is he lying to protect them?"

"Of course, Comrade Commander. But he'll tell us soon. He won't risk hurting his son."

"What of his wife?"

"Dead."

"Good. Release him, and tell him to butcher one of his precious pigs and let the word out. Send a squad of men there to hide. When the partisans arrive, spring the trap. This time, make sure they bring back a few alive. Meanwhile, I need you to get me some good maps. The ones I have aren't worth shit."

"Yes, Comrade Commander."

"When it's done, tell them to shoot Espertus. No one supports those bastards and lives."

Tadnik turned crisply on his heels and left the room.

At least two partisans were dead. But despite the interrogations, no one had told Zabrev the location of the partisan camp. Perhaps no one knew where it was, except the partisans themselves. He had to find at least one live bandit, and then he would have his information. One good tip could change things. That was all he needed.

In his hazy dream, Dana was standing in the interrogation room, pressing Zabrev's head down on the oversized desk, and swinging at his neck with a hatchet. Blood poured out. Dana kept hacking, but the Comrade Commander's head wouldn't fall off.

Dana jerked awake and groaned at pain that seemed to radiate from every part of his body. His throat ached from thirst, and his hand throbbed. His back burned like it was on fire. He was lying on something hard. He moved the fingers of his good hand over smooth dampness. From a window high up on the wall, moonlight filtered in through the bars. The room was small, and the air was unbearably stuffy. A cot stood against one wall, and there was a waste pail in the corner.

Dana arched his back at the pain. He remembered the whip, the interrogation room, the strange intimacy from Zabrev's face lingering inches from his, the interminable questions, the blows, the lights in his eyes, and the agony from his injured hand.

He wondered if his parents would survive the interrogation that was probably going on right now. His family was in danger because of him. The stark realization that he hadn't moved them away months ago hit him like a speeding train.

He had let his parents stay while the country crumbled around them, thinking he was immune to the plague of war. He had decided that the stories of brutality were exaggerated, and he would be spared just because he was Dana Ravas.

Of course, his parents wouldn't have wanted to leave. They had built the farm together, and it was their home. Instead of making them go, Dana had just ignored the Russians. He was too busy ordering the farmhands about to consider what might happen. He was too busy telling others that he owned the largest farm in Vilkija to believe that the Russians might take it away from him. He was too busy being angry with them for destroying his dream of practicing law to ever imagine they would go so far.

The raid had been inevitable, and he was stupid for not realizing it. Now it was too late.

Simas, Jurgis, and Vadi hadn't come in from the fields during the raid, saving their own lives instead of helping his parents. They didn't care. Nobody cared.

He didn't know anything about any damned partisans. People in town said they hid in the forest, and sometimes even in the open, melting into households as a brother, a cousin, or a friend. People disappeared for a while, saying they had gone to Vilnius to find work, but had come back saying there were no jobs. Some farmhands drifted from farmstead to farmstead looking for work. Maybe they were all partisans.

He had his suspicions about his farmhands, but they couldn't be partisans. One-eyed Simas was already slowing down, and his limp was getting worse. Vadi and Jurgis spent every free minute in the woods hunting, although they didn't always come back with something.

The farm was gone. The life he knew was over. The future was a stark unknown. Even survival was a question. He didn't think he could live through another round of beatings. He had to try to save his parents and himself, for no one else would.

He would tell Zabrev his suspicions about Simas and the others to save his own life. Zabrev would bring them in and interrogate them, but Zabrev would have to let them go, because they were just farmhands. Then they would all be safe.

All Dana had to do was talk.

Alone in his office, Zabrev thought about all the farmers he had interrogated this past week. Their refusal to cooperate had brought them pain, and for some, death. He had even let a few go, for they were simpletons and knew nothing.

From the way Ravas had spoken, it was clear that he had some education. He worked on a farm, but that quiet type of life wasn't likely to satisfy such a man for long. His defiance at the water pump showed pride and independence. Zabrev felt confident he could beat that out of him. Young people like Ravas tended to be arrogant, and think they were invincible. When they realized they weren't, they usually chattered like frightened schoolchildren.

Zabrev was sure Ravas knew about the Freedom Fighters, and probably had met some of its leaders. After all, he lived near the forests.

They had stolen guns from the soldiers, and had even used stolen uniforms as disguises. Zabrev had sent his men to look for strongholds where weapons might be stored. They had gone through barns, houses, sheds, chicken coops, and outhouses, but had found nothing. Men and guns can't just disappear. They had to be in the vast old forest or in the bog, the only places he hadn't searched. The bog was unlikely, because there was no dry ground. At least that's what the locals had said. But with these people, the unlikely was probable.

Zabrev would find the Freedom Fighters and make examples of them, no matter where they were. He would put an end to this nonsense.

He lit a cigarette, and pulled out the scrap of paper from his pocket. He had to find the man named Vargas, and learn why his name was on a list that had been buried in the Kudirka garden.

He put the paper back behind Ludmelia's photograph, thinking it funny that he had a photograph of a local girl in his pocket, but none of Sasha. He had made love to Sasha dozens of times. She loved anyone who provided her with food, clothing, and access to the social activities in Moscow. She would marry the man who took care of her the best. Years from now, he might see her walking along Tverskaya Street, clinging to another man's arm. She would smile, he would nod, and that would be all. He would save Gerta Ravas' amber brooch for someone else. If he married, it would be to a virgin. He would go no further with Sasha, especially since her mother was one of *these* people.

The piece of amber would stay hidden in the box beneath his papers in the bottom drawer of his desk, until he needed it.

Ludmelia though, was deliciously elusive. He was sure she would be wanton in bed, eventually. He would teach her to be. His stomach twitched as he considered the possibility that Ludmelia was a partisan, too. If she escaped to Kaunas, or went farther south to Vilnius, it would be difficult to find her. Many people lived there, and it would be easy for her to hide.

The thought of the old city brought to mind Mrs. Garin and another one of her damn stories. She had told him that long ago, Grand Duke Gediminas had been hunting in the forest near the River Vilnia. When night came, he fell asleep near a large rock at the base of a hill. The Grand Duke dreamt that a wolf clad in iron appeared on the hill and howled so loudly that the trees shook. In the morning, Gediminas returned to his castle and asked his advisors what the dream meant. No one knew, so the Duke sought the advice of the highest religious authority in all the land, who said the Duke would build a powerful fortress on that hill. It would become a city known throughout the world. Grand Duke Gediminas built the fortress that became the city of Vilnius.

"Our ancestors were like wolves and so are we," Mrs. Garin had said at the end of the story. "Fear the wolf."

What nonsense, thought Zabrev as he ground the cigarette into the ashtray.

CHAPTER 13

Ludmelia's head pounded from exhaustion as she pulled the oars through the water, gliding closer to the old forest with every stroke. She closed her eyes to the image of Mama stumbling to the cellar in the dark. "In here, Ludmelia," she called, opening the door. The room was jammed full of potatoes and crocks of *kopusta*. There was no place to hide, so Mama ran to the lake. Soldiers jumped out from behind the trees and shot her. Instead of falling, she floated up into the sky. Stretching her arms down, Mama said, "Come with me, Ludmelia. Give me your hand." Ludmelia reached up, but her fingers closed on thin air.

Ludmelia opened her eyes with a start. The forest was upon her. *Be careful,* came Papa's voice. Ludmelia pictured him smiling, for he always smiled at her. *Find a place where you can hide the boat.* His voice rang clear, and she was happy to remember him so crisply. She twisted around to the sacks of provisions, but Papa wasn't there.

The sky was brightening with the dawn as she veered away from the little beach and its tempting landing spot free of reeds. She pulled hard through tall grass, searching for a place to hide. Her shoulders burned, but being this close to the old forest fortified her, and already she felt safer. At a swampy area covered by overhanging branches, she secured the boat to a tree. She put the compass and blanket into her knapsack, along with the bread and cheese. She stepped out of the boat onto muddy ground.

As her footprints filled in with water, she noticed small pools in the shape of paw prints. *Wolves?* She shrank back, and looked around. *Don't be frightened, Ludmelia.* She smiled at Papa's voice, and thought back to a time he had taken her camping deep in the woods. She had just been an excited young girl, thrilled to be spending some time in the wild.

In the middle of a night glittering with stars, Ludmelia had woken up to see an animal the shape of a large dog, standing not five meters away. She didn't move. The animal came closer. Its bountiful fur and eyes that shone like jewels entranced her. "Papa, look," she whispered. By the time he reached for his gun, the animal had vanished. After that, Papa called her his wolf pup. He said the wolves knew there was something special about her, but Ludmelia thought he just didn't want her to be scared.

If Papa were still alive, there was hope they'd be together again someday. It was her nightmare that he would return to the house in Kaunas and find it deserted. She couldn't bear the thought of him searching through the streets, wondering if they were alive or dead. Mama had said he'd come right to their cottage in Vilkija, for that was the plan. But Mama was dead, and Ludmelia couldn't go back to the cottage. Still, Papa would search until he found her, no matter where she was, even if it took forever.

Though Papa fought best with a pen, he also knew the forest well and could use a gun. He was a warrior. She could be a warrior, too. Maybe she could find the partisans he wrote about in his pamphlets, and join them. At least she wouldn't be alone anymore.

Ludmelia threaded her arms through the knapsack's straps, threw the blanket over her shoulder, and headed for a hiding spot she knew would be good. It was a sea of ferns surrounding the ancient trees, just beyond an area of deep undergrowth, not far from the shore. Her permanent camp would be farther away, up the ridge and past a stream, to a small cave a kilometer to the east. Mama had found the best mushrooms there. Sometimes Mama had gotten on her hands and knees to examine the caps and stems to make sure they weren't poisonous. Sometimes she had cut into one with her knife to see the flesh before deciding whether to keep it or throw it away. Mama had said that picking mushrooms was like life. If you didn't make the right decisions, you might end up dead.

Ludmelia's stomach growled. She could almost smell the sweet, meaty scent of mushrooms, onions, and bacon cooking. She imagined dipping chunks of brown bread into the warm bacon fat and eating that, too, but there would be no mushrooms and bacon today.

Ludmelia passed little fir trees trying to grow in the shadow of their taller brothers. Her feet sank into the matted undergrowth, every step giving off the fragrance of leaves, and the glorious smell of the earth. Underneath, like a subtle ingredient in a complex stew, hung the sweet scent of pine.

She walked into a web of larger trees, stepping around the massive trunks of fallen oaks, and ducking under low branches spread out like welcoming arms. Heavy leaves glowed in the dim light, distracting her with their beauty. The old ones believed the woods were sacred, because of the spirits there. Ludmelia just thought it was a beautiful place. When she was a girl, the trees had reminded her of children's candy: giant sugary confections on wooden sticks. The memory made her heart feel lighter.

Ludmelia had the sensation of escaping to something familiar, and she already felt like a creature of the forest. She knew the area, but exhaustion made her slow down. *Keep going until you find a safe place to rest,* urged Papa. Ludmelia picked a careful path through the tangled growth, for a slip might mean a sprained ankle or worse. She remembered a young woman who had gone berry picking and had never come home. They had found her body next to an ash tree, with dried blood on her head, a fractured leg, and her foot trapped under a vine.

Light shone from behind the trees, although the sky overhead was still dark. She wanted to lie on the ground and sleep. *One more step.* Papa's voice rang clear. *Just one more step.* She grasped at branches, pulling herself forward. Mama and Matas were dead. Even if Papa were alive, there had been no word from him in years. She was alone. There was no reason to go on. There was no one left who cared if she lived. But she had to live, and kill the men who had hurt Mama. Ludmelia thought back to the cottage, and the names Denis and Uri. She thought of the soldier with the beautiful voice that had brought a chill to her heart. When she killed them, she would dip her hands in their stinking blood and rub it over her face to wash away the hatred. She didn't know how to find them, though. She didn't even know what they looked like. Maybe the partisans could help. Spilling Soviet blood would be good. Killing even one damn Russian would make her feel better. She was sure of it.

Keep going, girl. Ludmelia inched forward to the thought of Papa's hands stretched out to help. Heaving herself along, she yearned to go back to the little cottage. The soldiers would have finished their search for her by now. If she used the stove only at night, no one would see the smoke. She could hide there forever. Ludmelia chuckled. She could live in her own house for the rest of the war, and the soldiers would piss all over the countryside looking for her. Mama would laugh at the idea of her hiding at home, right under the Red Bear's nose.

Ludmelia pinched herself. It wasn't good to think of such things. She couldn't go home. She had promised Mama she wouldn't. It did no good longing for what she couldn't have. It wasn't part of the plan. The forest was her home now.

Before the sky became a shade brighter, she found her ferns. She carefully stepped through them to an oak tree with low branches. Ludmelia sat and ate some bread. After wrapping the blanket around her body, she lay down. The breeze through the leaves sounded like the whispers of lost friends.

Rest well, little wolf. I'm here with you. Papa's words comforted her. *Know where your things are. Have a weapon with you at all times.* She rummaged through the knapsack until she found Papa's pistol, and placed it at her side. *Two weapons are better than one.* She tucked the knife in her boot. Picturing his face, she closed her eyes and tried to sleep.

Well before dawn, Simas got out of his hammock in the partisan camp deep within the old forest. He put on his shoes and donned his gear: a German Mauser, a Soviet Tokarev pistol, grenades, and a pair of binoculars. He stiffly limped toward the nicest tent in the camp.

"Eda," he whispered. He listened for a moment before opening the flap. A blanket covered a bed of moss and leaves, next to a small pile of clothing neatly folded on top of a picnic basket. No one was inside.

His first thought was that Eda had run away, choosing the unknown rather than staying with him after the violence of their last lovemaking. But the sentries would have stopped her, and they would have woken him up.

The people at camp already knew Eda from town, and her frequent visits to the Ravas farmstead. They had invariably stopped by to see Simas on the pretext of a social visit, but really to talk about partisan business. They knew that he and Eda were going to get married. Simas winced at the thought that they probably knew about

Zabrev and Eda in Bablia's back room, for news traveled as fast as bullets, especially bad news.

They wouldn't know he couldn't bear to kiss her lips, or even look at her face anymore. They wouldn't know the stink he imagined every time he was near her. They wouldn't know how hopeless he felt, now that his feelings for Eda were gone and probably wouldn't return with Zabrev's death, or hers, or even his own.

What Mikas had done wasn't Eda's fault, but rational thought didn't matter. Simas was angry. He had already punished Mikas by taking Eda away from him. He needed to punish Zabrev. He wanted to punish Eda, too.

Even in the discipline of camp, people would guess at the anger and shame that filled every pore of Simas' body, and whisper about it behind his back. They'd wonder if he and Eda would stay together. They'd wonder if he'd hunt Zabrev and make him pay. He couldn't bear the thought of them talking about him. He couldn't bear that anyone knew that his love had been with a Russian. The chatter would erode his authority, and that might put them all in danger.

For everyone's sake, he had to pretend that things were fine now, and that he was still in love with Eda. He just didn't know how long he could do it.

The Bolsheviks had shattered his first love, and now that Russian Zabrev had destroyed his new love. It was happening all over again. The anger that had been simmering in his stomach for twenty years came to a full boil as he pictured Eda under the Russian.

Simas' thoughts were tearing his heart to shreds. He took a drink from his flask, and scanned the camp. Tall trees stood like towers next to camouflaged tents and barely-visible lean-tos made of intertwined branches and moss. Towels and guns hung from tree branches. Hammocks swayed between birch trees near the perimeter, their occupants sound asleep. The men lucky enough to have them preferred them for the comfort, and because they could be easily moved if the need arose.

He gazed at the cook tent where Raminta was tending a fire under a metal sheet protecting it from view. A large pot hung over the flame. Nearby, Eda was setting out cups on a rough-hewn table.

Eda's figure was slim and elegant as she worked, her white hair casting her countenance in a crown of innocence, but it was an illusion. Innocent Eda was gone.

Her simple act of lining up the cups brought him back to the last time he had gone to the Lankus' house for supper. Eda had leaned over the kitchen table the same way, gracefully setting glasses down and pouring vodka into them as Mikas stared at Simas.

Mikas downed his glass before saying that Communism would be good for the country. *The damned fool,* thought Simas.

"Don't misunderstand me," Mikas said, pouring more vodka. "I love my country. Communism is an economic matter, and I support the basic idea that all property is owned in common. Don't you?"

"The Ravas family worked hard for everything they own. Why should they give up their farm just because someone tells them to?"

"You're just a farmhand. When you can't work any longer, you'll have nothing. The Ravas' won't take care of you. No woman would marry you with that leg." Mikas glanced at Eda, and finished his drink. "But under Stalin, you'll live well. That is what he is trying to do; make it so everyone can live well."

"Communism is a bitter brew fit only for Russian stomachs. How can anyone who feels love for their homeland and pride in what they do accept this twisted ideology? Stalin's army kills our men and rapes our women, under a flag that's supposed to symbolize the common good of the worker, but it's just a damn bloody flag." Simas rose to his feet. "And I'll still be working long after you're in your grave."

Eda touched his arm. It felt like a soft breeze. "We're here for dinner, not for a political discussion," she said, looking paler than usual. Simas sat back down.

Mikas glared at his daughter. "I don't want you telling me what to talk about. I'm your father. I deserve respect. I will tell *you* what to do. *I* make the decisions in this family."

Eda turned her back as Simas swallowed a mouthful of vodka to keep from telling Mikas that he didn't deserve to have a daughter as gentle and beautiful as Eda. But for Eda's sake, Simas took a breath and asked, "What are we eating?"

"Kugelis." Eda explained how she had grated the raw potatoes, added bacon, eggs, and salt, and baked it. "The worse it tastes before it's cooked, the better it tastes when it's out of the oven. And this batch tasted terrible."

She took out the *kugelis* from the oven and put it on the table. Simas watched her while they ate, thinking how wonderful it would be to wake up next to her every morning.

His thoughts returned to the present. Now, he couldn't even bear to look at her.

Eda looked up as Simas approached the camp table. She gazed at him with soft eyes. Disobedient strands of her hair glowed like silver shavings. She hesitated for a moment before throwing her arms around his neck and kissing him. *"Labas,"* she said.

Simas pulled her hands down and picked up a cup. Eda blushed as she ladled some chicory coffee into it.

"I'm worried about Father," said Eda. "Is there anything you can do for him?"

Simas scowled. He put the cup to his lips and swallowed his contempt.

"I just want to make sure he has enough food. He's the only family I have," said Eda.

Sometimes family is one's heaviest burden, thought Simas. "These people at camp are your family now. Forget about your father."

"Maybe you're right." Eda brushed the tears from her cheeks and went into the cook tent.

Petra Sukas woke in his shack as the first rays of dawn filtered in through the cracks in the wall. He reached for the vodka, but the bottle was too far away. His hand dropped to the floor. He cursed the birds for chattering outside, aggravating the throb in his head. He stood and righted the chair next to the table. In bare feet, he opened the door, staggered out, and urinated into the weeds. He stepped back inside to the wood stove, poured the remains of yesterday's tea into a cup, and drank it cold.

He walked to the plow standing in a corner. Clumps of dirt clung to the blades, reminding him of the hours he had spent in the fields. But he was through working as a farmhand. His future was with the Party. Yet, if he didn't prove himself useful and find Ludmelia Kudirka, Zabrev might actually kill him. Petra felt like a trapped rat. He put on the clothes he wore yesterday: the shirt with dirt stains around the collar, trousers, and the jacket with red ribbons hanging from the lapel. When Zabrev appointed him to the Executive Committee, he would need a new suit. For now, he would manage with the one he had, for he had nothing else to wear, other than work clothes. The job at the Ravas farmstead got him food, the hut he lived in, and the vodka he bought at Bablia's, where he cavorted with other

Party members. It wasn't much of a life, but the Party had power, and would improve his station more than milking cows ever could. For years, he had sweated from dawn until dusk in the fields and the barn before walking home to his shack, while Dana lived in comfort in the farmhouse.

Petra chuckled, remembering the smoke he had seen rising above the treetops the day of the raid on the Ravas farmstead. The destroyers probably took everything they could carry off, as they always did, and burned a building or two to show their power. Now Dana would know what it was like to be poor, if he survived his interrogation. A position on the Executive Committee might get Petra a farmstead, even a wife. Maybe he'd hire Dana to sweat in *his* fields one day.

Petra sat on the bed and reached for his shoes. He remembered living in the Ravas farmhouse long ago, in the room off the kitchen. He had eaten his meals with the family. Petra's father and Bronai Rivas drank vodka in the sitting room after supper on Saturday nights. Sometimes, on warm summer afternoons, Petra, Dana, and Dana's little brother, Tomas, played together outside. Bronai had said that Petra would always have a home in the farmhouse, and he'd treat Petra like a son if anything ever happened to his father.

When Petra was twelve, everything changed. It was a warm summer day, and a rain shower had brought them in from the fields. When the sun came out, they had to wait for the ground to dry, so Petra's father, Isaac, took the boys on an impromptu excursion to Paunksmis Lake. The boys fished but caught nothing, and when they got bored, they asked to go swimming. Isaac said Tomas could go too, even though he was little, and like Petra, really didn't know how to swim.

As soon as the boys entered the water, Isaac found a place to lay down and take a nap.

Petra remembered the excitement of being in the lake, convinced he could keep up with Dana, who was bigger and stronger, although several years younger. They were a good distance from the shore when Dana stopped swimming and asked where Tomas was. Petra squirmed around, kicking hard to keep afloat. He couldn't see the little boy anywhere. "Tomas!" yelled Petra, as Dana dove under the surface. Realizing he was alone, Petra began to panic. He splashed frantically. Water hit his face. He gulped air. He glanced at the shore where his father lay sleeping, and screamed, *"Teti!"*

Isaac stood, moved toward the water, and stumbled. He got up, threw off his jacket, and fell again. He splashed into the water, kicking up foam as he swam.

When Dana came up for air, he had a look of terror on his face. Before Dana dove back down, Petra calmed a little, took a deep breath, and put his head in the water. He closed his eyes so there was no possibility of seeing Tomas' dead face, as he had to be dead by now. Petra was so scared he thought his heart was going to burst. He shivered at the thought of the dead body floating near him. Reeds touched his legs. He opened his mouth to scream, and water rushed in. Petra lifted his head and coughed as *Teti* reached him. Dana broke the surface. Petra put his face back in the water as the other two gulped air and dove down. Petra waited with his eyes closed for as long as he could before lifting his head for another breath of air.

Isaac eventually told Dana to stop searching. Dana cried as they swam back to shore, leaving Tomas behind. Petra wanted to cry, but he was too busy swimming as fast as he could to keep up.

Isaac followed the boys back to the farmstead. Their hair still damp from the lake, Dana and Petra sat on the front steps of the farmhouse, while Isaac went inside to tell Bronai that Tomas was dead. Soon, the boys heard shouting.

"I loved you like a brother, and you killed my son. Why didn't you stay with him? You knew he couldn't swim," yelled Bronai. "You still have a job here only because of the boy. I want you out of my house. You can live in the shack in the forest, with the other wild creatures that have no regard for human life."

Petra stared at his hands as the door creaked open, and his father came outside with Bronai.

"When you meet God, may He have mercy on your soul." Bronai beckoned Dana and they both went into the house, leaving Petra and his father alone on the porch.

Petra and his father moved into the hut that day. The place was old and dirty, but had a bed, stove, and a table. They hung the little clothing they had on the spare plow in the corner.

The next day, Petra sneaked back to the farm and hid in the barn, not knowing if he was welcome anymore. He just didn't want to be alone with *Teti,* who had spent the night in a chair, staring at the wall. When a group of men from Vilkija carried Tomas' body back to the farmstead, Petra watched from a crack in the barn door. Tomas seemed smaller than ever. His face was the color of ashes. Ever since, whenever Petra had a bad dream, it ended with Tomas dragging him down to the bottom of Paunksmis Lake. The memory haunted him every time he went there. Even as an adult, he could tolerate fishing from his rowboat only if it was close to shore. And if he hadn't needed the fish to eat, he wouldn't have gone there at all.

After Tomas' funeral, Petra's father sought solace in a vodka bottle. A year later, as Isaac walked home from Bablia's in the dark, a truck hit him and he died, leaving Petra alone and working for the family who was supposed to treat him like a son.

Petra gave a sour laugh. The workhorses were better off than he was. With Zabrev's help, Petra would be on top soon. He would have everything, and Dana would be beneath him. All Petra had to do was find Ludmelia Kudirka, even though he'd have to row across Paunksmis Lake to get to the old forest, where she might have taken her boat.

CHAPTER 14

As dawn was about to break, Simas watched the partisans row away, taking his guns, grenades, and binoculars. They were just following his orders, but still, standing on the Vilkija side of the lake, he felt naked without his weapons. He didn't need them today though, for he was playing the farmhand mourning the loss of his friends and employers. He glanced in the direction of the cove, even though the patrol boat had come in from its rounds hours before.

He found a place to sit, and waited for the sun to come up. His leg ached more than usual from the damp air. He pulled the flask from his pocket and took a swallow. It helped ease the pain a little. He was exhausted. Sleeping in the hammock was hard to begin with, although better than on the ground, but impossible when he seethed with thoughts of Zabrev and Eda.

As an owl hooted, Simas leaned with his back against a tree and eased into a light doze. In the cloud of a dream, he stood next to a priest, while Eda waited at the end of a long hallway. Ribbons in the traditional colors of yellow, green, and red danced in her hair. She wore an embroidered skirt and a white blouse. She smiled and walked toward Simas. When she was an arm's length away, he noticed that her belly was swollen with child. He glanced at the priest, whose face had transformed into Zabrev's. In a swell of anger and hopelessness, Simas put his hands around Eda's neck and squeezed. She disintegrated into dust. He awoke with a start, shivered in disgust, and took another drink. He stared at the sky as it brightened, his head throbbing.

When it was light, Simas pushed to his feet. He limped past a cluster of young fir trees and paused to scan the water. The old forest on the other side was quiet, as it should be. Despite his aching leg, Simas continued along the muddy road toward Petra Sukas' hut. He had a job in mind for the little rat.

Petra Sukas hurried down the road toward the lake, intending to cross it in the leaky old rowboat he kept hidden in the weeds. He hoped Ludmelia was close to shore, so he could find her without too much trouble. It was bad enough having to cross the lake, let alone search the many hiding spots in that dark and fearful place. If she went deep into the old forest, he might never find her.

He remembered seeing her once as he was walking past a field of rye, on his way into Vilkija. The sun had been low in the sky, and it seemed that a strange plant was moving across the field. He stared at it, thinking he had been out in the sun too long. But it was a woman, whose hair blended perfectly with the stalks. As she moved, her shirt billowed like a white cloud. She was almost out of sight before he realized it was Ludmelia.

"Hello, Petra," called Simas.

Petra jumped, startled out of his daydream. He turned toward Simas, wondering why he was at the lake so early.

"Where are you off to?" asked Simas.

"I'm going fishing." Petra winced at the lie, but it was all he could think of.

"In your best suit? And where's your pole and bait?"

Petra looked down. "I have no time for this."

"Of course you do. Come and sit with me. I want to talk to you." Simas held up the flask. "Let's have a drink."

With no choice but to comply, Petra joined Simas on a log overlooking the water.

"I'm glad to see you well after the raid on the Ravas farmstead yesterday, my friend," said Simas, handing him the flask. "Have some. We should celebrate being alive."

Petra took a drink, wiped his mouth on his sleeve, and handed it back. *Simas was being unusually pleasant,* thought Petra. *He must want something.*

"I need a friend," said Simas. "The Russians came to the farmstead yesterday. They burned down the barn and arrested Dana. And they murdered Bronai and Gerta. Thank God you're safe."

Petra resented the Ravas family for many things, but he never imagined the Russians would kill the old ones. He thought of all the meals he had eaten in the warm kitchen. The suit he was wearing was a gift from Gerta. It had belonged to her husband when he was young, and much thinner. When she had handed it to Petra, she had said that every man needed a suit.

Simas slapped his bad leg. "I tried to help. I ran toward the fire, but you know I can't go fast. When I realized what was happening, I hid. I should have done something, but they would have shot me. By the way, where were you?"

"You know I had the morning off to take care of some Party business."

"Ah, that's right. It was your lucky day."

"What did they want with Dana?" Petra toyed with the red ribbons on his suit.

"Can I trust you?"

"Of course." Petra took another drink.

"They say Dana knows about the resistance. You know, the Freedom Fighters, the Brothers of the Forest, the partisans."

"I knew it."

Simas looked surprised. "How did you know? Are you one of them?"

"Don't be ridiculous."

"Dana was always too smart, and too sly. He liked books too much. I think he's a partisan, and that's why the Russians threw him into prison."

Petra shivered as he considered the possibility of Dana finding out he was behind the raid. Then he realized that finding the partisan camp would even be better than bringing in Ludmelia Kudirka. "Where would they hide?"

"They say the partisans have a camp in the old forest. Their boats go across the lake to the far shore. Over there, right through the reeds. You can see the entire lake from there. A few men can defend that spot easily."

"How can you be sure?"

Simas leaned in close to Petra. "All I know is what folks say. The people in town seem to know what's going on."

"It's a big forest. There must be a lot of partisans hiding there." Petra twisted the ribbons around a finger.

"They say just a few. No more than five or six. I think others will join them in time, but it will be somewhere else. They say the partisans never stay very long in one place."

"Why has no one told the Russians? They're interrogating everyone."

Simas snorted. "It's alright for you and me to talk, but most people would rather die than tell the Russians anything. They hate the Russians. You know that."

Petra gazed at the far shore, his eyes dancing in expectation.

Simas shook his head. "You can't go there, you know."

Petra started. "Who said I'm going there?"

"I hear those partisans are vicious. Don't fool with them. And you'd better not tell Zabrev about this, either. If the partisans are gone by the time he gets there, he'll think you lied to him. Anyone who lies to the Russians is as good as dead."

"I have something to tell you," said Petra. The vodka had loosened his tongue, and his mouth seemed intent on talking, even though his mind told him it wasn't a good idea. "Zabrev took Eda into the back room at Bablia's."

Simas took a drink. "Oh?"

"It was the night the Communists threw a party for him. I was there."

"She's nothing to me."

"I thought you were going to marry her."

Simas' expression made Petra feel like he had turned into stone.

"I must be going." Petra jumped to his feet and headed for the road into town. Still jittery with excitement about his new prospects for success, he glanced back at Simas. His old foreman sat on the log watching him, his expression lifeless. Petra shivered again, and walked faster.

Soon, Petra was thinking about Zabrev's warning not to come back unless he had useful information. Petra's only avenue was to go to the old forest and see if the partisans were really there. He turned away from the road, and made his way to his rowboat. He wanted to cross the lake right away, but realized he should wait until dark. He didn't want the patrol boat to see him, for they tended to shoot before asking questions. He didn't want the partisans to see him either.

Petra found a dry spot to rest, but could barely keep still. His dreams were within reach. But if the partisans caught him spying on them, they might kill him. If he didn't find Ludmelia, Zabrev would kill him. He had to cross the lake, and images of Tomas' dead face made him shiver. He had never imagined success would take so much effort.

Hunger gnawed at his stomach. Soon, he would have more than enough to eat. He would have everything he wanted. Petra got up and searched the area for berries. After finding some, he went back to his hut to wait for the sun to go down.

CHAPTER 15

Ludmelia woke from a restless sleep, surprised to be surrounded by so many ferns. She glanced up at the sun sparkling through the leaves and guessed it was midday. She remembered her trip across the lake, and her hiding place in the old forest. Her arms felt heavy and tired as she scratched the bug bites. She knew she needed more rest, but had work to do before it got dark again.

As she pulled on her boots, she had the odd sensation that someone was watching her. She looked around, but noticed nothing unusual. Still, the prick of cold at the base of her spine wouldn't go away. She packed her knapsack and walked for a while, as if exploring the area, although she knew it as well as the fields behind the cottage. She found a spot with some cover and sat down. As she nibbled a piece of bread, she continued to scan her surroundings. She got to her feet and continued walking. She noticed no footprints, and no telltale signs of anyone there.

Ludmelia told herself it was just nerves, and went to the boat. She tossed the knapsack inside, and climbed in. She pulled hard through the reeds, turning farther away from the beach, as she looked for a better hiding spot. It was very slow going. When she found a good place, she tied the boat to a tree. She took off her boots, got in the water, and made several trips carrying her things to the shore.

When the boat was empty, she assessed her situation. It would be impossible to carry everything all at once up the ridge and deep into the forest, so she divided her possessions into bundles that she could retrieve later. First, she put the perishable food into an empty sack, along with the blanket and an extra shirt. It would be plenty to sustain her for a few days. She tied her winter clothing into a bundle. She put the jars of food into the hollow of a tree, and stuffed the bundle of clothing on top of it. She filled the rest of the cavity with leaves and sticks.

When her possessions were in order, she used the axe to chop bushy branches from a few nearby trees. She dragged the branches to the boat and arranged them over the vessel for more camouflage. She hid the axe in the tree with her clothing and food.

When she was done, the sun was already low in the western sky. Ludmelia was happy with her work for the day. After a night's rest, she'd begin her trek into the woods to her new camp. She picked up her sack, knapsack, and gun, and headed back to the spot where she would spend the night.

As soon as she had left the area near the boat, the feeling that someone was out there came over her again. She kept going, trying to show outwardly that everything was all right. She needed to be sure she was alone, as she couldn't risk someone following her to her new camp. She'd never feel safe. If someone were watching her, she'd have to take care of it.

She reached her sea of ferns just before dark. She spread her blanket over some leaves, making it look like she was lying down. Silently, she moved away to the safety of the trees. She sat on a rock, held the pistol in her hands, and waited.

When she was a girl, the forest had been a place for excitement and adventures with Papa and Matas. They had often camped in the woods near Kaunas. They went to the forest near Didmiestis, and to the woods around Paunksmis Lake, including the old forest. Papa taught them how to track, trap, fish, and make a shelter. They could start a fire without matches and leave the ground so pristine no one would ever know they were there. They knew how to skin an animal. They practiced shooting. Occasionally, they hiked deep into the woods, and Papa let Ludmelia and Matas lead the way back, knowing they enjoyed the game.

They even played hide-and-seek. Once, Ludmelia hid by draping herself along the branch of a tree right next to their camp. Papa and Matas had searched for her for hours. When they returned, Ludmelia climbed down. Papa realized she'd been there the whole time, and he laughed until tears rolled down his cheeks.

When Ludmelia was little, their excursions had been a game. As she grew older, Papa's obsession with the forest became almost fanatical. He said their lives might someday depend on living there, as their ancestors had done. When Papa talked about military tactics and hunting men instead of animals, the forest became much more than a playground.

Now, in the old forest, hiding in the dark because she suspected someone was watching her, Ludmelia realized she had been studying all her life. It was time for her examinations, and failing meant death.

"Ludmelia," said a voice.

She jolted upright and pointed her pistol at the sound. She was right. Someone *was* following her. Still, the realization that she wasn't alone hit her like a slap in the face. She put her finger on the trigger.

"It's me, Vadi."

"Come out where I can see you." Ludmelia got up and moved behind a tree as footsteps crushed the ferns near her bed. Soon, she recognized Vadi's sizeable form.

"How did you know I was here?" she asked.

"One of the men has been watching you all day."

Ludmelia thought of Mama, steeled her stomach, and gripped the gun more tightly. She didn't think anyone had any interest in her except the Russians, but a woman alone in the woods might be a target for any man.

"We're doing some work here tonight. You have to come with me," said Vadi.

"I'm not going anywhere with you or anyone else."

"Give me your pistol."

"You're insane."

"Please. Simas wants you to come with me."

"Simas is here, too? Fine. But I'll keep my gun."

Another man stepped out from the trees, pointing his rifle at Ludmelia.

"I'm sorry," said Vadi. "We can't take any chances. We don't want to hurt you, but you can't carry the pistol where we're going. You've seen us, so we can't just let you go. Please Ludmelia, put the gun down."

Ludmelia remembered the knife tucked in her boot. If they tried to rape her, she would defend herself. "Alright, I'm setting it down. Don't shoot."

She held up the pistol and slowly dropped to one knee. She carefully set the gun down and stood back up.

Vadi walked forward, knelt, and picked up her gun. He tucked it under his belt.

With the stranger walking behind her, Ludmelia followed Vadi past the black trees, dreading that each step took her closer to an inevitable doom. Soon, she smelled smoke. They stopped at a campfire where several men waited. All had guns. She couldn't defend herself against so many, and if she ran, they would shoot her. But when she recognized a few of them as visitors at the Ravas farmstead, she relaxed a fraction. The man standing near the light, wearing an eyepatch, was unmistakable.

Simas swore. "What are you doing here?"

"Hiding," said Ludmelia. "The soldiers came to the cottage. They killed Mama. I hid in the attic and ran away after they left. Why aren't you at the farmstead?"

"The Russians took Dana away and killed the old folks."

More Russians to hunt and more deaths to avenge. "Who did it?" Ludmelia's eyes stung as she blinked away fresh tears.

"Denis and Uri Mastev."

Ludmelia flinched. *Mama's killers.*

Simas moved in so their faces were only inches apart. Ludmelia's instinct was to step back, but she didn't. He spoke. "There are three kinds of people. Those who collaborate with the Russians, like Petra Sukas, those who cower and hide, and those who fight back. Which type are you, Ludmelia Kudirka?"

"I want to fight."

"Then you've come to the right place."

At dark, Petra began rowing across the lake where Tomas Ravas had died. Petra desperately tried to think of anything but the little boy's ashen face. First, he worried about the patrol boat, and hoped to be at his destination before it left for its rounds. Next, he worried about Zabrev, and what the Comrade Commander would do to him if he didn't find the partisans or Ludmelia.

As he pulled farther away from shore, he felt even worse. He tried to focus on his plans. If he managed to find the camp, Zabrev would think him a brave man and give him the position he wanted. If he didn't find the camp, he could still search for Ludmelia. She couldn't be that hard to find. After all, she was just a woman. If he found either her or the partisans, his dreams would come true.

Halfway across the lake, a chill shook him. It was bad luck rowing over Tomas' soul. Petra scanned the surface, expecting the boy's ghost to pop out of the water. The image of dead Tomas followed him all the way to the old forest, where the gray-blue moonlight cast the trees in eerie tones. Petra stepped into the shallow water and pulled the bow of the boat onto shore.

It was just bright enough for Petra to see basic shapes as he stumbled his way over the little beach and into the woods. The dark trees loomed over him like evil trolls. Shadows swayed as wild creatures growled. Creaking branches hid the moans of the dead waiting to grab him.

He tripped on a root and fell. He lay still for a moment, cursing his clumsiness, his life, the partisans, and the damn woods. He got up and moved farther inland. He could see a dim light through the trees. His breath quickened. Soon, Petra heard a voice. There it was again. The light grew brighter. He had to be sure. He had to see guns and faces. He had to know.

Petra moved from tree to tree. His foot sank into oozing mud that held his shoe fast. He pulled to work himself free. As he got closer to the light, he could make out figures standing around a campfire. At last, he had something that Zabrev wanted. This was enough proof even for him. By noon tomorrow, Petra would be Secretary of the Executive Committee. Life would be wonderful. Petra stretched his neck out from behind the tree, and felt the touch of cool steel against his throat.

"Don't move," growled a voice.

"I'm a friend," Petra whimpered.

Someone tied a cloth around his head, covering his eyes and blinding him. His hands were pulled back and tied. He was pushed forward until he tripped and fell. He felt the heat of the campfire on his face. Hands pulled him to his feet.

"Please don't kill me!"

CHAPTER 16

Hiding with Simas behind some trees a short distance away, Ludmelia watched the scene unfold at the campfire. She didn't have her pistol, as it was still tucked in Vadi's belt. At least she could run away if she had to, for Simas could never catch her. Feeling both excitement and dread, she was certain that her life was about to change yet again.

"Don't hurt me. Who are you?" said a voice tinged with desperation. Ludmelia immediately recognized it as belonging to Petra Sukas.

His oversized jacket and pants billowed as the men jerked him in different directions in front of the fire. He was blindfolded.

As Simas stood, he motioned Ludmelia to stay where she was. When Simas got to the fire, Vadi stepped forward and took hold of Petra's belt.

"Stand still if you want to live," said Simas, deepening his voice, disguising it. Ludmelia fixed her gaze on the one-eyed man, surprised that he was able to hide his voice so well.

"Please don't kill me!" Petra squeaked.

Vadi pulled Petra's pants down. Ludmelia narrowed her eyes in confusion.

"What are you doing?" Petra tried to break free. Vadi caught him and shoved his head down, forcing him to bend at the waist, and holding him there.

"Are you partisans? I want to join you. I want to fight for freedom," cried Petra.

Laughter. Simas pulled something out of a knapsack. Firelight glinted off the jagged surface of a small rectangular object that looked like a potato grater. He scraped it against Petra's naked ass. Petra screamed and jumped away, but his feet tangled in his pants and he fell.

More laughter.

"Why are you hurting me? I can help you." Petra clumsily got to his feet.

Vadi seized the back of Petra's neck. The little man hunched his shoulders.

"Please, no more! I can tell you what Zabrev's planning. He knows me. He'll tell me his plans, and I'll tell you. I can even tell you what he is thinking, because I know him so well. Zabrev and I are like brothers."

"Tell us now," growled Simas.

Petra paused. "Well I don't know anything, but I will go back and find out."

Simas scraped the object against Petra's ass again, and the skinny man screamed like a girl. Vadi took a handful of something and rubbed it against the bloody skin. Petra screamed once more.

"Shut him up," snarled Simas. Vadi struck Petra in the mouth, knocking him to the ground. Petra moaned.

A pine knot popped in the fire. The flames sizzled and dimmed before leaping up again.

"Because of you, we'll have to move camp tomorrow," said Simas.

"No you don't. I won't tell anyone," whimpered Petra.

"You'd better not. And if we ever find you here again, you're a dead man." Smiling, Simas turned to Vadi. "Take this piece of filth back to his boat."

Vadi took hold of Petra's collar and dragged him away.

His backside was too sore for him to sit, so with his knees grinding against the wood in the bottom of the boat, Petra rowed like a madman. He prayed to get away. He was certain they were following him. If the partisans captured him again, they would kill him. When he was a good distance from the old forest, he stopped for a moment to catch his breath. He looked back, and saw that he was alone. He was exhausted and relieved to be alive, but ashamed and angry.

His ass was raw and screaming with pain from the grating. His knees ached from the hard wood. Petra sobbed and curled up in the bottom of the boat, despite the several inches of water that had collected there. Zabrev would have his information soon, but how Petra had suffered for it. Zabrev had better appreciate his sacrifice, and make it worth his while.

Realizing the patrol boat might come upon him at any time and shoot before he could say anything, he picked up the oars and started rowing again. His strokes were quick but inefficient, and he cried the entire way.

Finally at the far shore, Petra took off his pants, and stepped out of the rowboat into the shallow water. He waded until it was up to his waist. The cold chilled him to his core, but the pain gradually dulled to a throb. He tied up the boat, dressed, and gingerly made his way to the road leading into town. There were no trucks out this late, so he walked the five kilometers to the prison. With every step, he told himself that once he talked to Zabrev, things would change for the better.

As Petra walked along the empty streets approaching the prison, the lights shining above the dark walls surrounding the place made it look like it was floating. Despite his painful backside, Petra ran to the gate. He pulled the rope. A bell rang, and a moment later, a piece of wood the size of a small window slid open in the door. A guard peered out. He looked sleepy, like he'd been dozing, and he appeared surprised to see Petra. "What do you want?"

"I must see Lieutenant Zabrev," wheezed Petra.

"Too bad. He's asleep. Come back in a few hours."

"It's urgent. Wake him up."

"And risk getting shot? No, thank you. On your way."

"I must see him. I have information about the partisans. I know where they are."

The guard paused and looked at him. "Stay here. Don't move." He closed the window. The gate opened, and Petra walked in. The guard waved to someone within the compound, and another soldier approached. They conversed in low whispers. The soldier glanced at Petra, crossed the courtyard, and entered a building. A few minutes later, the soldier returned and motioned for Petra to follow him. The guard stepped aside, and Petra walked behind the other soldier into the structure. Their steps echoed down a long, dimly lit corridor.

Soon, more footsteps sounded, and Tadnik appeared, buttoning his jacket.

Petra blinked. "Where's Zabrev?"

"Sleeping, as I should be. What's this nonsense you're trying to peddle?"

"I found the partisan camp. I want to speak to Zabrev."

"Where is it?"

"Across the lake. I saw them in the forest."

Tadnik chewed his lip as he gazed at Petra. "Fine. I'll wake him, but you'd better be telling the truth, fool, or you'll be dead before breakfast."

Petra wrung his hands as he stood next to the soldier, waiting for Tadnik to return. Soon, the outside door slammed against the wall, and Zabrev stormed down the corridor, followed by Tadnik.

"This had better be good," Zabrev growled, as he went into his office.

Zabrev sat behind his desk and stared while Petra shifted his weight from one foot to the other. Tadnik stood to the side.

"I found the partisan camp in the old forest, just a few hours ago," said Petra.

"How did you get there?" said Zabrev.

"I rowed across in my boat."

"You have a boat?"

Petra felt sick. "Yes, Comrade Commander. When I got to the shore, I saw light from a campfire through the trees, so I moved closer."

"Why were you in the old forest?"

Petra hesitated. "I was looking for the Kudirka girl, as you requested."

"As I *ordered*."

"Yes, Comrade Commander, as you ordered."

"What were you doing searching for her in the middle of the night?"

Petra hesitated again. "I wanted to get an early start."

"Did you find her?"

"No, but I found the partisans. It was dark, and I couldn't get close, but I'm sure it was them. They had guns." Petra was about to tell of his abuse at the partisan hands, but he had a rare flash of insight. Zabrev was suspicious of everyone and everything. If he knew Petra had actually spoken to the partisans, he might think Petra was one of them. He couldn't take the chance that Zabrev wouldn't believe him, so he would keep his martyrdom to himself for now. Perhaps someday he would tell Zabrev the full story, over a few glasses of vodka. Petra hadn't actually seen anything, because of the blindfold, but he had to make the story good. He shuddered as he thought about what more to say.

"What kind of guns?"

"I don't know. Rifles, mostly."

"How many men?"

"It was hard to tell. I think there were five or six of them." Petra winced. He had no idea. But Simas had mentioned the number of partisans living in the woods, so it must be right.

"Did you recognize anyone?"

"No, I couldn't get that close. They'd have killed me. It was a miracle I got in and out without them shooting at me, but I was just one man in a little boat." Petra looked down at his hands. "I overheard them say they were moving camp tomorrow."

Zabrev lit a cigarette and looked at Tadnik. "What do you think?"

Tadnik shrugged. "He might be telling the truth."

"Draw a map," said Zabrev.

Petra sketched a diagram on a piece of paper, but his hand shook so badly, he had to turn the page over and start again. He handed it to Zabrev.

"These are the etchings of a child. Tell me why I shouldn't just shoot you now," said Zabrev. He passed the paper to Tadnik.

"I barely escaped with my life." Petra's face glowed red.

"If this information isn't good, it will be your last day on earth."

"It's good Comrade Commander," Petra stammered.

"Get the men up," said Zabrev. "Take everyone available and check it out. If this is true, it's our chance to crush them for good. Even if it's only five or six men, I don't want any to get away, and I want them alive. They can tell us about the partisan organization and we can destroy it. And get him out of here."

Tadnik opened the door and shoved Petra into the corridor.

"Sit," said Tadnik, pointing to a chair. "A guard will come and take you out."

"No, thank you."

"Sit!"

Petra slowly sat, the dull throb in his buttocks erupting in pain. When he looked up, Tadnik was gone.

A guard took Petra outside the gate. Petra had been up all night, and was tired and hungry. He wanted a drink, but couldn't go to Bablia's, because he didn't have any money. He set out on the road home, hoping to get a ride from someone. He would come back later to congratulate Zabrev.

As he limped along, Petra rubbed his hands together in happy expectation. Soon, he would be a wealthy man, a leader, a revered Communist. Soon, he would live the way he was meant to live.

CHAPTER 17

It was still the middle of the night as Ludmelia and the others waited near the shore, watching the patrol boat make circles on the dark water, its engine growling like a bear. In her hat and Matas' jacket, she was dressed like the other men. Simas, who was sitting next to her, was so still she thought he was either sleeping or dead. As the rumble of the engine grew louder, Ludmelia worried that soldiers would come to the little beach. She remembered hiding in the reeds from the same sounds just last night. The rumble grew dim, and the chirp of a cricket kept her company.

Finally, the patrol boat went back toward the dock. Without a word, the men got up. They went into the reeds near the shore. Ludmelia heard the rustle of leaves and the crack of branches. Soon the men came back in rowboats.

Ludmelia asked Simas where they were going.

"Across the lake," said Simas. "Petra will have told Zabrev everything he knows by now, and we'll see if the Russians take the bait."

"There's no point in taking her on the raid," said Vadi.

"She can't stay here alone. She'll go with us to the Espertus farm, and wait there until we return. Some men might need patching up after the mission," said Simas.

"I'm not a doctor. I want to kill Russians," said Ludmelia.

"You'll do as you're told," said Simas.

Ludmelia wanted to say more to convince him to take her on the raid, but at least she was going part way. "Why the farm?"

"He supplies us with food, and he keeps his mouth shut. You should do the same." Simas pointed to a boat. As she climbed in, a lone wolf howled from atop the ridge. The wild cry settled into her bones, as if warning her of danger.

As the boat glided away from the doleful sound, Ludmelia quivered in expectation. She was part of something full of purpose and vitality. She dragged a finger through the cool water. All the time spent hiding in the cottage with Mama had been a waste. Now, surrounded by partisans, she felt like she had discovered sunshine.

Four Studers carrying Russian soldiers raced out of the prison gate and turned onto the road out of town. They passed the open fields near the Ravas farmstead, where the headlights briefly shone on the startling ruin of the barn and the abandoned house. Squatters might settle there soon, but for now, it held only the spirits of those who had died there. Farther along, they sped past a cluster of trees hiding a little cottage. The foliage grew denser as they passed some hillocks. At the Espertus farm, the stink of the pigsty swept in through the open windows of the trucks. Inside the barn and house, a half-dozen soldiers weary from another night of boredom, craned their necks at the sound of the engines. But the trucks sped by without stopping.

The foul smell cleared, and the trucks bounced over deepening holes in the road. The uneven motion jostled all within. In the back of one truck, an old soldier took a drink from his flask and almost spilled some.

Zabrev stared out the window into the blackness, pleased with his swift transformation of Petra's information into a workable plan. Speed wasn't always good when planning a mission, but his force vastly outnumbered half-a-dozen measly partisans. Even if there were more than he expected, Zabrev was prepared. Further, he would approach the camp through the bog. The partisans would never expect it. Surprise would be his ally. He would capture them all. He had nothing to worry about. Still, he frowned as he recalled his conversation with Tadnik, just before getting into the trucks.

"But do the Mastev brothers know this particular bog?" Tadnik had asked.

"Of course they do. They're from the area."

"If they don't know the path, we may not make it through."

"If it turns out they're lying, they know I'll have them shot."

"Then it will be too late for us, Comrade Commander."

"It's just a swamp. The legends of the bog swallowing up entire armies are exaggerations told by ignorant people intent on intimidating us."

Zabrev put his elbow out the window. Tadnik was too timid and too cautious. He would never go far. Later, when they defeated the partisans and destroyed their camp, Tadnik would understand the genius of Zabrev's plan. It was going to be a great day.

The truck hit a rut, jolting Zabrev from his thoughts. He looked up at the sky. The men would have to walk through woods before getting to the bog, but the nearly full moon provided enough light. Nothing could hide from them.

The Studers flew past groupings of trees and a patch of heavy underbrush, where the prone figures of Simas and the partisans waited out of sight, not thirty meters away.

Simas and the others waited for the sound of the truck engines to fade before continuing their journey down the road to the Espertus farm. Once there, Simas made his way to the top of a hillock overlooking the place, while the rest of his troop waited under the protection of the trees. Moving away from the crest so he wouldn't be seen from below, he lay on his stomach, observing the house and barn through his binoculars. Kazys was a loyal friend, but the unexplained absence made Simas wary. Kazys was never away for an entire day. It was healthy to be suspicious.

Smoke rose from the chimney, which meant Kazys was home. Across the yard, the barn door was ajar, and the outside entrance to the loft was open. Usually, Kazys closed everything up tight, like most farmers, to keep out the birds and small animals. It was possible he just got busy and forgot. Simas could make out the shape of the truck next to the barn. He would use it to get the men into town, once he was sure it was safe. The pigpen was dark, but a sigh from a contented sow assured Simas that pigs were there. It seemed peaceful enough, but he had to be sure. After watching for a time, Simas climbed down and joined the others.

"Ludmelia, go to the house and look inside. Say you heard he killed a pig, and you're there for some meat. If he's alone, come back out and wave to us," said Simas.

"And if he's not alone?" asked Ludmelia.

"Make up an excuse and leave. You're just a girl. Nothing will happen to you."

"Can I have my gun back?"

Simas shook his head and pulled her cap off, stuffing it into his pocket. Her amber locks fell to her shoulders. "It's better if you go in without it. If there are soldiers there, they'd shoot you for having a gun."

As the sky brightened to a red dawn, Ludmelia walked into Kazys' yard. If soldiers were there, Simas should have noticed some sign of them. He would never knowingly put her in any danger. He was just being cautious. Still, she felt like a target, and wished she had the pistol. At least she had the hunting knife tucked into the side of her boot. Simas didn't know about that. She anxiously glanced at the open door of the barn as she cut across the yard. She stepped over a broken pail, her foot landing in mud. She didn't bother to wipe it off.

She stepped up to the faded brown door in back of the house, took a deep breath, and knocked. When it opened, the fragrance of roasting pork wafted over her. Her stomach growled.

A stream of sweat ran down the side of Kazys' face as he stood inside the doorway. Ugly bruises marked his cheek and chin. He held a cloth to his cut lip. One eye was almost swollen shut, the other blackened from some injury. "What the hell do you want?"

Ludmelia forced a smile. "We heard you killed a pig. Mama wanted to know if I could do chores in exchange for some meat."

Kazys shook his head. "I don't have any to spare. Go home. Get out of here."

"You must have plenty. I can smell it."

As Kazys stepped back to close the door, his gaze went to the yard. Ludmelia saw her chance, and slipped past him into the warm kitchen.

"Come back here!"

Lamplight washed the walls in tones of amber. A stove dominated the room. On it stood a large black pot, and next to it, a bin full of wood. A roast lay on a wooden table, along with two plates holding bits of pork and half-eaten chunks of bread. Two of the four chairs were pulled away from the table. The narrow hutch along the wall held a stack of dishes and mismatched glasses. A door stood ajar to the right, the edge of a rumpled bed barely visible. A long green curtain served as a room divider to a sitting area. Through the partially open curtain, Ludmelia could see chairs and a small table. The material gently swayed.

"Alright. I'll give you some, as long as you leave right away." Kazys went to the table and began cutting from the roast.

"What happened to your face?"

"An accident. I was chopping wood when a piece flew up and hit me right between the eyes. I was lucky it didn't blind me. You should always be careful when wielding an axe, but I'm just a stupid pig farmer." Kazys laughed and nervously glanced around the room.

"A piece of wood did such damage?"

"Look who we have here," said a voice.

Kazys let go of the knife. It clanged to the floor.

Ludmelia turned to see a grinning Russian soldier pointing a rifle at her. A hand opened the curtain to the next room, and another soldier, unusually tall, walked into the kitchen. He held a pistol in one hand as he stepped to Ludmelia and smiled down at her. He was still chewing his breakfast. Her heart raced as her gaze darted from one soldier to the other.

"She's just a girl from town. She's nothing," said Kazys.

The shorter soldier turned and pointed his rifle at Kazys. "Saving her for yourself? Maybe we'll give you a turn when we're done with her."

Kazys let out a high-pitched giggle. "No, it's just that I know a woman in town who would be much better for you. She knows men, and knows how to please them. What do you want with a stupid country girl? Come, let me give you some more to eat. Would you like a drink?"

"Shut up, fool."

Kazys whimpered and wrung his hands.

The tall soldier slipped Ludmelia's jacket off her shoulders and let it fall to the floor. He looked down at her breasts and took a deep breath. She stepped back. He took her by the arm and dragged her into the bedroom. As she pulled against his grip, her insides coiled so tightly that it hurt. He slammed the door shut with his foot, and shoved her onto the bed. The sheets held the same dank stench of the pigpen. He held the pistol in one hand as he undid his belt buckle with the other, all the time watching her.

"Take your pants off," he said. He set the pistol on a battered bureau, unbuttoned his trousers, and pulled them down.

Ludmelia stared at him as she undid her pants. *Survive for me, Ludie.* The soldier leered at her. A blast of gunfire exploded outside.

"What's going on?" the soldier yelled, as he hurriedly bent down to pull up his pants.

Ludmelia drew the knife from her boot and pushed off the bed. She leaped onto his back like a tigress and jammed the knife into his flesh. It hit something hard. She pulled it out and stuck it in again. He moaned as he slid to the floor with Ludmelia still on top of him, ramming the knife in again.

The soldier from inside the kitchen yelled, "Get the hell in here!" More gunfire blasted through the house.

Ludmelia pushed against the lifeless body and stood. The air seemed very cold. She quickly fastened her pants, grabbed the pistol from the bureau, and ran to the door, flinging it open. She fired a shot at the soldier crouching at the window.

He turned to her with a look of utter disbelief before collapsing to the floor.

Ludmelia ran to the window and squatted down to exchange the pistol for the dead soldier's rifle. Shots blasted through the glass, shattering it to pieces. She glanced outside to see a soldier firing from the barn's loft. Her bullet hit him in the forehead, and he dropped like a sack of potatoes.

She stayed at the window as gunfire boomed outside. When it stopped, Simas shouted her name.

"The ones in here are dead," yelled Ludmelia. "I'm coming out."

She stood, still holding the rifle. She picked up the pistol as Kazys sobbed from under the table. She opened the door and stepped outside.

A partisan scavenging a body stopped what he was doing when she appeared. Another man noticed. Others paused and stared.

Simas pulled out a submachine gun from under a dead Russian. "Why are you stopping?" A man pointed toward Ludmelia.

Ludmelia's eyes smoldered as the dawn's light covered her skin in the colors of flame. Her golden hair glowed, and her shirt was drenched in blood. With a rifle in one hand, and a pistol in the other, she looked like a warrior on fire.

Simas recovered first, and limped to her. "You're covered in blood."

"I'm fine." Ludmelia looked down at her chest, while Simas took a step back and watched her expression. He didn't know whether she was going to run away, cry into his shoulder, or toss him a gun and tell him to get moving.

"They were waiting for us," she hissed.

Ludmelia went back inside, and Simas followed. Kazys was crawling out from under the table.

"How did the Russians know we were coming?" Simas said to Kazys.

"Thank God you're here," said Kazys. "They had my son. If I didn't help them, they were going to kill him. Look at me. They beat me." The sweat and tears made Kazys' face look like it was melting.

"You know what happens when you betray us," said Simas.

"I had no choice!"

"You could have come to us. We would have helped you."

"How could you have helped me? They have my son! They would have killed him if I had gone to you."

"It doesn't matter now."

"What do you mean? Please, Simas."

Simas raised his gun and fired a burst into Kazys' torso. As the sound hung in the air, the pig farmer spun around and crashed to the floor.

"Simas!" The cry came from outside.

"It's alright," Simas shouted.

Two of the others came into the house. They paused at Kazys' body and exchanged a glance. One man went to the soldier lying near the window, and started going through his pockets.

"Was there another one?" asked Simas.

Ludmelia nodded toward the back bedroom.

Simas went into the other room, followed by the two men. They all emerged a minute later. The two partisans stared at Ludmelia. Simas wore a grim smile as he handed her the knife. "I think this is yours."

Ludmelia took the knife. It was already wiped off. She slipped it into her boot.

Simas handed her a clean shirt. "Good work. Now wash up, and put this on. At least it doesn't have any blood on it." He and the other two took the roast from the table and went outside.

Alone with the bodies, Ludmelia pulled off her bloody shirt and hurled it against a wall. She went to the sink for some water. As she rinsed off her arms and face, she tried to pretend the bodies weren't there, that she hadn't just killed three men, that the water dripping from her arms wasn't red from their blood. When she reached for the clean shirt, her gaze went to the bodies. She couldn't help it. The soldier at the window was laying face down. He could be asleep. But Kazys was on his back, his brutalized face visible, his eyes frozen open, and his mouth twisted in a look of horror.

Ludmelia leaned over the sink and vomited into a dirty pan. When the heaving subsided, she held onto the counter and took a deep breath. She rinsed her mouth out with water and put on the fresh shirt. It was big for her, so she tucked it into her trousers. She picked up her jacket from the floor and put it on. Holding the two guns, she went outside.

Vadi was sitting behind the wheel of Kazys' truck with the engine idling. The dish holding the roast was empty and lying on the ground. The partisans were climbing in the back, and covering themselves with a piece of dirty canvas.

"So how does it feel to kill Russians?" said Simas, turning to Ludmelia.

She didn't answer, but handed the rifle up to one of the partisans. He bowed his head.

Simas nodded. "You ride up front with me. It'll be less suspicious if we meet anyone on the road."

CHAPTER 18

The dawn was still an hour away when the Studers carrying Zabrev, Tadnik, and the Russian soldiers stopped at a dense growth of trees. The men climbed down from the back of the trucks. Forty-year-old soldiers huddled next to those barely old enough to carry a gun, as they waited to begin their trek.

One young soldier stood to the side, shuffling his feet and glancing over his shoulder.

"It'll be alright, Grigory," whispered a soldier with gray hair. "There are a lot more of us than there are of them. Besides, after today, you'll be an experienced soldier."

"I just don't know how those two can do the terrible things they do." The young man nodded toward the Mastev brothers standing next to Tadnik. "And now we have to follow them through the bog."

"Some think they can do whatever they want because the people should be grateful we drove the Nazis out."

"I hope this is over soon." Grigory hunched his shoulders.

"Who's at home waiting for you?"

"My mother, and two younger brothers."

"Eh, no sweetheart?"

"There's a girl in the village." Grigory looked away shyly.

"Good. Just follow orders and stick together. It's how we stay alive."

Within minutes, Tadnik commanded the men to fall in line. They began their march through a long expanse of trees made into threatening shapes by the moonlight.

When the Russians arrived at the bog, the sky was giving way to shades of scarlet, revealing a landscape stretching out in desolate detail. Decaying trees stood like giants. Pools of water shone red under the bloody sky. Black branches, bushes, and strange weeds covered patches of earth. Some areas were choked with green vegetation. In other places, dull pools of mud gave the illusion of firm ground. Nothing moved, except for swarms of mosquitoes. The warm air smelled of rot.

Tadnik ordered the men forward, and got in behind Uri and Denis, who were leading. Zabrev stayed near the rear. Even with their first steps, the ankle-deep mud pulled at their boots, releasing obscene sucking noises and dank odors. The men pushed on over ground that grew watery, sometimes rising to their thighs. They lost their footing on the uneven bottom and scrambled to recover their balance. In spots, they rested their submachine guns on their heads to keep them dry. Men breathed in and coughed out bugs. They gave each other worried glances as they struggled on, each step more difficult than the last.

At the dim ripple of far-off gunfire, Zabrev smiled. His soldiers were probably capturing the partisans who had gone to Kazys Espertus' farm for food. As he struggled through a dense patch of weeds, he was still certain it would be a great day.

One hour became two as the soldiers fought the hostile terrain. The slow traverse became slower. The men panted from exertion, and pulled at the collars clinging to their necks in the damp heat. Some mumbled with dissatisfaction each time Uri turned away from the most direct route through the bog.

After skirting a barrier of grass growing on dirt too weak to support the weight of a man, Uri paused and glanced back. Lines of worry creased his face. He wiped his brow with the back of his hand, leaving a swath of brown.

"What is it?" asked Tadnik.

"Nothing, sir." Uri breathed in, and took a hesitant step into a pool of mud. He sank to his waist. The men behind struggled through a thigh-high mess of weeds crisscrossed with dead tree limbs. Some left the line in hopes of better footing and shallower mud. In the rear, Zabrev slowed, too.

"Stay together," called Tadnik. He hunched his shoulders and took another step.

A lone soldier off to the left yelled as he fell. His face emerged, covered in mud. He struggled to move. "Help!"

"Get a rope," shouted Tadnik as he lumbered in the direction of the stricken man.

A few lines were thrown.

"Get him out of there!" yelled Zabrev from behind.

Tadnik barked commands as they formed a human chain along the lengths of rope. Even the rescuers began to sink.

"Tie this around you, Grigory," shouted an old soldier as he threw an end to the sinking man. Grigory's arms moved slowly, heavily, as he clasped the rope.

"I can't . . ." Only Grigory's shoulders and head showed.

"Stop thrashing," shouted another voice. Soldiers at the far end of the rope sank to their thighs.

"Hurry," shouted Zabrev.

Mud was up to their waists, and still the soldiers pulled.

"Get out of there," yelled Tadnik, as one of the soldiers sank up to his chest.

Hands grasped hands among urgent shouts as the soldiers desperately pulled a would-be rescuer free from the muck, and another and another, all trudging away in relief. Now, only Grigory's head was visible, his face a brown mask of horror as he clung to the rope. The others pulled with determination from weak footholds, while trying to avoid the trap of mud.

Tadnik pulled with the others, his hands constantly slipping.

"Pull harder!" shouted Zabrev.

Mud covered Grigory's chin.

"Hang on!" yelled a voice.

Tadnik tried to get a footing, though none was possible. His face lined with strain as he pulled. Then Grigory let go. The rope pulled free. Tadnik fell into the mud, along with the soldiers. Men got to their feet and scrambled away on trembling legs, while spitting out gobs of filth.

"Don't leave me!" cried Grigory.

Tadnik lunged forward. Hands clutched his boots and legs. He lifted his head and swabbed the mud from his eyes. He stretched his arms out into the muck, but Grigory was too far away. Mud covered Grigory's nose and eyes. His brown fingers wiggled from the surface. Only the hair on top of his head showed, until that disappeared too.

Tadnik heaved the heavy mud away with his arms, but it just filled in again. "Grigory," he yelled, gagging.

Another second passed, and the men pulled Tadnik back to safety. Shaking from the exertion, he bent at the waist, and coughed up brown bile. Weak and spent, he stared in disbelief at the void left by the soldier. With all the men and all their resources, they couldn't muster the rescue of a single man from this muddy hell.

"Why didn't you save him?" yelled Zabrev, finally at the scene of devastation. "I can't afford to keep losing men."

A few hours later, the soldiers reached the outer edge of the bog, and the protective covering of the trees. The solid ground was a welcome relief from the hot hell where their dead comrade lay. Zabrev ordered the Mastevs ahead to scout, and the others to rest while they waited for the brothers to return. The soldiers collapsed to the ground in exhaustion. The air reeked with the stink that still clung to them from the bog.

Zabrev drank some water, disgusted with Tadnik's ineptitude. He would deal with that later. He pulled out Petra's crude map and examined it again, even though he had already committed it to memory. Their plan was in place. Despite their troubles in the bog, Zabrev could almost taste victory.

He looked up at the light filtering through the leaves in hazy streaks, while the men lingered in nervous expectation. The density of the trees reminded him of a fortress. With a feeling of apprehension, Zabrev remembered the story Mrs. Garin had told him of Trakai Island, where the Teutonic Knights had laid siege against the Lithuanians. The mighty Knights began losing their strength there, and it declined until their miserable defeat at the Battle of Grunwald years later. The Teutonic Knights would never rise to power again. The siege had marked the beginning of a long, slow death.

Zabrev wondered whether Mrs. Garin was predicting his own decline. He was glad he would never see her again. The old woman's stories were more than he could stand. *Crazy old witch.*

Zabrev looked around. Even in the company of armed soldiers, it felt like someone was watching him. Several more minutes of unease went by before the Mastev brothers returned.

"We found a campfire, but no one was there. The embers were warm, so they couldn't have left long ago," said Denis.

Damn! Zabrev ordered the men to their feet. With the Mastevs in front, they went deeper into the forest. The woods became denser, and the ground more dangerous as they proceeded to the campsite.

Boots trampled plants that slanted toward the sun, near moss-covered rocks. Occasionally, a soldier tripped over the vines that snaked along the ground and up around tree trunks. One man's foot caught in a root and he fell hard, crying out.

A soldier came forward, opened a backpack of medical supplies, and began tending the injury. He turned to Zabrev. "It's his ankle, Comrade Commander. He'll need to be helped."

Zabrev gestured to another soldier. "Take the clumsy fool to the shore and come back. Stay out of sight." He ordered the men on.

Finally at the clearing that matched Petra's map of the camp, Zabrev took account of his surroundings. Four hastily-crafted lean-tos stood to the left. In the middle, a circle of rocks held blackened wood, still burning red in the ashes. A kettle stood next to the rock. A few blankets lay on the ground.

Damn bastards had to be somewhere nearby!

Tadnik came forward, his clothing and face caked with dry mud.

"Any sign of them?" demanded Zabrev.

"No."

"I know they're here. I can smell them."

On their right, something shifted. Tadnik sank to the ground, pulling a startled Zabrev down with him.

Silence followed. Tadnik and another soldier made their way around the underbrush. Soon, they returned.

"We didn't see anything. It might have been a deer, or some other animal," said Tadnik.

The soldiers continued through heavy vegetation, to the foot of a ridge. Halfway up, soft earth held the remains of roots that had survived a recent mudslide. Some trees leaned against the rising terrain. Others formed a casual pile, forming yet another barrier that had to be conquered in order to get to the top.

Zabrev summoned the Mastev brothers.

"The undergrowth is so thick up there, a camp would be impossible," said Uri. "They'd have to go farther in."

The soldiers within earshot exhaled in relief.

"They've got to be here," said Zabrev. "What's beyond the ridge?"

"It's been some time since we've been here," said Denis.

"You're supposed to know this place," said Zabrev.

"It's relatively flat, but there's no good place for a camp, at least not near here," said Uri, giving Denis a nasty look. "It might take days to find them."

"And you're just telling me now?"

The brothers exchanged an uneasy glance. Uri opened his mouth to speak. Zabrev cut him off. "I'll deal with you later."

Even though the path up led into gloom, Zabrev was there to find partisans, and so he would. Maybe the Mastevs knew what they were talking about, and maybe they didn't. He'd find out for himself. *He was surrounded by incompetent fools.* Zabrev ordered the men forward.

As endless clouds of biting bugs circled their heads, the men sweated and tramped for an hour up the ridge, climbing over broken limbs, making slow progress through the tangled undergrowth. Some men slid backwards, and had to scramble to regain their footing.

A gunshot rang out and a man fell.

After a split second of stunned silence, the soldiers hit the ground, crawling toward the sparse cover. Some fired back without waiting for an order.

"It's from up there," Tadnik pointed into the ever-darkening woods.

"Get them!" shouted Zabrev.

The soldiers attacked. Zabrev sensed he was closer to victory with every breathless shout, with every crashing boot, and with every bullet spent. They pierced deeper into the forest, firing at shifting shadows that made every tree look like a partisan, and every branch a gun.

But something was wrong. No one was firing back. Zabrev poked Tadnik's arm. "Where are they?"

"I don't know, sir."

Quickly, the pang of realization grew into full-blown rage. Zabrev had pulled all his men for this mission, leaving only a skeleton crew at the prison. The partisans weren't *here.* They were *there.* The farmers had tricked him. *Mere farmers.*

That damned Petra Sukas was the cause of this charade. Zabrev would strangle him, shoot him, hang him, and have his skin sliced off so people could see what happened to partisan agents. Petra was supposed to be working for *him,* not *them.*

"Radio the prison," Zabrev ordered. The moments until Tadnik returned hung like weights around Zabrev's neck.

"No answer," said Tadnik.

Zabrev swore. "Have the patrol boat pick us up. We've got to get out of here!"

CHAPTER 19

As Kazys' truck bounced along the road toward the prison, Ludmelia kept picturing the faces of the Russians she had killed. She shook her head to dispel the image. She had to ignore those few moments in Kazys Espertus' house, because they would take over every dream, and every conscious moment, if she let them. She couldn't afford the distraction. She had to remain alert and ready to use a gun. She wondered what Simas had in mind for her next.

Vadi stopped on a deserted side road just down the street from the prison. Ludmelia got out of the truck after Simas.

He looked at her. "You're going to be my prisoner. Jurgis, you too. Here, wrap this around your head." Simas handed the wiry man a strip of cloth.

Ludmelia tucked the dead Russian's pistol inside her jacket where it wouldn't show.

Dressed with white armbands identifying them as members of the People's Militia, Vadi and Simas headed toward the prison. Vadi trained his gun on Ludmelia and Jurgis, who walked ahead, with their hands loosely tied in front. Wearing the bandage, Jurgis looked like he had a severe head injury.

At the gate, Simas pulled the bell rope.

A small piece of wood in the door slid open to reveal a guard with a cigarette dangling from his mouth. "What do you want?"

"People's Militia." Simas patted the armband.

"Go away. You have no business here."

"But I do, my friend. I have a few lowlifes for you. This one attacked us." He shoved Jurgis viciously into the gate. "This is his woman." Simas stroked her hair. "Not bad, eh?"

The guard smiled.

"I bet you a month's pay that they're partisans. That is, if we ever get paid." Simas laughed.

"Alright. Bring them in."

The gate opened. Vadi followed Ludmelia and Jurgis into the courtyard. Simas entered last.

"Where do you want him to put these scum?" asked Simas.

"Our men will take care of them."

"He can do it. Over there, right?" Simas pointed toward the wing holding the jail cells. He began pulling a bottle of vodka out of his knapsack, but paused and looked over his shoulder. "Is the Comrade Commander in?"

The guard shook his head.

Simas smiled as he took out the bottle. "Hell of a breakfast, I know, but my bones are tired. Perhaps you'll join me?"

The guard hesitated for a moment. He waved another sentry over, who accompanied Vadi and his two prisoners into the building.

Simas went to the fountain and sat on the edge. "Do you mind if I wait here for my man?"

The guard nodded.

"I heard the party they threw for Zabrev at Bablia's was really something. Were you there? No? I wasn't either. It's a shame that officers have all the fun, while the rest of us do all the work.

"I know you aren't supposed to drink when you're on duty, so I'll have a sip and leave the rest for you to enjoy when you have the time and opportunity." Simas smiled, and opened the bottle. He was about to put it to his lips, but held it out to the guard instead. "Perhaps we should all toast Lieutenant Zabrev. After all, what harm could it do?"

The guard stubbed out the cigarette and took a drink. Another guard joined them. They talked for a few minutes. Vadi appeared at the door of the jail wing, and nodded to Simas. As one of the guards lifted the bottle to his lips, Simas smiled, took out his pistol, and shot him in the head. He fired another round into the other guard. Vadi shot the guard in the tower, and ran to the gate, pushing it open.

The partisans rushed in as soldiers emerged from the barracks, shooting. Bullets pinged against the stone fountain near Simas. The partisans cut the guards down. Simas rushed into the prison wing, with Vadi at his heels.

Dana started at the gunfire outside his window. The Russians must be executing the prisoners. Maybe he was next. He wouldn't even mind, because he couldn't take any more torture. A bullet would be merciful. It would stop the pain. He wouldn't have to think, or worry anymore. It would save him from making up stories about his friends, and he wouldn't have to face himself afterwards. Dana put his good hand over his face and sobbed.

The cell door clanked open, and a lean, dark figure stood in the doorway. Dana couldn't make out the face of his torturer, but he didn't care anymore.

"Shoot me, and be done with it." Dana turned his face to the wall.

The figure came in and knelt by his side. "Would you like to get out of here?"

On hearing a woman's voice, Dana thought he was dreaming. He closed his eyes and pictured an angel looking down on him, but something about the voice seemed familiar.

Ludmelia smiled. "Hello, Dana."

He gaped in disbelief, grasping her arm. "Can it be?"

Ludmelia nodded. "Can you walk?"

"I think so."

Ludmelia helped him to his feet. Dana took a step and collapsed. "Vadi!"

A man the size of an oak tree came in, and slung Dana over his shoulder. Dana groaned as he watched Ludmelia go into another cell.

Dana's chest bounced against Vadi's back as they walked to the courtyard. Every motion brought pain, but Dana was so relieved to be out of the cell that he didn't mind. He was free, and Ludmelia had saved him. He pictured her face, and her fresh beauty. He wouldn't have to betray anyone because of her, but his willingness to do so was a secret he would have to keep for the rest of his life.

As Vadi put Dana down on the edge of the fountain, Kazys' truck rumbled into the prison yard. Another truck, a Studer, pulled into the yard from a shed behind the prison. The driver waved at Simas, who was walking to the fountain.

"You're here, too?" asked Dana.

Simas shrugged as prisoners stumbled by. They moved as if awoken from a bad dream. A tall, muscular man with stooped shoulders shuffled over to them. It took Simas a moment to recognize the man through the bruises on his face. His left eye was badly swollen.

"Edvard Urba," said Simas. They embraced.

"They just brought me here late last night." Edvard pointed to his eye. "This was their welcoming kiss."

Simas smiled. "The Russians are still repairing the phone lines you cut. Did you tell them anything about us?"

"No." Edvard straightened his back. "My brother and his family are in Vilkija. If the Russians come looking for me there, they'll kill them all."

"Don't worry. We'll take care of them. Get into Kazys' truck. You're coming with me."

Edvard nodded to Dana, and walked toward the truck.

Across the yard, Ludmelia cleaned the fresh blood off her knife with a rag as she stepped out from the prison wing. She hadn't vomited this time after killing the guard. Maybe she was getting used to it. She noticed two of Simas' men entering a long, low building, and followed them in, hoping to find something out about the Russian with the beautiful voice.

As other men emerged from the prison wing carrying armloads of weapons, and headed for the trucks, Simas struggled up to the edge of the fountain.

"Everyone, listen to me," said Simas. The parade of prisoners stopped, and hopeful faces looked up. "Those of you who need a ride, get in one of the trucks. We'll drop you outside of town. If any of you have to go home, go quickly. Gather provisions and fan out. Take your families with you, but get out of Vilkija. And good luck to you."

"God bless you," said a man as he passed the fountain.

As Simas climbed down, a young man with a filthy leg cast limped over, using a broom as a crutch.

"Have you seen my father?" Kazys' son gazed at Simas. The raw burns from cigarette butts mottled both arms.

"He's dead," said Simas. "The Russians laid a trap for us at the farm. He was killed."

"I want to fight with you."

"No."

"But I didn't talk. I didn't say anything. Please. For my father's sake."

"We don't want people like you and your father. Get out of here!"

The young man flinched.

Simas went over to the soldier lying nearest the fountain. As Simas leaned over him, the soldier opened eyes that were the color of borscht.

"This is what we do to Russians," said Simas as he cut into the man's neck. At first, the red mark looked like a smile. Blood flowed, and the soldier stared at Simas until he died.

Two women clung to each other as they passed Simas, their expressions distressingly blank, their movements wooden. A man with blood caked to the side of his head let out a cry and ran to them. "My God you're alive," he said, leading the two women to the gate.

Damn those Russians, thought Simas. He took his rifle and smashed it into the dead soldier's face. It wasn't enough. He smashed it down again. He went to the man next to him and did the same. The crunch of bones was like kindling to a fire as Simas continued to beat the men.

Ludmelia came out of the office wing, carrying a satchel with pieces of paper sticking out from the side. She cringed as Simas delivered blow after blow. She hadn't hesitated when she stuck the guard in his belly inside the prison wing. She hadn't even flinched when Vadi and Jurgis killed the other two guards. She remembered the bedroom at the pig farm, and stabbing the soldier with her knife. That Simas was hitting dead soldiers shouldn't bother her, but his rage made her stomach twist.

Simas straightened up and glanced around him. The prisoners who had stopped to stare moved on, as if they had seen nothing.

In his hut, Petra awoke with a start. *Zabrev must be back by now.* He pulled on his shoes, grabbed his jacket, and rushed out the door, almost giddy with excitement. As soon as he got to the road, a farmer gave him a ride into town in the back of a rusty old truck.

As Petra approached the prison, all he heard was a chorus of grasshoppers singing from the nettles. That was odd, for normally the place was bustling with activity in the morning. The gate was wide open. Petra straightened, ignored the feeling of dread, and went into the prison yard.

At first, he thought the guards lying on the ground were asleep. As he moved closer, he noticed the gashes at their necks, and the blood under their heads. He gagged at the smell.

It was Simas. Simas had planted the idea that the partisan camp was in the old forest. Like a fool, Petra had told Zabrev, and it had ended in a massacre at the prison. The partisans had used him. They might even be hunting him now. Certainly, Zabrev would be hunting him soon.

Petra turned and ran out the gate as if the devil were chasing him. He turned left at the corner, and headed toward the forest. His head churned as his feet hit the ground, the throb in his backside blazing into pain. When he couldn't run anymore, he slowed to a walk, snatching glances back down the road. He heard someone coming from behind a grove of trees, and dove into the ditch. He looked up from the mud to see an old woman chewing a stalk of grass while walking beside a horse. Petra shivered with relief as he picked himself up and wiped the mud off his jacket. He continued down the road, feeling more alone than ever before.

His father had been the only person who ever cared about him. Bronai and Gerta didn't care, not after Tomas died. Neither did Dana, Simas, or the other farm hands. They all looked down on him, and left the worst jobs for him. He was the one who had to clean the pigsty and the barn. He was the one who had to spread manure in Gerta's garden. His father had been the only person who ever loved him. Petra thought back to when he was young, taking long walks with *Teti* in the woods.

One afternoon, they had walked through the forest until they found a clearing where they sat and ate lunch. Petra's father stretched his legs out and closed his eyes.

"Can I go exploring, *Teti?*" Petra asked.

"No. Stay with me so you don't get lost."

"There's nothing to do."

"Take a nap."

"I'm not sleepy. Please *Teti*. I won't go far. Please?"

"You wear me down, son. You can explore the clearing while I close my eyes for a few minutes. Don't go far."

"Yes, *Teti.*"

Little Petra walked around the clearing, but there wasn't much to see, except grass and weeds. The forest was more interesting. *Teti's* head rested against the rock, his mouth open and eyes already closed. Petra took a few steps and listened for *Teti's* voice telling him to come back, but all he heard was the wind shaking the leaves, and the birds singing. He ran up a hill behind a cluster of trees. The clearing where *Teti* slept was over his left shoulder. A tree grew out from under a large rock on his right. He climbed up on the rock, jumped, and made the tree shake. Petra climbed another tree and explored a bird's nest. He walked along a rotten log, waving his arms for balance.

Everything in the woods was alive and exciting. When he realized he should be getting back, Petra didn't know how. The clearing that had been over his left shoulder was gone. There were just gigantic trees moving toward him through the mist, as if they were going to capture him and take him away.

"*Teti*, where are you?"

No answer. Petra ran, hitting branches, barely breathing. He raced to the right. *Teti* wasn't there. He ran to the left. He climbed a tree so he could see farther, but more trees surrounded him.

"*Teti*," Petra cried. Wraiths, *baubas*, waited in the shadows to capture him and carry him off to their caves, where they would eat him. Petra ran. Branches and bushes cut his legs. Leaves lapped at his face. Tears blurred his sight.

Petra sank to his knees, sobbing, promising God that he'd be a good boy forever if only *Teti* found him. He heard a sound. It was nothing, just an animal. No, it was a voice. It was his name. *Teti* was calling for him!

"*Teti*, over here!"

"Stay where you are."

Petra leapt to his feet.

"Don't move, Petra."

Soon, *Teti* stood in front of him like a big friendly bear. Petra jumped into his father's arms.

"It's all right, little one. You're safe now."

Petra wiped his eyes with a muddy sleeve as he shivered from fear at his uncertain future. He had to get away. He felt lost, just like when he was a boy. This time, there was no one trying to save him. He was on his own, and he wasn't safe anywhere.

CHAPTER 20

In the prison yard, the pebbles crunched beneath his feet as Zabrev walked toward the bodies that lay like downed tree limbs. Despite the yells of Tadnik and the soldiers running past him, the place held a strained stillness.

Zabrev paused at the fountain, where spongy gray pulp lay amid the smashed heads of the two soldiers lying there. Their throats had been slashed, and they rested in pools of blood. Both men were missing their boots, belts, hats, and guns. One had no pants. Zabrev gazed around the yard at the soldiers, going from body to body, looking for survivors. The doors to all the buildings were open. A body lay sprawled in front of the prison wing. Another lay in the doorway to the barracks. The sense of dread he had felt in the forest settled in his stomach like a meal of dirt.

"Comrade Commander," called a soldier from the tower. "Up here."

Zabrev went to the ladder and climbed up to a small platform surrounded by a waist-high wall of wood.

"He's alive," said the soldier.

The injured man's face contorted with pain. Blood covered his shirt and the floor beneath him.

"Did you recognize any of them?" said Zabrev.

"People's Militia," wheezed the injured man.

"How many?"

"Tell my mother I love her."

"How many?" shouted Zabrev.

The man didn't answer. His face became still. The soldier bent down and closed the man's eyes.

As Zabrev climbed down, the scene of death and blood shook his very core. The partisans had showed a cunning and hatred that stunned him. Those bloodthirsty savages had done this to *him*. They were destroying his *future*. He had to put an end to this, and he didn't care how much blood it took. He would show them what happened when anyone tried to fool a *Russian*.

He looked toward the shed next to the prison, and noticed that they had even taken the last Studer.

With Tadnik following him, Zabrev strode inside the building that housed his office. Stray paper littered the floor, some sheets marred by muddy footprints. A filing cabinet was toppled, the drawers open, and the contents strewn across the floor. Everything useful was missing, even the typewriter. Tadnik bent down and began picking up papers.

Zabrev stepped through the open door to his office. Books lay on the floor under the overturned bookcase. All the maps were gone. His desk drawers lay strewn about the room. He picked up the torn sheets of music to *L'elisir d'amore* and looked at them for a moment before letting them fall to the floor. The gramophone had been shattered, and the records broken to bits, just like his youthful dream for a different life. He looked up at the ceiling and cursed God for his assignment to this desolate place.

The partisans had tricked him into going into the woods with the soldiers. They knew how much time they had. They had been watching him all along. Even though walls surrounded the prison, Zabrev went to the window and pulled down the shade.

He noticed a book of Pushkin's poetry on the floor and picked it up, seeking distraction and solace in the words.

The storms of ruthless dispensation
Have struck my flowery garland numb,
I live in lonely desolation
And wonder when my end will come.

Zabrev slammed the book shut and threw it against the wall. It nicked the shade, which rolled up, making the sound of a flat tire slapping against a road.

Tadnik entered, as if summoned by the odd sound.

"Clean this mess up," said Zabrev. He pulled out a cigarette from his pocket and lit it.

"Yes, Comrade Commander," said Tadnik.

"Find the criminals who escaped, and get them back here. Arrest anyone who helps them. Kill anyone who resists. Stack the bodies in front of the school. I want everyone, even the children, to see what happens to those who help the partisans. Make it a night they won't forget."

Tadnik turned on his heels.

"Take the Mastev brothers with you, and let them loose. And find my truck!"

Tadnik nodded and left the room.

Zabrev righted a chair and sat among the mess. Armed with the victory here and the weapons from the prison, the partisans would be stronger than ever. Zabrev needed names and information, but no one in Vilkija was telling him anything useful.

He had to report to his superior and mentor, Colonel Karmachov, but admitting a defeat at the hands of peasant farmers was more than Zabrev could bear. If he told the truth, his career would be over, and probably his life. Russian top command never tolerated failure. If he lied, at least he had a chance to make reality match his vision of success. The words Zabrev chose would mean the difference between survival and death. The truth didn't matter anymore. He was in a gamble against time. When Colonel Karmachov found out the truth, Zabrev's past failures would be readily forgiven, as long as he obliterated the partisans.

He found some fresh paper and began to write. His hands were shaking so badly he could barely get the words down. He crumpled the first piece and threw it away. He tried again.

4 August 1944. Soviet forces continue to annihilate partisan encampments in the area of Paunksmis Lake. Thwarting a brutal attack against the Vilkija prison, Soviet troops seized victory from enemy forces.

Petra dashed across the road like a scared rabbit. No one was in sight, but he wasn't taking any chances. He took the long way around to the Ravas farmstead, just in case someone was following him. It was the one place where he would be safe, for Zabrev had already been there.

As he crossed the road to the farmyard, Petra cried out at the blackened remains of the barn standing as a monument to destruction. Charcoal dust covered the ground and the side of the house nearest the barn. Two overturned pails lay near the water pump. The place was quieter than he had ever known it to be. Even the rooster was gone.

Dark stains marred the ground near the steps to the house. Petra shivered, stepped over them, and went inside. He headed for the kitchen. The cabinet doors were all open. Broken dishes, cutlery, and pots lay on the floor. Petra picked through the mess, looking for food.

He checked the drawer where Gerta kept the bread, but it was empty. He searched the shelves for the block of fresh cheese that had been there just a few days ago, but it was gone. He worked the pump at the sink until water ran, and stuck his head under the cold stream. He filled the kettle and was about to light the stove when he stopped. *Someone might see the smoke.*

To his relief, Petra found a plate of boiled potatoes under a cloth on the shelf over the stove. Although dry and cracked, he ate them, wondering why the Russians had to take absolutely everything.

Somewhat revived, he pushed against the door to the dark hallway that led to the room he had shared with his father long ago. He prayed with all his heart to see *Teti* sitting in the chair by the window smoking his pipe. He stepped over the threshold, to a room empty of both people and ghosts.

Two narrow beds rested along opposite walls, the bedding tossed to the floor. An empty, battered trunk stood open between the beds. Clothing lay in a crumpled mess on the floor. The room held no memory of him or *Teti*. Nothing was left to show that Petra had spent years living there. There was nothing to confirm that once, long ago, he had been part of a family.

He ached for the dream of Bronai forgiving *Teti* and growing old with him, as Dana and Petra grew up to be men. Petra pinched himself in the arm, for it was best not to think of what might have been.

He sank to his knees and poked through the clothing: nothing but old work shirts and trousers. Petra considered taking a few things, but he didn't want any part of that life anymore.

Petra closed the lid and went up the stairs to the bedroom where Bronai and Gerta Ravas had slept. That room, too, was in shambles. He was too tired to give it more than a casual glance. He opened the window a crack before taking off his jacket, shirt, and pants. He left them on the floor and climbed into the bed.

In moments, he was luxuriating in warm comfort. No one was ordering him to milk the cow, feed the pigs, or sweat in the fields. He had a glimpse of the life he deserved. Petra was in a fine house with abundant comfort. All he needed was food. He pictured himself relaxing in the sitting room, enjoying Bronai's pipe, and sipping the vodka that was probably still hidden behind an old crate in Simas' tiny room. He could stroll through the fields and view the domain that was now his.

He sighed and smiled. If he could somehow find a way to get some food, he could hide here for the rest of the war, and life would be fabulous. Petra closed his eyes and drifted off to sleep.

In the middle of the night, he noticed a flutter of white at the window. He bolted upright and yelled.

"Gerta, is that you?"

The figure moved.

"Don't get mad. I didn't think you were home. Here, the bed is warm for you. Don't tell Bronai I was here."

The figure didn't speak.

"I'll be going now, Gerta." Petra swung his legs over the side of the bed. He glanced at the window again, and the curtain moving in the night breeze. He let out a strained giggle, and snuggled back under the warm blankets where he lay awake until dawn.

Tadnik swayed in the passenger seat as the truck slowly passed through the center of Vilkija, his skin prickling with the dour expectation that the night would ripple with death. Lights shone from a few windows, while most houses were completely dark. A dim amber glow showed Bablia's front door. Farther down the street, the empty stalls of the market gave Tadnik the feeling that something evil was lurking.

Faced with the grim task of filling the prison cells again, Tadnik did what he always did: his duty. Tonight, it meant finding the escapees and others. It meant killing those who resisted, whether they supported the partisans or not.

At least when soldiers faced soldiers, they fought for objectives, such as a hill, a village, or even a country. The prison break had been a partisan objective. The Russian soldiers had given their lives to protect the prison, and that should have been enough for an instant of solace before their hearts stopped beating.

Tadnik wondered what a teacher or dairy worker might think of when faced with death. Perhaps they remembered their families, or felt satisfaction from their life's work. Maybe they became angry or dumfounded.

He ordered the driver to stop at the house owned by Edvard Urba's family. Even though Edvard was a baker who lived in Latvia, his brother lived here. Having escaped from the prison, it was the natural place for Edvard to hide. Tadnik got out of the truck and motioned for the Mastev brothers to follow him to the door.

Tadnik knocked. No one answered. He motioned Uri to break the door in. The house was dark, and a search revealed that no one was home.

Standing on the front step, Tadnik wondered where the family could be. Next door, a soft light shone through a window above an empty flowerbox. The shade moved, as if someone was trying to peek out.

Tadnik gestured to the men to follow him. He went to the next house, and knocked. As he was about to motion Uri to kick the door in, it opened a crack. A man in his late thirties looked at them fearfully, as he ran a hand through a crop of messy brown hair.

"We're looking for Edvard Urba," said Tadnik.

"His brother lives next door."

"Who are you?"

The man hesitated. "I'm Rokas Teviskis. I live here with my wife and children."

Uri pushed the door open.

"I've done nothing. What do you want with me?"

Denis sneered and pointed his gun. The man turned to run, but Denis shot him and stood over the body until it stopped moving.

A woman screamed, and Uri muscled past his brother. When Tadnik found them in a bedroom off the kitchen, Uri was on top of her, pressing her into the mattress.

"Leave her alone," said Tadnik.

Uri shrugged, and stood. The woman scrambled off the bed, picked up a lamp, and swung it at Uri's head. He shot her twice in the chest. Blood spread over her nightgown as she collapsed to the floor.

Young voices screamed for their Mama from another room. Denis and Uri ran toward the sound, and two more gunshots exploded in the house.

Tadnik found the two dead boys in a back room on a bed next to the wall. His lips curled in disgust. *There had been no need to kill the children.* He turned his back to the Mastevs, angry that he had to tolerate these thugs because Zabrev had ordered it.

"Search the house," said Tadnik, holstering his gun. He closed the door quietly as he left the room, as if not to disturb the little ones. He went to the small sitting room across from the hallway, where Rokas Teviskis lay dead on the floor.

Soon the brothers returned, chewing on the remains of sandwiches. They had found nothing valuable in the house.

"Load the bodies," said Tadnik.

The Mastev brothers stuffed the last bites into their mouths, and dragged the bodies outside, where the driver helped lift them into the truck.

Tadnik went outside to the front step and closed the door behind him. He walked slowly to the truck, and climbed into the front seat. As they drove toward the gymnasium, he noticed that every house had gone dark. No doubt every door was locked, and every quivering soul inside was praying they wouldn't be next.

At the school, the windows gleamed like eyes in the glow from the headlights. The driver turned the truck around and backed up to the front steps. Tadnik got out as Uri and Denis threw the bodies down from the back. The adults went first, their flesh making a loud thud when they hit the hard ground. The children landed on top of their parents in a pile. Tadnik was the last man to climb back into the truck. He nodded to the driver, and they left to find more victims.

CHAPTER 21

The room was so dark Dana thought he was dead. A light appeared around a woman: Ludmelia. She floated to him, and tenderly kissed his lips. He opened his eyes and was surprised to be outside and under a tree. Shafts of moonlight shone down through the leaves. He smelled pine. He was fully dressed under the blanket. He had stockings on his feet, but they were numb from the chill. He moaned, remembering his parents and the fire. He thought of the whipping, the beating, the prison escape, and Ludmelia.

He sucked in the fresh air as he propped himself up on an elbow, wincing from pain. He noticed the bandage and splint covering his injured hand, and wondered who had taken care of him.

Simas sat on a nearby stone. The deep black of the eye patch contrasted with his pale features, making him look threatening in the dim light.

"Where are we?" asked Dana.

"The old forest, across from the lake," said Simas.

"How long have I been sleeping?"

"A few hours. How do you feel?"

"Terrible, but I'll live, thanks to you."

Simas looked at him for a moment and stood. "I'll have Raminta bring you some tea."

Dana struggled to sit up against a tree.

A young woman wearing a dark skirt and a shawl approached. She favored one leg. "Welcome," said Raminta, handing a cup to Dana.

Simas came back and sat down again.

"Are my parents here?" asked Dana.

Simas shook his head. "It was those damn Mastev brothers. They shot your mother and father after you were taken away. They're both beyond all this now."

Raminta shook her head and spat. "The bastards."

"Zabrev told me they were alive." Dana's hand shook so badly, hot liquid spilled over the side of the cup. Raminta took it from him and set it on the ground.

"You can't trust what the Russians tell you," said Simas.

Dana covered his eyes with his good hand. "I should have made them leave years ago."

"They wouldn't have gone." Simas handed Dana his flask. Dana took a drink, and choked from the sting.

Simas spoke quietly. "After the Russians left, we buried them in the potato patch, next to the orchard. One grave for the two of them. We didn't have time for anything better. Jurgis marked the spot with a rock." Simas took a drink before putting the flask back in his pocket. "What did you tell the Russians?"

"Nothing." Dana winced as he shifted against the tree. His heart beat so fast he thought he was going to be sick. *He had been a hair's breadth from indicting them all, with nothing more than suspicions. Only time and luck had prevented it. Simas must never know.*

"During interrogation, some people make things up, but the Russians don't like it."

"I told you I didn't lie. I didn't say anything," Dana snapped.

"Good. I'm proud of you. You stood up to a whipping in the farmyard, and you got through an interrogation. It's made a man out of you. I can see it in your eyes. We can use men like you."

"What?"

"The Brothers of the Forest. I'm their leader." Simas smiled. "Join us."

"I don't want to be a soldier."

"The war makes us all do things we never intended. You can kill Russians if you want, and make them pay for what they did to Bronai and Gerta. Or you can stay in camp to cook and clean, like the women, although some of our women also kill Russians. Ludmelia just joined us, and she has several kills already. Everyone does what they can."

Dana looked at Simas in disbelief. His farmhand, an aging cripple, was leading a resistance group, and Dana had an opportunity to join them. His family was gone. He couldn't return to the farmstead, for he had escaped from prison, and the Russians would surely be looking for him. He needed a place to rest, recover, and decide what to do.

"How were you able to get past the guards at the prison?" asked Dana.

"I told a songbird the location of a fake camp in the old forest. Zabrev came with his soldiers, and one of my men did just enough to keep them there searching for us. Only a few Russians were left at the prison. Jurgis and Ludmelia masqueraded as our prisoners, and the guards let us in. After freeing you and the others, we took clothes, food, guns, and ammunition; everything we could carry. Ludmelia took forms, identity papers, and maps from the offices inside. We even got a typewriter, so we can make more pamphlets. We would have taken the furniture, if we had a means to carry it off. The Freedom Fighters struck quite a blow."

"When I saw Ludmelia, I thought I was dreaming."

Simas gestured to a figure lying under a blanket on the edge of camp.

Dana leaned his head back against the tree. Mere hours had changed him from a prosperous landowner to a fugitive. His speculations about Simas had been true, and if he had told the Russians, they might all be dead. He had no choice but to stay and become a partisan. Once again, the war was tossing him toward a future he didn't want.

Hours later, the guard went to Simas' hammock. "We have a visitor."

Simas gazed into the darkness, his eye socket aching from dryness. His back hurt and his leg throbbed. He draped his sore leg over the side of the hammock, and reached for his rifle leaning against the tree. He used the gun as a crutch to get to his feet. He picked up his boots and carried them to a rock. As he sat with a heavy sigh, a boy with strawberry colored hair approached.

"Jonai Gabe. Why are you here? Is your father alright?" asked Simas.

"Papa's fine. He said to tell you that the soldiers killed a family. The children, too. The Mastev brothers carried the bodies out, just hours ago, and dumped them at school."

"My God."

"The Russians went through Vilkija in the middle of the night, arresting everyone they could find. Papa said it isn't safe anywhere."

Simas nodded.

"Papa doesn't want me to come into the woods anymore. He said it's too dangerous. He doesn't even want me to go to school. He said no child should have to see such things, even in wartime."

"Ask him for me, to let you do this a little while longer. Just a little while. Until I can find someone else."

"Sure, Simas."

"Tell your father to invite the Mastev brothers for a drink at Bablia's tonight."

"Alright."

"It's important. Tell him to make sure they're there."

The boy nodded.

"You did well. Have Raminta get you something to eat."

Simas smiled, and the boy went to the cook tent. As leader of the partisans, part of Simas' obligation was keeping families safe. Some wanted nothing to do with him. Others supported the cause, and Simas tried to protect them, even though it was impossible to be everywhere at once. If Simas got word where the Soviets would strike next, he warned the family and helped them escape, as he had done with Edvard Urba's family. If a Russian family took over a deserted farm, Simas had them driven out, at gunpoint if need be.

Sometimes, Simas just didn't know what the Russians were planning. But this time, for killing a family, he would bring them to their knees, whatever the cost. He would start with the Mastev brothers.

The churn in his stomach told him that sleep would be impossible, so he stumbled into the tent containing the supplies they had stolen from the Germans and the Russians. He reached behind a box of grenades, and pulled out the bottle he had hidden there.

When Dana woke up again, his back still stung, but the pain in his hand had diminished to a dull throb. He was cold and hungry, but at least he was alive, and in a forest instead of a prison cell. He shivered as he pushed to his feet.

As dawn appeared through the haze, figures wafted about, doing various jobs. Their motion was purposeful, but somehow lethargic, as if they carried burdens on their shoulders. Few people spoke. Others still slept under blankets, scattered about like leaves. Even the rocks reflected a sense of solemnity. The camouflaged lean-tos and tents were barely visible, unless one got close. Some people already sat at rough tables near a tent with its flaps open. A man lugged boxes marked with Russian lettering into a larger tent standing a short distance away.

Just off the center of the clearing, two shirtless men carried sacks of dirt out from a bunker. One man was well muscled, and worked with mechanical regularity. The other had the thin, underdeveloped body typical of a student. Dana smiled at the memory of his time at university, and the hours spent with friends discussing politics and philosophy. They had debated the ideas of the time with intellectual passion, but practical ignorance. They had talked about Hitler's policies, and speculated on his intent. They had reviewed the principles of Leninism, and some thought it might even help some countries economically. They argued with conviction and naivety. It would be years before they would see firsthand the effect of Hitler's death squads, and feel the impact of the Soviet hammer.

"Did you sleep well?" asked a woman. Her brown hair was pulled back. She had round cheeks and soft eyes. The face seemed familiar, as if he had seen it in a dream. Dana shook his head.

"You were barely conscious when they brought you in after the mission. I took care of your hand, and your back. They did quite a job on you." She gently took his arm and examined the bandage. "I'm Dr. Vera Alexas."

"Thank you."

"We'll have to keep a close watch for infection. We have to make do with herbs, salt, and vodka, because there's very little medicine. A few days of rest, and you'll feel much better. You'll be glad to know they only broke two of your fingers. You should be able to use a gun."

They circled around to the cook tent, where Raminta was heating water under a metal sheet that served as a roof.

"The forest here is large and dense, so we can light fires, but we only do it for a brief period of time," said Vera.

Jurgis and Vadi emerged from the forest, and nodded to Dana. "Sorry about your parents."

"So you're partisans, too," said Dana.

"We've been helping Simas for a while," said Vadi.

"You've known me for years, and you didn't trust me enough to tell me?" Dana felt a sting. Even though he knew nothing, he had been ready to accuse them both.

"If we didn't trust you, you wouldn't be here. Besides, you can't tell the Russians what you don't know."

"You were working for me."

"We take our orders from Simas."

"You take your orders from *me!*"

"Not in the forest."

"Gentlemen," said Vera. "None of us know everything. That way, if we're captured, we can't say much. There are just over two dozen people here at camp. There are other groups, but we don't know who they are, or where they are. Partisan leaders even use code names."

Vadi and Jurgis sat down.

"Who are all these people?" said Dana.

"Most are from Vilkija, and from many different professions. We have farmers, an office worker, a teacher, and even a baker, although he's from Latvia. Some, like Simas, have military experience," said Vera.

"Don't forget that we have a doctor," said Vadi.

Vera smiled.

"I'm impressed," said Dana, glancing at Vera. "How long have you been here?"

"Since the Germans left, but Simas had the foresight to begin hoarding supplies long before that," said Vera.

"At least the Germans paid for the food they took," said Vadi.

"The Germans devastated the Jews, and for the rest of us, they were just as brutal as the Russians," said Vera. "In wartime, bad people do terrible things. The tragedy is that good people are driven to do bad things, too."

"Nothing is as bad as the Soviets."

"How can a few farmers and office workers take on the Russian Army?" said Dana.

"The Russians won't be here for long. The West won't allow it," said Vadi.

"In 1941, we fought with the Germans against the Soviets. The West may not forgive us for that," said Vera.

"The West won't condone communism. It's against their principles. Once the Germans are defeated, they'll move to defeat Stalin. All we have to do is survive until then," said Vadi.

"Now you sound like Simas," said Vera. "If you're here to hide and wait for someone to come and save you, you've picked the wrong place."

"Before anyone saves us, I have an account to settle with one Russian in particular," said Dana. "Zabrev."

"I saw how brave you were during the raid on the farmstead. And Simas said you didn't talk during the interrogation. Maybe you'll get your chance." Vadi gently put his hand on Dana's shoulder. Dana winced, and Vadi removed the hand.

"At least we're in the forest where we have the advantage," said Vera. "We know the old paths and short-cuts through the bogs and woods. We'll be alright, as long as we have faith in ourselves, and fight for our freedom as long as we need to. *We* need to decide our fate and declare that the Red violence must stop. Patriotism was something we learned about as children, but now it's more than just poetry and songs."

"If we don't stop the Red terror, it will roll through Europe like a Russian tank," said Vadi.

"We could be fighting for a long time," said Jurgis.

Ludmelia awoke to the sound of voices. She remembered coming to the camp with Simas and the others last night, and relaxed. She felt the ground for the pistol, and didn't find it. Her pulse quickened as she stood and lifted the blanket. *No gun.* She thrust her hand into her knapsack. *Not there.* She rummaged through the leaves that made up her bed, until she felt the cool metal. She breathed a sigh of relief, and tucked the pistol under her belt.

A morning mist hung in a gray curtain through the trees. A glistening layer of dew covered everything, including her blanket. Ludmelia noticed the forms and shapes of figures moving like ghosts. Some were already working, while others drifted to tables near a tent and campfire.

Blended into the hushed sounds of the camp were bird songs, the melody of the wind through the oaks, the scratches of squirrels running on ragged bark, and the sound of a distant stream. She closed her eyes and took a deep breath, wishing Papa was with her.

Dana sat on a nearby rock, sipping from a cup. She sensed he was watching her, and she didn't like it.

"Why are you staring at me?" she asked.

"Hello, Ludmelia."

His clear eyes and broad, open face brought her back to the Ravas farmstead, and the afternoons with Mama in the kitchen. Occasionally, Dana had come inside for tea. He had nodded to her, but had said little, acting as if he had forgotten all the times they had played together as children. He had always been arrogant, but since leaving school, he had become angry as well, ordering Simas and Bronai about with stubborn determination. Still, once she had caught him bandaging Gerta's hand with surprising tenderness after she had burned it on the stove.

"It really was you in the prison?" asked Dana.

Ludmelia nodded.

"Where's your mother?"

"Dead."

"My parents, too." Dana told of the raid on the farmstead, and Zabrev's brutal orders.

Ludmelia recoiled at Zabrev's name. It seemed that everyone knew the Russian. "Your parents gave us food when we had nothing. They gave Mama work when we were desperate. I felt more at home in your mother's kitchen than I ever did in the cottage."

"Living in camp is going to be different from the farmstead." Dana managed a faint smile.

"I'm glad you're alright."

Dana looked toward the cook tent. "I see they're making breakfast. Let's get something to eat."

They approached a wisp of a woman leaning over a cauldron, ladling coffee into cups.

"Eda?" said Ludmelia.

The woman turned and smiled. She put the ladle down and hugged Ludmelia, who smiled at the memory of the two of them chatting in the farmstead kitchen while Ludmelia had waited for Mama, and Eda had waited for Simas.

"Mama's gone," said Ludmelia.

"I know."

"And Bronai and Gerta Ravas."

Eda brushed a tear from Ludmelia's cheek. "I know." She let Ludmelia go, and hugged Dana.

"When did you get here?" he asked.

"Simas brought me a few nights ago."

"And already you look like you belong," said Ludmelia.

Eda smiled and left, returning with cups of coffee. She placed them on the table and returned to help Raminta.

Ludmelia and Dana sipped in silence, until Vera came to the table and sat down.

After introductions, Ludmelia spoke. "Why didn't you leave the country before things got bad, Doctor? You must have had the contacts and money to escape."

"There weren't many doctors in Vilnius, and I was needed. Every morning, I thought I'd stay for one more day, and then I ran out of days. They came for me in the night and brought me to a prison."

"Why?" asked Ludmelia.

"Who knows? They were arresting everybody. Maybe it was because I have family in the United States. Maybe it was because my eyes are blue."

"How did you escape?"

"When Simas heard I had been captured by the Russians, he rescued me."

"He seems to be doing a lot of that lately," said Dana.

"Sometimes I yearn for clean sheets and a soft bed, and have to remind myself that many people have it much worse. Some have lost everything and everyone," said Vera.

Ludmelia looked down into her cup.

Vera watched for a moment as the younger woman brushed a tear from one cheek, and then the other. "Dana, excuse us. I want to show Ludmelia around camp."

As the two women walked, Vera threaded her arm through Ludmelia's, and spoke. "After the Soviets arrested me in Vilnius, they raped me. It's something no woman should ever have to bear. They kept me alive because I'm a doctor, but that didn't stop them from doing what they did."

"How can you bear to talk about it?"

"Women must talk, for their own good, and because others must know what it's like for us."

"They did things to my mother."

"And you?"

"I got away, but the Russians will pay for what they did."

"I knew women who killed themselves because they were raped. They could never get past the shame of it. They thought their lives were ruined. If we take our own lives, the bastards win."

"The war has ruined our lives anyway."

"I don't agree. Strife brings out our true selves, and besides, we're fighting for our freedom. Nothing is more important than that. Not every generation has such an opportunity."

"Or such a burden."

"The war has given many women scars that no one can see."

As a man approached them, Ludmelia noticed he was missing three fingers on his left hand. The stubs were swollen and red. Only his index finger and thumb remained.

He nodded to Vera.

"Did the Germans or Russians do that to his hand?" Ludmelia whispered when he had passed.

"Neither. It was a farm accident. Simas lets him stay because he can still handle a gun."

CHAPTER 22

Ludmelia paced the ground next to her bed of leaves, thinking about what had happened to Vera and to Mama. She was almost raped at the pig farm, so she knew something of the terror. If it happened to her, she didn't want it to change who she was. Someday, she would find one man to love, no matter what happened to her during the war.

Seeking distraction from her thoughts, she looked around and noticed a man sitting alone at the camp table. He had the lean strength of an athlete. His face was handsome, even under the bruises. She recognized him from the prison break. Ludmelia sat down and introduced herself. He said his name was Edvard Urba.

"Where are you from?" she asked.

"My father is from Riga, Latvia, and that's where I live. My mother is from Lithuania, a village near Memel. We spent our summers there. When I was little, my cousins stayed with us. We spent hours roaming the beach and digging in the sand. They used to tease me, because I was so small."

Ludmelia laughed. "It's hard to picture you ever being small."

"Well, maybe I've grown a little. Sunsets on the beach are the most beautiful thing in the world to me, and I miss them."

"I stayed at the seashore once, when I was a girl. I still remember waking up to the scent of salt in the air. The water was cold, though."

"I like the cold. It makes feeling warm and comfortable all the sweeter."

Ludmelia rested her chin on her hands. "If you're from Latvia, why are you here?"

"My brother married a local woman and lives in Vilkija. I was spending a month with them, when the Russians came and arrested me."

"And you know Simas?"

"My brother knew Dana Ravas. We spent many hours hunting in the woods behind the farmstead, and that's where I met Simas. It turns out Simas and I have similar political interests, and recently, I did some work for him." Edvard glanced at the rifle leaning against the bench.

Ludmelia crossed her hands. "What do you do when there's no war to fight?"

"Before the war, I was in the Latvian military. Now, I'm a baker."

"After this is over, I guess you'll be going back to Latvia?"

"I don't know. I'll have to wait and see what the future brings."

"I hope we have something left when the fighting stops."

"We'll have the forests, the land, and the sea, as always."

"I like the forests the best. My father and I went camping often."

"The kind of camping we do here is different from spending a pleasant night out in the woods." Edvard smiled.

He stood, and held out his hand to help her up. When she took it, Ludmelia felt a tingle race through her arm.

Simas limped past the partisans, who were standing in groups or sitting on logs, watching Jurgis hook two corners of a flag to a tree. The breeze caught the cloth and it unfolded, revealing the wide swatches of amber, green, and red of the Lithuanian flag.

The swearing-in ceremony Simas was about to start was a necessity, even though a partisan risked death if he talked, whether or not he had taken the oath. Promising allegiance before God drew them closer together, for words and promises were all they had left.

Simas stepped up on a stone, his back to the flag, and said, "Let's get started."

Voices hushed, and faces turned to him. Most of them had weathered the storms of war for years, but everyone looked young to Simas. He wondered how many would live to see the next year, or even the next day. Every moment it became a little harder to keep them alive through the insane war that had forced them into the woods.

"Those of you who are new to camp, come up here," said Simas.

Dana, Ludmelia, and Eda stepped forward.

"Are you ready?" asked Simas. The three faces beamed up at him like children to a teacher, and they nodded their heads.

"Repeat after me. I swear to fight for the freedom of Lithuania, and in the presence of God, I swear to give my life to my country. I swear to protect my brothers and sisters." He waited for the trio to finish. "I swear to obey the orders of my leader, to avoid all association with the enemy unless ordered to do so, to report anything and everything to my superiors, and to uphold a tradition of silence. If I break this oath, may God punish me with death."

When the voices faded, Simas continued with the Lord's Prayer. When it was over, he pulled out the pistol from its holster, and held out the barrel to Eda. She looked at him with a confused expression on her face. She took the gun, and put into the pocket of her skirt.

Voices chuckled.

"Give it back to me," whispered Simas.

Eda handed it to him.

"Kiss it."

"Kiss what?"

Laughter rippled through the camp.

Simas held out the barrel again.

She kissed it. He held out a corner of the flag. She looked up at him, and kissed that, too. When Eda stepped away, her cheeks were bright red.

Next, he turned to Dana, who also kissed the gun and the flag. Simas shook his hand and said, "I'm proud of you."

Dana's gaze darted nervously around the camp as he stepped away.

After kissing the gun, Ludmelia pressed the tricolor to her face. When she lifted her head, Simas was staring down at her. "I'm proud of you, too."

The crowd pressed in to congratulate the new partisans. Dana watched with narrowed eyes as Edvard kissed Ludmelia on both cheeks and smiled at her. Dana went to congratulate her too, when Simas began to sing. His voice wasn't good, but everyone stopped to listen to the country's anthem, which the Russians had declared illegal. One by one, the partisans proudly joined in, singing loud enough for the angels in heaven to hear. For a few minutes, they didn't care if the Russians heard, too. Dying with the words of the hymn on their lips would be all right. For with those words, they determined to stand together and follow the path of truth and light.

They sang their resolve to live in this land of heroes, and accept nothing less than a life of freedom, even if it took their lives.

At the end of the song, Dana turned back to Ludmelia, but she and Edvard were gone.

After the ceremony, Simas had some of the partisans join him around one of the camp tables.

"Where are Ludmelia and Edvard?" asked Simas.

"Here," said Edvard as the couple came in from the edge of camp.

"We've got work to do. A team is going with me to pay a visit to the Mastev brothers tonight."

"I want to go," said Ludmelia.

"Don't you think it would be better if you stayed behind?" said Vera.

"Not after what they did to Mama. Besides, I killed three Russians at the farm, and another at the prison."

Vera turned to Simas, an angry look on her face. "She's just a girl."

Simas considered his options. The last time he had seen Victor Kudirka was in the Ravas kitchen. Victor spoke of both children with pride, but Ludmelia was his joy. "She is the best among us," said Victor. "She's a natural leader, and never misses a shot. If she chooses to fight, if it comes to that, guide her, Simas. Teach her, and give her the chance to prove herself." Simas had agreed, never expecting Victor's wishes to become reality.

Ludmelia's eyes blazed. "You've seen what I can do."

"Fine. You can go," said Simas. "Edvard, I want you with us. Jurgis, Antanas, you're going, too."

Simas glanced at Dana, remembering his promise to Bronai. "Heal quickly. You'll be going with us soon."

At dark, Jurgis, Antanas, Simas, Edvard, and Ludmelia crossed the lake in search of the Mastev brothers. Antanas and Simas sat together in the boat, reminiscing in low voices about their time together in the Lithuanian Army, while Jurgis and Edvard rowed. Once ashore, they headed for Kazys' truck that Vadi had hidden in the woods after the prison raid. The Studer they had stolen, with the prominent Soviet stars on both doors of the cab, was still hidden in the woods on the opposite side of town.

Edvard pulled off the canvas and leafy branches that covered the truck as Jurgis got in behind the wheel. After some coaxing, the engine turned over. Simas and Ludmelia climbed in. Edvard and Antanas got in the back. The cab smelled of pigs. Simas rolled the window down. As they drove over the rough terrain, the jostling caused Ludmelia's hips to bump into Jurgis'. She moved away, only to bump against him again the next time the truck hit another mount of dirt.

Just outside town, they parked the truck behind a barn. They got out, checked their pistols one last time, and walked toward the road. Soon, dim light from windows cast the streets of Vilkija in an ominous glow. The partisans passed Mr. Poonas' bread shop, and the market with stalls that looked like coffins in the dark. They heard someone approach, and hid between two buildings. A lone soldier turned the corner and went down the street.

They walked on. At the sound of Russian voices, they flattened themselves against a wall hidden in shadow, and two more soldiers marched by.

At last at Bablia's, Antanas and Jurgis found a nearby place to hide and provide cover if needed, while Simas and the others waited out of sight in an alleyway where they could watch the front of the grog house. The night was hot and stuffy. Ludmelia clenched her fists as she thought of the time she had spent in the attic hiding from Denis and Uri, and of what they had done to Mama.

Occasionally, soldiers came out a few at a time, swaying down the steps. Each time the door opened to a swell of voices, Ludmelia caught her breath, but the Mastev brothers didn't appear. She grew impatient, wondering if they were even inside, but Jonai Gabe's job was to bring them there. She knew from Simas that Jonai invited the Mastevs to drink with him often, and they rarely declined, especially after a heavy day of interrogations and beatings.

Still, Ludmelia tensed each time the door to Bablia's opened, and relaxed only a little each time it slammed shut. She was about to ask Simas if they should leave, when Edvard touched her arm and pointed. There they were.

At the top of the steps, the Mastev brothers halted for a moment in the light from the open door. She had imagined them to be ugly and big like trolls, but they weren't. They were just two men, taller than average and very thin, like everyone else. She wanted to run out into the street and shoot them, but that wasn't part of the plan.

Ludmelia slipped off her jacket and hat. As she handed them to Simas, he quickly pulled the gun from her belt. She tried to snatch it back, but Simas wouldn't let it go.

"If they find this on you, they'll kill you," he whispered. "We'll protect you."

With those words, Simas pushed her into the street. She took a deep breath. At least she had the knife tucked into her boots. She stepped into the light cast from Bablia's windows, and thought of Mama.

Already at the bottom of the stairs, the brothers turned and walked in the opposite direction. They hadn't even seen her. *They were getting away!* Soon they would be gone, and she would spend the rest of her life killing them only in her dreams.

Ludmelia unfastened the top buttons of her shirt, put her hands on her hips, and began singing a bar song as she staggered toward the brothers. They stopped, turned, and exchanged a glance.

"An angel has found us," said Uri.

"She won't be an angel for long," said Denis, laughing as he took hold of Ludmelia's wrist.

Ludmelia hissed and snatched her arm away.

"I like it when they put up a fight," said Uri.

The brothers towered over her like a wall of Russian stone. Instinctively, Ludmelia dropped her hand to her belt. If only she had her pistol, she could kill them both. She didn't care if the soldiers inside the bar heard the shots. She didn't care if she died, as long as the Mastev brothers died, too. But before she could bend down to get the knife in her boot, the brothers came closer. She backed away. They followed her into the alley.

The brothers closed in. The certainty of what they intended shook her bones as Ludmelia pressed her back against the wall. Denis bent his face to her neck. His uniform felt rough. His stubble scratched her skin. She jerked her head away and it hit the wall. Ludmelia bit her lip from the pain. She tried to kick him in the groin, but he was too close. She gagged at his stink of stale beer and body odor. She smashed her fists into his ears.

"Bitch!" Denis pressed one hand against her throat as the other reached down to grope between her thighs. She couldn't breathe, couldn't swallow. She frantically scratched at his face. Then he sagged as if the strength had disappeared from his legs. Ludmelia slid down under him, his weight crushing her. She pushed against his shoulders, unable to breathe, and desperate to get away.

Then the weight was gone, and Edvard was leaning over her. He took her arm and helped her to her feet. She put her hand to her throat, still feeling the pressure. She looked down at Denis' prone body, his neck dark with blood. Nearby, Uri lay on his back, his neck also bloody.

She glanced up at the stars. *They're dead, Mama.* Edvard pulled her arm, but she wouldn't move. She stared at the bodies, waiting for feelings of relief and joy but they didn't come. All she had was a sense that Vilkija was better off now. She spat on Uri's body, and wiped her mouth on her sleeve. She kicked Denis violently in the side. *That's for Mama.*

"Let's go," whispered Edvard.

"I'm not done," said Simas. His mouth curled into a snarl as he wiped his knife on Uri's shirt, and put it away. Simas pulled a piece of paper from his pants and tucked it into Uri's front pocket.

Ludmelia gazed down at the bloody sight. She swallowed bile at the sight of their bloody necks, but she believed they deserved it. Edvard took her elbow, and they quickly moved down the alley to the cross street where Antanas and Jurgis were already waiting. From there, they made their way out of town.

By the time they arrived at the barn where they had parked the truck, Ludmelia was past the shock of the last hour. The Mastev brothers needed to die, and she had the satisfaction of helping, but her stomach quivered at the memory of what had happened. Even though she had suffered more from the Mastevs than Simas or any man ever could, the image of their bloody necks remained wedged in her mind.

Ludmelia remembered the look on Simas' face as he had stared down at the bodies, as if they weren't dead enough, and there was something else he needed to do to hurt them. She wanted to know what was on the note Simas had left in Uri Mastev's pocket, but seeing that same look still on his face, she didn't dare ask.

CHAPTER 23

With only the moonlight to brighten his path, Vadi climbed the hill and headed through the old forest toward camp, patrolling yet another area of the vast space. All the partisans shared guard duty. It was their job to know the forest as well as their bedrooms at home, but most of them didn't have homes anymore.

The moonlight made the way easier and less foreboding, but he didn't need the help. When they were younger, he and Jurgis had spent hours in the woods hunting and exploring, just to avoid going home.

When the boys were barely teenagers, their father had hit his head falling off a horse. The boys found him lying unconscious on the side of the road, a short distance from their house. They carried him inside and put him on the bed. Their mother, *Motina,* was frantic. *What will we do if he doesn't wake up? How will we survive?* Jurgis went for the doctor, while Vadi stayed with Father, watching his eyelids for a flutter, and his fingers for a twitch, indicating he was still with them. Vadi prayed that he would just wake up and be well again.

"There's no medicine for this," said the doctor. "He might get well, and he might not. We just have to wait and see."

Throughout the night, the sons stood vigil at the bedside while *Motina* wailed in the kitchen. Early the next morning, fresh with the hope that comes with first light, Vadi called to Jurgis who was asleep in the chair. "I think he's waking up."

The boys leaned over the bed as Father opened his eyes and smiled. Jurgis clasped Vadi around the shoulder and uttered a cry of joy. Father's eyes closed, and his face relaxed. Vadi put an ear to his father's chest and waited for a sound, but heard nothing.

Within a month, *Motina* was fussing over a man from a nearby village who had taken Father's seat at the head of the table. After that, Vadi and Jurgis spent every spare moment out in the woods.

Eventually, they found jobs at the Ravas farmstead. Gerta cared for them as if they were her sons. They ate their meals with the Ravas family, and slept on cots in the room downstairs near the kitchen, where Petra and his father had once lived.

The years working with Simas, and the discussions about fighting the Russians had been the best of Vadi's life.

As Vadi approached the area around camp, he looked for the sentry. As usual, he didn't see anyone, for the men knew how to hide. Vadi called out the password. A sentry appeared, not five meters from where Vadi stood, and smiled. It was a constant challenge to see how close they could get to the men coming in from patrol. Vadi nodded and made his way to Simas' hammock.

"I'm back," said Vadi.

"Help me up." Simas rolled out, and Vadi helped him stand.

Simas limped to the latrine outside camp and unfastened his trousers. His hand shook, and his piss came out in an uneven stream. He glanced at Vadi, who was undoing his own pants. The Mastev brothers were killers, thieves, and rapists. Simas had enjoyed slitting their throats. If he had time, he would have beaten them, too, just like at the prison. Maybe he would have even done more.

Now, Simas needed to focus all his attention on Zabrev. Part of him dreaded to see that Russian, but the bigger part couldn't wait until the bastard came into the forest. The note in Uri's pocket had invited the vicious bear to tea.

Simas fastened his pants. "Petra is of no use to us anymore. In fact, he knows too much already. Have Raminta track that boot-licker in the morning, as he's probably still sniffing around. Tell her to take her bow and arrows. If she finds him, she knows what we do with informers."

Zabrev paced the floor in his office, incensed from Tadnik's report of the dead soldiers found at Kazys Espertus' farm. Their guns and equipment were gone. Even the pig farmer was dead.

Even worse, he had just received word that Colonel Karmachov would be in Vilkija next week. The Colonel was impressed with his reports of success, and wanted to congratulate Zabrev in person. When Karmachov discovered what was really going on, Zabrev was as good as dead. His night of terror had yielded a jail full of prisoners, but the interrogations had produced little useful information. All he had left were a few days to find the partisans, and end this sensation of a rope slowly tightening around his neck. He had to act fast. He was running out of time.

Tadnik knocked and entered, his eyes laced with fatigue.

"What happened?" Zabrev braced himself for more bad news.

"Denis and Uri Mastev were found stabbed to death outside Bablia's, and their throats cut. The partisans, of course."

The Mastev brothers were just thugs, but the partisans had gone too far.

"We found this on one of the bodies." Tadnik handed Zabrev a piece of crumpled paper.

Zabrev unfolded it and read.

I'm in the old forest, you Red bastard. Come and get me.

Zabrev slammed his hands down on the desk. Tadnik jumped. Zabrev wanted to order the men to kill everyone in the entire town, but it would be a mistake if he acted rashly. He had to crush them, but he couldn't afford to make another error. Zabrev needed men to guard the prison and continue the interrogations, for some of the captives must be partisans. They had to be. They weren't saying anything useful yet, but they would. He would make them, even if he had to beat every damn one of them to death.

Now, at least he was certain that the partisans were in the old forest. Still, he couldn't destroy them until he knew the location of their camp.

Zabrev lit a cigarette and sucked in the smoke. His soldiers were dying, yet he had inflicted no damage on the damn bandits. He had barely fired a shot. He needed facts. He needed names. He had to assume that everyone was a partisan, including his own men. He couldn't trust anyone.

Zabrev's gaze went to his aide standing there, giving the impression of strength and competence. He would have to keep an eye on Tadnik, too.

Every man Zabrev could spare would go into the old forest immediately. They would blow the forest apart with bullets and bombs. He was out of options, for once Colonel Karmachov realized what damage the partisans were inflicting, Zabrev may as well stick a gun in his mouth and squeeze the trigger. Finding them was the only way he could stay alive, even though the thought of going back there filled him with dread.

In the dark of night, the partisans were already preparing. The weapons had been handed out. A few people were still chewing the remains of a hurried breakfast. Vera had placed their rudimentary medical supplies into backpacks, and was hoisting one over her shoulder.

The men and women gathered around him, and Simas spoke.

"The Russians will be here soon, fifty or even sixty men, probably. We'll be outnumbered, but we know the forest, and they don't. We have a chance to defeat them and get the Russians out of Vilkija, at least for a while."

The partisans murmured their approval.

"I expect Zabrev to be with them. I want you to bring him to me. Under no circumstances are you to harm him. I want him alive. I don't care about anyone else."

"Why don't we just kill him, too, Simas?" asked a partisan. "The bastard hurt enough of us already."

"Sooner or later, a division from the Red Army will arrive, and that will be a different situation entirely. I need to know when, and I need to know what equipment they're bringing. I need to interrogate him," Simas lied. He just wanted Zabrev for himself.

Dana glanced at Edvard, who was standing next to Ludmelia.

"I'd like to go, too. I'm ready, and I can still shoot," said Dana, lifting his bandaged hand, wiggling the thumb and index finger.

Simas glanced at Vera, who nodded.

"Alright," said Simas. "I'm putting you with Vadi and Edvard. They'll keep an eye on you. Besides, we need all the men we can get."

Ludmelia bit her tongue. She had spent years in the woods learning its ways. She could shoot better than any of them. Yet in every mission so far, Simas had used her as bait. He treated her as if she could be replaced as easily as a worm on a fishhook. Dana wasn't nearly as capable. He was still moving stiffly, after only a few days of rest. Simas said Dana had grown up, but Ludmelia had her doubts. She didn't know whether it was possible for someone like Dana to change so quickly.

Simas startled her out of her thoughts by handing her a SVT-40 semi-automatic with an optical sight. "This is for you," he said. "I know you're a crack shot. Today, you're a sharpshooter. I want you in Vadi's group. Pick off as many Russians as you can."

As dawn broke, Petra marveled at the beautiful view of the rye fields from the window in the Ravas' bedroom. The room was still a mess though, with the bureau drawers open and their contents thrown to the floor. Petra got up and searched for a fresh pair of socks. He found a dark pair, with something stuffed in the toe. He stuck his fingers inside and extracted a roll of rubles. Petra laughed. This was his lucky day.

With the socks on his feet and the money in his pocket, he padded down the hallway to Dana's room. A colorful quilt lay on the floor, next to a bed and a broken chair. A mirror hung over a set of drawers with the contents spilling out over the side. Books lay all over the floor. Some bindings were broken, as if someone had stomped on them with a heavy boot.

Petra opened the closet. Two shirts and a tie hung inside. A suit lay on the floor. Petra picked it up and slipped on the jacket. The gray satin lining felt cool against his skin, but the sleeves hung down beyond the tip of his fingers. He rolled them up and admired himself in the mirror. He straightened his back. Yes, he would have made a fine Secretary of the Executive Committee.

Petra held Dana's trousers up to his waist. The cuffs lay on the floor. The pants were far too long for him.

He remembered that Bronai was short. Maybe his clothes would fit better. Petra let the trousers fall to the floor and the jacket slip from his shoulders. He went back to the room where he had slept. This closet held a brown suit and a tie. More clothing lay wrinkled on the floor.

Petra put on the pair of trousers. The length wasn't bad, although the waist was far too big. He searched for a belt, and found a pair of suspenders hanging from a hook. He clipped them to the pants, pulled up the straps, and moved his hips in a dance.

Petra rifled through the items on the floor for a shirt, and his fingers brushed against a black dress. The cool fabric chilled him, for it felt like the touch of Gerta's hand.

He went back to Dana's closet for a pair of shoes, but the ones he found were far too big. Petra skipped to the other bedroom and tried on Bronai's shoes. They fit perfectly.

Petra laughed aloud. He loved being rich.

He settled for Bronai's suit, shirt, and shoes. He also wore Dana's dark blue tie. He moved the roll of money to the pocket of his new trousers, and placed Bronai's brown cap on his head, cocking it to the side. He unpinned the red ribbons from the old suit and was about to move them to the new jacket, but thought better of it. It was time to forget the past and to start over.

Petra felt like a new man. He was going to miss this place.

He left the house carrying a knapsack with all the food he had found: a few barely ripe apples, some raw potatoes, and half a loaf of bread he had found in the slop bucket for the pigs, although they were gone, too.

Petra closed the back door behind him, and with a spring in his step, headed down the stairs.

CHAPTER 24

Vadi led the partisans along the ancient path through the forest, pointing out hiding places he had forged under tree roots and bushes. Ludmelia had no idea he was so clever.

They arrived at the little beach as dawn broke. Following Simas' instructions, they split into groups and positioned themselves so they had cover, as well as a view of the shoreline, and a good field of fire. Vadi led Dana, Ludmelia, and Edvard to a spot on an upsweep of land near the ridge. Groups of men waited to their left, and others took positions to the right. Simas, Vera, and another man stayed farther back.

Ludmelia lay on her belly alongside Dana and Edvard, while Vadi peered through binoculars at the lake. Moisture seeped in through her pants. A bug crawled up her ankle. Insects hummed. Edvard shifted to his side, and Ludmelia sighed. She pinched herself in the arm to stop a daydream from even starting. She glanced at Dana, who was scowling at Edvard, and she wondered why. Edvard didn't seem to notice.

Her stomach growled. Breakfast had been hours ago. She remembered the bread in her pocket, but she couldn't eat it now. It was there in case she had to spend the night away from camp. She remembered the fragrance of pork roasting in Kazys' kitchen, and how it had turned sour when mixed with the scent of blood. The grotesque expressions of the dead Russians lying on the floor became more vivid in the recollection. Yet the explosive strength she had felt when she killed them still empowered her. In that instant, no one could have hurt her, and it felt good.

She had spilled Russian blood, and that felt good, too. Her mind drifted to Denis. She shivered recalling his touch, and felt relief knowing that he and his brother were both dead.

Dana slapped a bug on his cheek. Ludmelia pinched his arm. He rubbed the sore spot and smiled at her. His eyes looked sleepy.

"Stay perfectly still. If the bugs want to eat you, let them," she whispered.

"Quiet," said Vadi.

"No one's here," said Dana.

"Do as you're told."

Ludmelia felt Edvard's gaze on her. Her face got hot.

At first, the distant hum of the patrol boat's engine blended in with the sounds of the forest. Soon, its growl was all she heard. The minutes passed by faster the closer it came, until the boat stopped near the shore, its engine still rumbling.

Ludmelia expected to see soldiers exit the boat, but the seconds of inactivity made her wonder what the Russians were doing. Then the bombardment started. The explosions were so loud, Ludmelia thought that the earth had cracked open. Machine-gun blasts from the patrol boat riddled the area. Small trees fell to the ground. Bits of leaves and bark flew into the air. Mortar rounds pounded the earth. The noise seemed to go on forever.

Ludmelia wanted to burrow into the dirt to get away from it all. She pressed her body to the ground and covered her head against the bits of bark and wood falling down on her. The Russian's sheer power in slicing through the forest made her think that she and her brothers and sisters might not survive.

"Go, go, go!" shouted Zabrev from the patrol boat, as his men scrambled and thrashed through waist-high water to the shore.

By the time Zabrev stepped onto the muddy beach, the soldiers had secured the area. The shore was his. Soon, the entire forest would be his.

The patrol boat sped back to the dock for the next wave of soldiers, as the small craft could barely accommodate twenty men. He expected to see dead partisans, but the shore was deserted, except for a few birds that had been blown apart in the assault. Already, his feeling of strength began to fade.

As Zabrev ordered the men into the woods, he had the odd feeling that his nightmare was just starting.

Settled into their spot, Vadi, Dana, Ludmelia, and Edvard waited for the barrage to end. When it did, Vadi looked through the binoculars, and handed them to Ludmelia.

"They're coming. The skinny one is Zabrev's aide," he whispered. "Comrade Commander Zabrev is the big one to the left. Remember, don't kill him."

She gazed through the lenses at a broad-shouldered man who stood half-a-head above the rest. She couldn't see his face clearly because of the helmet, but she would remember his physique for the rest of her life. She looked to either side at the wave of soldiers advancing.

Ludmelia returned the binoculars and glanced at the others. Edvard waited calmly, but Dana looked terrified. His face was pale, and she could see his hands shaking.

She moved away from them, and took aim at a spot in a soldier's path, feeling like a she-wolf stalking her prey. She waited for Simas to take the first shot.

When it came, the soldiers scattered, but one came into her sights. She brought him down, and then quickly rolled to her right. *Take the shot and move. If you don't, you're dead,* said Papa. The rain of return fire started, but still a few partisans managed more shots.

From her new spot, Ludmelia tried to glimpse her companions. Not far from their original hiding place, Vadi was tying a bandage around Dana's leg. Edvard lay on the ground, his chest covered in blood. Stunned, Ludmelia stared at him. *Get up, Edvard.* He didn't move. *Oh God, please no!*

Vadi dragged Dana behind some trees, and motioned for Ludmelia to follow. She shook her head. Vadi motioned again, but Ludmelia didn't move. Vadi shrugged, picked Dana up, and they disappeared through the trees.

Within seconds, she thought she had just made the stupidest decision of her life. She was alone. Edvard was certainly dead, or Vadi would have tried to move him. She didn't know where the others were, and the Russians were still shooting. *Make a plan and stick to it,* said Papa.

Gazing at Edvard's lifeless body one last time, she became drunk with the prospect of blasting the Russians to hell. She wanted make them suffer, to make them pay. She thought of Edvard's strength and his touch. She thought of the thrill after the swearing-in ceremony, when he had taken her behind a tree and kissed her. She hadn't known him well, but sometimes anticipation can leave a stronger mark than reality. If she had time to mourn for him at all, it would have to wait. Her sadness would have to wait, for she was hunting Russians.

Zabrev didn't know where the shots were coming from, at least not with certainty, for they seemed to come from every direction. He had already sent groups out to find the snipers. His was the last group left, and there wasn't time to wait for the patrol boat and more men before moving again. As they ran for the protection of the trees, gunshots broke the silence, and another one of his soldiers fell down dead.

As they approached the spot where they had assaulted the phantom camp, there came another explosion, much louder than the rest. Zabrev dove for cover. The smoke cleared to reveal Tadnik kneeling by a soldier.

The man's side was a mass of raw meat. Blood covered what remained of his leg. A crater the size of a grave lay next to the injured soldier. The man's weak whimpers shook Zabrev, and for a moment destroyed all sense of strength and control. *It was just one man*, thought Zabrev. *Just one man.*

As Tadnik frantically wrapped a tourniquet around the bloody leg, the injured soldier became quiet and still. Zabrev looked at his men. Their faces held the same hollow expression of imminent death that he had seen in the troops at Stalingrad.

"They planted mines," hissed Tadnik.

Ludmelia moved toward the explosion, scrambling for a new hiding place recklessly close to Zabrev and the group that remained with him. She knew it was foolish to be there, but she didn't care. She felt like a starving woman feeding a hunger. She steadied the rifle and took aim. Zabrev's head was the first thing that came into view. It made a lovely target, but the soldier next to him pulled back his helmet to wipe his brow. *He was the one who wanted to die.* She felt power. In that moment, nothing mattered but killing the soldier.

Aim, hold your breath, steady, steady, fire. Go!

She moved immediately. Return bullets hit the dirt, but she was gone. She was Ragana, the goddess of the trees. She could slip through the forest undetected. She could determine life or death.

The Russians didn't think she was a spirit of any kind, for they came after her like angry bears. As Ludmelia ran, the trees protected her, some absorbing Russian bullets and others deflecting them.

"Dammit," shouted a voice. Roots tripped Russian boots. A man fell to the ground. Twigs slapped against Russian faces, slowing them as Ludmelia raced away.

The clamor of gunfire seemed to wilt even the leaves on the trees.

You're the best shot, Ludie, said Papa.

She stopped, turned, aimed, and fired. She was running again before the soldier fell, and the others crashed through the underbrush in pursuit.

It took only a moment to get to the hiding place, a little bunker forged in the ground under a rotting tree. Vadi had pointed it out just hours ago. Ludmelia crawled inside and shifted the thick branches back over the opening. She waited, her chest heaving from the exertion.

A black deeper than the richest velvet surrounded her. The damp air smelled of earthly decay. Ludmelia lay on her side and hugged her knees to her chest. Bullets hit nearby branches, while others zinged into trees, their sounds strange and fearful in the complete darkness. Ludmelia's heart beat wildly, and she pushed her fist into her chest so that it would pound more quietly. *She was going to die.*

Dirt fell onto her head and face. The sweat dripping down her cheeks felt like worms crawling on her skin. She barely breathed for fear of making a sound.

She had made it convenient for the soldiers by crawling into her own grave. She remembered the attic and the blackness that had hidden her. She remembered the rhythmic squeak of the bed and Mama's agonizing death. She had survived. She might survive again.

The gun blasts sounded even closer, and then they stopped. Footsteps approached, and heavy Russian voices. "Where is he?"

"It was an army."

"Are they gone? Oh God, are they gone?"

"Did you see them?" The words sounded so close, they startled Ludmelia.

"They disappeared like ghosts."

She pointed the gun at the entry to her hiding place. If they found her, more Russians would die, and she would, too.

"They're picking us off," said another voice. Ludmelia imagined wiggling her gun through the dirt and shooting the man.

"The bandits shot Boris."

"Fedya, too."

"They blasted Sergey to bits."

"I'm not going to stay here and die like a dog."

"Zabrev and Tadnik are worried."

"Remember how the bandits cut Denis and Uri."

"The partisans will kill us for sure, and cut us, too."

"The officers don't care about us. They never do."

"Run man! Save yourself."

Boots pounded the earth.

"Stop," shouted yet another voice. It was softer and farther away, yet somehow familiar. Shots rang out, followed by cries of pain. Bodies thudded to the ground, and rolled. Ludmelia stared into the black.

"Commander Zabrev, what have you done?" cried another man.

"No one disobeys me and lives."

The voice's rich tone made Ludmelia think of a rushing stream, but she had heard it before. It was the voice from the cottage, the one without a name. It had ordered the others to *finish it*. There was no doubt. This soldier had ordered Mama's death. Hatred filled Ludmelia so completely she thought she would explode. She didn't care what Simas wanted. One more shot was all she needed, but if she came out now, she might miss, and Commander Zabrev might live.

The voices faded. When she thought it might be safe to leave her hiding place, she waited some more, fearing a trap. If Zabrev was in the forest, she could track him, no matter how much time had passed. Still, waiting to emerge from the little bunker was one of the hardest things she had ever done.

The light hurt her eyes when she finally moved the branches aside and crawled out. It took a moment for them to adjust. No soldiers were in sight, other than the dead ones at her feet. Ludmelia stepped over a body, and set off to find Zabrev.

She spotted him some time later with Tadnik, both crouching behind a pair of spruce trees a good distance away. They waited with their pistols drawn. A woodpecker tapped a tree and Zabrev jerked his head upward. Tadnik didn't even move. No other soldiers were in sight. Either they were hiding, dead, or they had all run away.

Ludmelia waited, still shaking from her frenzy to kill. In those moments, she hadn't even thought of the risk she was taking. She hadn't thought about anything but killing. She could never act so foolishly again if she hoped to survive.

Zabrev nodded at his companion, and they left.

Ludmelia followed them, but remained a good distance behind. As the light faded, she sensed them before seeing them. Tadnik's dark figure was standing guard, while Zabrev lay stretched out on the ground. She shimmied under the branches of a pine tree, the scent of resin sharp and clean. Her stomach growled. She reached into her pocket for the bread, and wondered if Dana was all right, and how far he and Vadi were from camp. She thought of Edvard, and hoped he was at peace with God. She hoped his last minutes hadn't been painful. She wouldn't let herself think about him anymore, because she couldn't afford to. She had to stay focused. Ludmelia chewed slowly to make the food seem like more of a meal. She drank water from her canteen. When she had finished, she moved to a spot even closer to the men.

CHAPTER 25

In his new suit, the knapsack on his back, and the roll of money in his pocket, Petra felt like a rich man going on a trip. As he descended the back steps of the Ravas' house, his gaze drifted to the potato patch and a rock topping a wide mound of fresh dirt. *The old folks might be buried there.*

A shiver ran down Petra's spine, and he ran through the fields. When he slowed, faint footsteps crunched the plant stubble behind him. Petra felt a wave of panic and spun around, but no one was there.

He continued through the fields paralleling the road, not far from trees where he could hide if he had to. He started at another sound, but saw nothing. If the footsteps were more than just his imagination, it was certain they weren't Russians. Russians would have already killed him.

As Petra admired the open tract of land, imagining that it was part of his own estate, it didn't feel like he was alone. At the cold chill of fear, he broke into a run again and headed toward the woods. There, he slowed to a walk. He paused by an elm tree to listen, but his heart was beating too fast to hear anything. He ran some more. Branches whipped his face. He stumbled over rocks and climbed over dead tree trunks. He tripped on a vine, and rotated his arms for balance until his step was sure again. He ran until his lungs ached. He stepped on a rock covered with moss, and fell hard.

He moaned as he got to his feet, gulping for air. Blood pounded in his ears. He jumped at another sound. It might be Zabrev. It might be the branches shuffling in the breeze, the partisans, or an evil wood nymph. It might be his imagination. It was best to keep moving.

He stopped at a clearing, too tired to go any farther, and peered out over the grass. It was just like the clearing he had visited with *Teti* when he was a boy and life was easier. He shivered from sweat and the moisture that had seeped into his trousers when he fell. He turned his face toward the crystal sky. The scent of pine made every breath feel fresh. Petra leaned against a tree and closed his eyes. He was a vessel, and the sun was pouring life into him.

Maybe he would find a farmhouse with a grieving widow and leave the hardships of the war to others. He wasn't meant to live a difficult life. He was born to live as a wealthy man.

A pain shot through his chest. His father had had a weak heart. Maybe Petra was having a heart attack. He tried to take a step, but couldn't move away from the tree. Somehow, he was pinned to it. A wooden rod with feathers at the end protruded from his chest. He wrapped his fingers around the rod and tried to pull, but he was too weak. Raminta stood on the other side of the clearing. *She had been following him.* She held a bow in her hand.

"Help me, Raminta," whimpered Petra.

"This is all the help that traitors and informers get." She took an arrow from the quiver on her back, placed it on the string, pulled, aimed, and fired.

"No," shouted Petra. He put his hand up to stop the arrow, but it blasted through his flesh, nailing the arm to his chest. His body shook from another bolt of pain. His hand felt wet. *Raminta wouldn't let him die, would she? Would she?*

Zabrev lay next to a flat rock, gazing up through the trees. He and Tadnik had traveled far and had seen nothing, heard nothing. Yet, it felt like someone was out there. Zabrev twitched at a sound, and sighed in relief as a mouse ran to a bush.

If they were alone now, it was certain they wouldn't be alone for long. It was time to change the game. It was time to track the partisans. It was time for *him* to be the aggressor and pursue *them*. Zabrev pulled a flask from his pocket and took a drink. The liquor left a warm path down his throat.

Colonel Karmachov might be at headquarters already. He would be wondering why Zabrev had lied in his reports. He would want an explanation for all the disasters that that his guards no doubt, would have mentioned by now. Maybe Colonel Karmachov would have him shot on sight.

Zabrev could say that the partisans were more resourceful, deadlier, and there were more of them than they had predicted. It didn't matter, though. Zabrev was dead unless he destroyed the partisan camp, and even that might not be enough.

A Communist official, a commissar, might be there, too, demanding an accounting. Zabrev wouldn't survive an inquiry, even from a pasty-faced official who had never even fired a gun. His only chance at survival was here, where partisans were undoubtedly looking for him.

"Comrade Commander, should we leave the forest?" asked Tadnik.

"No," said Zabrev, scowling at the interruption. "We'll stay until we find them."

"Yes, Comrade Commander." Tadnik squatted down, and continued peering into the trees.

Dana moaned as Vadi lowered him onto a makeshift table already red with blood from other wounded men. Simas had returned, along with Vera, the injured, and those who had carried them to camp. The men who were able, had already left to join the others hunting the Russian soldiers scattered through the forest.

"Where are Edvard and Ludmelia?" asked Simas, as Vera hurried over. Patterns of blood stained the apron tied around her waist. She immediately began tending to Dana's leg.

"Edvard's dead."

"Not him, too."

"Has Jurgis come in?"

"Not yet."

Vadi took his cap off and looked down at his feet. "Ludmelia stayed, and kept shooting."

"What?"

"There was nothing I could do. I had to get Dana back here, and she refused to come." Vadi nodded toward Dana. "He was jittery, but at first, he kept his head and I thought he was going to be fine. We even managed to get a few shots off before he went crazy. Like an idiot, he got up and started running toward them, firing his gun. A regular one-man army. Edvard went after him. Just as he was tackling Dana, Edvard got it in the chest. Dana took one in the leg." Vadi spat and squashed the spittle with his foot. "If Dana had just stayed put, Edvard would be alive. Dana wasn't nearly as ready as you had thought."

Simas rubbed the stubble on his jaw. "Damned fool."

"Dana didn't even realize what he had done until I told him. Edvard died saving him. At least Edvard could fight."

Simas looked at the wounded man before him, and turned back to Vadi. "Have something to eat, and get back out there."

Vadi nodded, and walked to a table where Eda was already dishing out a bowl of potatoes flavored with small bits of boiled beef. He sat down on the bench.

"Zabrev's in the forest?" As Eda handed the bowl to Vadi, her hand shook.

Vadi nodded and surrounded the bowl with his arms as if he was worried that someone might snatch it away. He spooned food into his mouth. After a minute, he sat up, gave a great sigh, chewed, and huddled back down for more.

"Will they ever leave us alone?"

"If we capture Zabrev and Simas makes him talk, we might survive for a while, at least."

The moonlight made the trees seem even taller than they were, and Ludmelia felt safe. The constant low hum of insects soothed her. She had settled down under a fir, close enough for a slightly obscured view of the two Russians, and just within earshot.

Tadnik bent over a backpack and pulled something out, handing it to Zabrev. Ludmelia's stomach growled as she watched the men chew.

Despite all the time she had spent with Papa in the woods, she had never dreamed she would be tracking Russians in the forest. If it weren't for the war and all of Papa's training, would she be a different woman? She couldn't imagine Zabrev as a different man.

Focus, Ludmelia. Don't let your mind wander.

Yes, Papa.

"I have no doubt we're alone. They can't track us in the dark, anyway," said Tadnik. He surveyed the surrounding brush, and handed Zabrev a flask.

Zabrev took it and glanced over his shoulder. The air felt thick and heavy. Branches hung listlessly from the dark trees, while the moon lurked behind them like a giant eye. Zabrev watched it as he took a drink and waited for his body to relax. The partisans knew his every move. Maybe they were watching him now. Maybe one of Zabrev's men had been helping the partisans. His skin prickled. He looked up at the trees. They seemed a little taller, and a little darker. He took another drink.

"Damn them," said Zabrev.

"I'm sorry?"

"Damn them to hell. If they had offered us a bite of food and a bit of information, we wouldn't have to take anyone to prison. There would be no need for interrogations. We wouldn't have to be here in the middle of the night hunting the partisans. They're too stubborn for their own good. They don't understand how important it is to cooperate in order to survive. They need to understand that the Motherland will never give them up."

Zabrev took another drink. "Didn't you find them insolent when you lived here?"

Tadnik shrugged. "I found them to be a lot like us."

"Don't make jokes." Zabrev's head began to pound. "You said the locals helped you when you were hiding in the forest."

"A few, yes. One family was originally from Russia."

"These people are like animals. I know because in Stalingrad, we lived like animals in the ruin of a factory, or in the rubble of an apartment building. One night we dug through wreckage to get to a cellar where we thought we'd be safe. In the morning, a few of the men refused to come out. I made them though, at gunpoint. When they saw the sky, they ran." Zabrev laughed. "They actually thought they could escape."

"I heard about soldiers running, just like today." Tadnik's lips pressed into a thin line.

"And they were shot, just like today. They were deserters. Cowards. They deserved what they got. No one can escape. Not you, not me."

"Some of the boys who ran today were in school last week, going home to their mothers at the end of the day."

"And what would you suggest I do, let them go?"

Tadnik waited before speaking, as if bolstering his courage. "Instead of going after the partisans here, we could go back to headquarters, and figure out a way to flush them out of the forest so we can overpower them."

Zabrev took another drink as the night pressed into his chest. Tadnik had hidden in forests not thirty kilometers away. He knew these people. He admitted that they had helped him. Now, Tadnik wanted to leave. He wanted to go back to the shore. Maybe partisans were waiting there to ambush them.

Though Tadnik had killed a couple of partisans who were hiding in a bunker in the woods, his trap at the Espertus pig farm had been a disaster. He had let a man die in the bog, and had let another walk over a mine. Tadnik had failed. Tadnik was useless. Zabrev would have to pay for Tadnik's failures.

Zabrev wondered if Tadnik had written the bloody note luring them here, that he claimed to have found in Uri Mastev's shirt pocket. Perhaps Tadnik was supplying the partisans with information because they had saved his life.

He could tell Colonel Karmachov that Tadnik was a traitor. Zabrev could blame the failures on him. Zabrev could say his aide was out of control, and had written the false reports. Those years hiding in the woods had turned Tadnik into one of *them*.

When Zabrev got back to headquarters with knowledge of the partisan camp and the information that a traitor had been among the soldiers he commanded, Karmachov might even promote him for triumphing over great odds.

Tadnik continued. "We can regroup, and get reinforcements."

"Perhaps." Zabrev put his hand on the pistol in his hip holster.

"We could even kill one prisoner a day until the partisans surrender, or someone talks. That would at least pressure them to come out of the forest."

"Perhaps." Zabrev shifted his weight so Tadnik couldn't see him slide the gun out of the holster.

"Why don't we go back to headquarters and think of a plan?"

"You can leave if you want." Zabrev pointed the pistol at his aide.

"Comrade Commander?"

"Confess, traitor!"

"What?"

"You've been working with the partisans all along."

"No."

"Don't lie to me!" Zabrev shot him twice in the chest. Tadnik collapsed like a puppet cut from its strings.

Zabrev winced at the sound, immediately regretting the noise. At least Tadnik wouldn't lead him into a trap anymore. Zabrev got up and holstered the pistol. He slung his knapsack over his shoulder, and picked up his Thompson.

As clouds rolled over the moon and a soft rain began to fall, Zabrev groped his way through the trees like a blindfolded child. He stumbled along for hours before stopping to crawl under a bush.

CHAPTER 26

In the dead of night, Simas paced in front of the campfire and relived the events of the day. The bombardment had been vicious. Two of his men were dead, and possibly even more. He just didn't know. His men were still out hunting down the soldiers. All the injured men who could walk were trolling the woods. Those who couldn't walk but were able to hold a gun were posted as sentries.

A feeling of desperation settled into his stomach. He yearned to fill it with a drink, but he couldn't. He had to stay alert, in case any Russians came close to camp.

Guided more by an instinct for self-preservation than intent, Simas walked the path to Eda's tent. She kept him from putting a bullet through his head, yet every time they were together, he punished her with violence that surprised even him. She tolerated it though, as if she wanted him to hurt her, and sought absolution from it.

"It's me," he whispered, as he opened the flap and went inside. The mattress of leaves crackled as Eda made room for him. Simas put the gun down, took off his boots, and lay next to her.

She sighed. "Those poor men."

"They knew the danger."

"How can you say that?"

Simas put a hand behind his head.

"What about the bodies?" asked Eda.

"The men have already brought them to camp."

"We'll have to tell the families."

"They'll know soon enough."

"Until they do, wives will go on pretending their husbands are alive, and children will wait for their fathers to come home."

"I can't spare anyone. I can't risk someone going into Vilkija and being captured. Don't you understand?"

"I would give anything for it never to have happened."

"I don't have time to waste thinking about what might have been."

"That's all I have left, Simas." She touched a finger to his cheek, and paused. "I love you, and want to marry you, if you'll have me."

"We can't get married. There's no room for love in wartime."

"And when you decide you don't want me anymore, you'll toss me aside?"

"We don't have a priest."

"If we had one, would you marry me?"

"The woman is not supposed to ask the man."

"When are you going to stop punishing me?"

Simas propped himself up on an elbow and looked down at her. All he could see was the faint outline of hair that was as light as snow. If he dared to pretend, maybe all the bad memories would disappear. Maybe he could forget. She put her hand on his cheek, and he covered it with his own. He remembered the honey-scented Krupnika liquor, and the smell of drying hay. Simas reached out to embrace Eda in the relief of love, as he had that day in the rye field before all this started. Maybe he could forget. As he sank into her flesh, Zabrev's image came back, jeering at him, teasing him. Simas bucked into Eda as the tent filled with the memory of smoke, vomit, and beer. As soon as he finished, he rolled away. Eda turned on her side, her back to him, and cried.

Without a word, Simas left her and went back to his hammock. Sleep continued to elude him, as it did most nights. He couldn't remember the last time he had truly rested. He wondered if Eda spent her nights that way, too. At the first rays of dawn, Simas got up, wincing at the pain as he stood. He reached for his boots and his gun, and limped to a rock.

Jurgis waved to him from the edge of the clearing and came into camp. The normally spry man moved like an eighty-year-old.

"I was close, so I wanted to report," said Jurgis.

"Good."

"There are no Russians in the immediate area. We shot the ones we could, and the rest scattered like rats. We found a few who were wounded, and they're not a problem anymore."

"Did you see anyone from camp?"

"Jokubas, Antanas, and a few others. Is Vadi here?"

"He was, but I sent him out again. Go and get some rest."

"I just want some food, and I'll go back out."

Simas watched Jurgis walk to the cook tent. His men were exhausted, stressed, dirty, hungry, and still they wanted to do more. All they needed was to survive until the West came to save them, whether it was in another week, another year, or another lifetime. But no one would arrive in the next few days to rescue a group of weary partisans.

He had fooled Zabrev once. He wouldn't fool that Russian again. Simas might win a battle or two if he called on support from the partisan camp near Didmiestis, and its leader, Lightning. But once the Red Army troops arrived in force, survival would become a bloody game of numbers that overwhelmingly favored the Russians.

If they captured Zabrev, he might tell them something they could use. At best, it would delay the inevitable onslaught. At least Simas would have the satisfaction of ending the man's life. He had to do that for his own sanity.

Maybe Zabrev was already dead. Maybe Ludmelia had killed him. She had been a girl in the Ravas kitchen, but a woman had killed those Russians at Kazys Espertus' farm.

Simas thought of his old friend, Kazys, the father of the boy he had watched grow into a man, the lonely widower whose wife he had helped bury. None of that mattered. History didn't matter. Feelings didn't matter. Kazys had betrayed him, and had to die.

Simas got to his feet and shuffled to Dana's tent, where he opened the flap. Dana's injury meant there was one less man to fight, and one more man to slow them down if they needed to leave camp quickly. Dana was one more person who needed to learn everything about surviving in the woods, for it was clear now that he knew nothing.

"You alright?" asked Simas.

Dana nodded. "My leg hurts terribly."

Simas' leg throbbed, too. The difference was that Dana's would eventually heal, but Simas' leg would hurt for the rest of his life.

"You know about Edvard?" asked Dana.

"Of course."

"Are you going to let me stay?"

"Should I?"

"Maybe it would have been better if the Russians had killed me instead."

"That's not what happened."

"I had to pay them back for what they did." Dana wiped his eyes.

"And you were going to do that by running at dozens of armed men?" Simas thought back to the raid on the Ravas farmstead. Dana's actions weren't brave. They were cocky. Simas was glad Dana hadn't been privy to their plans, for he probably would have talked during the interrogation. Dana had no idea what it took to be a man after all. Now Edvard was dead, and Simas was left with his promise to take care of Bronai's son. Simas didn't even want Dana in camp.

"Where's Ludmelia?" asked Dana.

"If she's alive, she's still out there fighting."

Dana covered his face with his hands. "I'm sorry, Simas."

Simas closed the tent flaps. He needed every man to fight like ten, and every bullet to hit its mark. *Damn that promise.*

Simas motioned to Jurgis, who handed Raminta his bowl and kissed her lips before coming over.

"Go find Ludmelia," said Simas. "If she's still alive, bring her in. If you find any Russians, kill them. Kill them all, dammit."

At dawn, Zabrev was still lying under the bush, so Ludmelia pulled out the last of the bread from her pocket and chewed it, pretending it was sweet *pyragas* filled with golden raisins.

Zabrev awoke and crawled out from his sanctuary. He stood, shook his shoulders, and stretched. He urinated on a tree. Ludmelia made a face and turned away.

Zabrev pulled a piece of paper from his knapsack and examined it. Then he crumpled it into a ball and threw it on the ground. He pressed it into the dirt with his foot, spat on it, and walked away.

When he had moved off, Ludmelia retrieved the paper. It was a hand-drawn diagram of the area of the old forest nearest the shore. She put it in her pocket and followed the Russian.

When Zabrev stacked three small rocks together, Ludmelia realized it was a location marker. After he left, she threw the rocks into the undergrowth. Later, Zabrev broke a tree branch and left it hanging down, pointing along his path. When he was out of sight, Ludmelia tore it loose and tossed it aside.

When Zabrev stopped to rest, Ludmelia found a hiding spot, and aimed the rifle at his head. She caressed the trigger. One twitch was all she needed to avenge Mama's death, Edvard's death, and the deaths of Bronai and Gerta Ravas. One tiny movement would repair her frayed heart.

She could tell Simas that Zabrev was about to kill her. She could say she had no choice but to shoot. Simas would understand. It would be easy. Ludmelia held her breath and closed one eye. She remembered that Zabrev might know something that would help them, and lowered the gun.

Zabrev put his face in his hands, and mumbled, "Go away!"

Ludmelia held her breath, worried that he had seen her.

"Leave me alone!" Zabrev sprang to his feet, snatched up a stick, and lashed at the bushes with a force that made Ludmelia wince. He threw the stick down, and slumped to the ground. A few minutes later, he got up, checked his compass, and moved on.

Ludmelia wondered if she was dealing with a lunatic as well as a murderer. Whatever he was, if she could maneuver Zabrev to the east, she might be able to deliver him right into Simas' arms.

As the day wore on, Zabrev tried to remember the vague images of the young men in Stalingrad fleeing from the fighting. He remembered shooting his gun. He had fired at Germans. He had fired at the Russian soldiers under his command as they ran away. He had watched men die. He was a Communist and a Soviet officer. They had to respect him. His was the voice of authority. He gave orders that others obeyed, and when they didn't, they paid with their lives.

He had never thought about the men he had killed, until now, in this cursed forest. For the first time in his life, the lined foreheads, moles, scars, good teeth, bad teeth, thin cheeks, and fat cheeks swirled into images that were both frightening and familiar. One by one, the faces came to him in the delicate twigs of a bush, in the graceful slope of a branch, and in the creases on a rock. He had no idea there had been so many faces.

Zabrev took a sip of vodka from the flask. There wasn't much left. He should distance himself from the faces. They were watching him.

He didn't want to shoot, because the partisans might hear the noise and come after him. He would fire at the faces if they came too close.

A breeze shifted the leaves on a bush and a face lunged at him. "Leave me alone!" Zabrev beat the branches until the face went away. He threw down the stick and ran. He jumped and weaved as the forest whirled past. He tripped on a root. He crashed to the ground, and crawled to a log. He waved his gun, but had no target.

He held his breath and listened. The trees creaked like the knees of old men. The wind whispered in voices of the dead. He got up and ran again, not caring about the direction, stopping every few minutes to listen to the forest taunting him.

Zabrev wandered for hours looking for his markers, not finding them, and making more. Finally, he sat down with his back against a tree and his gun on his lap, waiting for the ghosts to find him.

Ludmelia had trailed Zabrev's wild path easily, and found a place in a thicket where she could keep an eye on him. If Zabrev continued going in the same direction, he would be at camp soon. Ludmelia considered going ahead to warn Simas, but the sentries would be alert and tell him they were coming.

She wondered why Zabrev had beaten the bushes with such fury. Maybe he was lashing out at phantoms, or maybe he was just insane. Earlier, when he had rested with his face in his hands, she had thought he was in agony.

He deserved to suffer. He was a killer, and so was she. The war had turned them both into killers.

If Papa were here, he would tell her to be strong. He would tell her to protect her family and the people who mattered to her. He would tell her to fight for her country. He would tell her he loved her.

She stared at a gap between two trees, praying for Papa to appear, when something moved. At first, she thought the swath of blue was a bird, but it was too big. When she realized it was Jurgis' beret, she exhaled in relief. She caught his attention, put a finger to her lips, and pointed in Zabrev's direction. Jurgis nodded.

A minute later, as Ludmelia pointed the rifle at Zabrev's head, she felt powerful and angry, but above all righteous. The urge to shoot was overwhelming. *Be calm,* said Papa.

"Get up, you son-of-a-bitch," she said.

Zabrev opened his eyes. "Ludmelia."

She started at the sound of her name, shaken by the familiarity it brought. She lowered her gun. Just by saying one word, he had snatched away her thoughts of death. *How dare he!* She hit him in the mouth with the butt of the gun. A shocked Zabrev fell to the side and spat out a bloody tooth.

Jurgis glanced at her, took away Zabrev's rifle, and handed it to Ludmelia. She slung the Thompson's strap over her shoulder.

"Take off your belt," said Jurgis.

Zabrev unbuckled his belt and holster while staring at Ludmelia. He held it out to Jurgis, who strapped it around his hips. Jurgis tied Zabrev's hands together with a cord, pulled him to his feet, and gave him a shove.

Ludmelia had missed her chance. She told herself that Simas wanted Zabrev alive, that he could help the partisans survive. It didn't make her feel better, though. It felt like Zabrev had hurt her again.

Ludmelia led the way, not bothering to double back, or hide the path in any way. It didn't matter that Zabrev knew where camp was, for he would never leave the forest alive.

As they got close, Ludmelia noticed subtle movements. They had reached the sentries. Jurgis had her wait with Zabrev while he approached the guards with the password.

Zabrev's head kept darting from side to side, as if his enemies were going to pop out of the trees. At the sight of the lean-tos, he straightened his shoulders and marched like a soldier while Ludmelia held a gun to his back.

Men with bandaged heads and arms in slings silently watched as Zabrev walked into camp. Ludmelia was relieved that some had returned, and worried that many hadn't.

Raminta stepped up and spat in Zabrev's face. "That's for my neighbor you tortured."

A man leaning on a crooked stick, spoke. "Enjoy your time with us, Zabrev. I'll want a few minutes to interrogate you myself."

"I could kill you now with my bare hands," jeered another.

"Have a good time in interrogation."

"You killed my father, you bastard!"

The battered partisans limped toward Zabrev, surrounding him, striking him with their arms and canes, kicking him, and spinning him around.

He roared. "Get away from me!"

CHAPTER 27

Alone in the munitions tent, Simas sat with a bottle in his hand, squeezing the neck, imagining it was Zabrev. He tried to concentrate on what the Russian might know and how they might use the information. It could be significant. It had to be. He thought about interrogating Zabrev, and the questions he would ask. He thought about how he would make the Russian talk. Most of all, he kept returning to how he was going to kill Zabrev.

At a commotion in the normally quiet camp, Simas went outside to see Zabrev marching as if he were leading a dress parade. In that moment, Simas forgot everything except the room at Bablia's, where Zabrev had taken Eda.

One bullet would free Simas from this torture. He pulled the pistol from its holster, but partisans surrounded Zabrev, and there was no clear shot.

Zabrev strained against the rope tying his hands together as he kicked the partisans pummeling him. At least this time, his enemy was real. Some kicks brought the satisfaction of hitting flesh, and it compelled him to kick even harder. Zabrev grunted and growled, and the partisans retreated. He was victorious. He was Russian. He was superior!

They came at him again, like hungry wolves.

A fist to his face. "That's for my brother!"

Arms gripped Zabrev. A stick jabbed his stomach, and a fist slammed into his jaw. Zabrev struggled against them.

"This is for my husband!" said another voice. Fingernails tore furrows into Zabrev's face.

Zabrev moaned like a wounded bear. When he sank to the ground, the partisans fell on him. A woman drew back her leg and kicked him. Arms hammered down amid cries of anger, pain, and the dull thud of flesh hitting flesh.

"You said we need him alive," said Ludmelia as she clutched Simas' arm, his pistol still pointed at the crowd. "You had better stop this."

Simas ignored her, his gaze fixed on the angry horde.

She pushed down, lowering the gun. He snapped. "Don't tell me what to do!"

Simas glanced at Eda standing alone, away from the fight. Strands of hair stuck to her cheeks. Her face shone wet with tears as she sobbed with her mouth open, her body shaking. Her cries pierced him like daggers.

"They'll kill him," said Ludmelia.

"I thought you wanted him dead, too."

"I was going to kill him. But you said he had information that could help us survive."

"Fine, then. Take care of it." Simas holstered the gun.

Somehow, she had to find the strength. "Stop!"

The beating continued.

Ludmelia looked for Jurgis. She found him with his arms wrapped around Raminta, guiding her away from the violence.

Vadi would help. He had to, but even he was moving in to join the fray. Ludmelia reached into the crowd for a bandaged arm. Its owner cried out in pain as she pulled him away from the others. She stepped into Vadi's path. As he raised his hand to push her aside, she slapped him in the face. He blinked. She slapped him again, and he turned away.

"Stop them!" she said.

As if recovering from a trance, Vadi worked with her, pulling the men and women off Zabrev, and moving them to the side as if they were sacks of feathers.

Once away from Zabrev, the passion left the partisans. They rose to their feet, and helped others get up. Some stumbled away, their shoulders slumping, their bodies reflecting the suffering they had endured, and would endure, until their lives, in all likelihood, ended in violence.

The only sounds came from Zabrev, who moaned as he lay curled up on the ground, his body still flinching from blows that no longer came. Blood dripped from his nose. He coughed, and more blood trickled down the side of his mouth. One eye was already swollen shut. His lips were puffy.

"Stand up, you bastard," hissed Vadi, but Zabrev stayed on the ground. Vadi dragged Zabrev to a tree as Ludmelia followed them.

She called to one of the partisans and pointed to Zabrev. "If he tries to run, shoot him in the legs. Just don't kill him, not yet."

Vadi checked the cord still around Zabrev's hands before slipping a rope around Zabrev's neck. Vadi tied the end to the tree. Zabrev had acted like a dog, and now he was tied up like one.

Ludmelia had stopped them from killing Zabrev, and now she was angry. She wanted him dead as much as they did. *The wrong people were dying.*

She caught up with Vadi halfway to the cook tent. "What happened to Edvard back there?"

Vadi told her.

Ludmelia's restraint left her. She searched the crowd for Dana, and finally noticed him sitting on the bench with his leg bandaged, staring at Zabrev lying under the tree.

Ludmelia ran to Dana and hit him in the back with a fist.

His spine arched at the pain. The line of red appeared on the back of his shirt. He turned and looked at her with an expression of agony on his face.

She hit him in the jaw. "How did he die?"

"They shot him, that's all. It wasn't my fault!"

Ludmelia hit him again.

"He didn't have to go after me. I didn't ask him to. He could have stayed where he was." Dana lowered his gaze and wiped his nose with the back of his hand. He turned away and put his head down on the table. His whole body quivered.

She wanted to hit him again, but he looked pitiful. Ludmelia ran to the edge of camp, where she sat on a rock, hugging her knees to her chest. During those minutes with Edvard, she had forgotten about the war. Now the war was all she had left. She wanted to cry, but the tears wouldn't come. She wanted to run, but her legs wouldn't move.

Zabrev's face throbbed from the pounding he had received only minutes before, yet it was a relief knowing that he wasn't among ghosts anymore. He could take flesh and blood.

A man with an eye patch approached. Although he had a limp, his most distinct quality was an air of sadness. The war did that to people.

"Ask your questions, or shoot me and be done with it," said Zabrev.

"The lieutenant is a bit edgy, eh?" asked Simas. It took every ounce of strength he had to keep his composure. Vadi stood behind Simas like a shadow.

Zabrev spat out more blood. "Don't mock me, traitor."

"Traitor? I'm defending my homeland." Simas wanted to squeeze the Russian's neck as badly as he wanted another drink.

"You were part of Russia for a very long time. After the Revolution, you had a few years of independence, and you forgot who you are. Your loyalty belongs to Russia. We're all Soviets. You belong with us. Give up this nonsense before there's nothing left for you to protect. Give up before we crush you."

"Tied up like this, with my men all around, I don't think you'll be crushing anyone."

"My soldiers know where I am, and they'll be coming after me." Zabrev blinked at his own lie.

"Many of your men are already dead. The ones who survived are running away from us like frightened children. You are alone. No one is coming to save you. Besides, you're going to tell me everything you know. Believe me, you'll talk. We learned our interrogation techniques from the very best."

"The Germans, of course."

"A little, but a lot more from you bastards." Simas nodded to Vadi, who untied the rope around Zabrev's neck and dragged him to his feet.

"Bring him," said Simas.

Vadi shoved Zabrev toward the edge of camp.

Ludmelia looked up as the three men trudged past her and into the woods. Still angry and armed with more words, she went to the cook tent to find Dana again. He wasn't there.

"Bring this to Simas, so the Russian pig can be revived when he passes out." Raminta handed her a pail full of water.

"I'm looking for Dana."

"Do what I say. This is important. It's for the interrogation."

Ludmelia took the pail, and caught up with Simas just beyond camp. "Raminta said to give you this for when he passes out." She handed him the pail. "I want to watch. He had them kill Mama."

Simas didn't order her to leave, but when he turned and held up his hand, she stopped and found a place to sit.

The three men proceeded a short distance away, to a log near a thicket. Vadi handed his gun to Simas, and pulled out a short length of rough rope with a knot on the end. He put it in the water.

"Take your clothes off," ordered Simas, pointing his rifle at the Comrade Commander. Vadi untied his hands, but Zabrev didn't move. Vadi shoved him, but the Russian wouldn't comply. When Simas touched the end of the barrel to Zabrev's head, the Russian undressed, placing each piece of clothing carefully on the ground.

Black hair covered Zabrev's back and legs. His buttocks shone like pale moons. Ludmelia was past being embarrassed. In the last few days, she had seen and heard enough intimate moments to give her nightmares for the rest of her life.

Vadi retied Zabrev's hands in the front, and hit him in the face. Ludmelia couldn't make out the words when Simas spoke. The Comrade Commander spat something out.

Vadi held the wet rope up in front of Zabrev before lashing it across his face. Ludmelia jumped at the slap. The Comrade Commander staggered backwards.

The next snap of the rope hit Zabrev's neck, leaving a red welt. A moan came from deep within his throat. Vadi crashed the knot across Zabrev's shoulders, down his ribs, and back across his upper thighs.

Zabrev screamed when the rope lashed his penis.

Simas placed his hand on Vadi's arm, and the lashing stopped. When the Comrade Commander straightened, his body was so tense that Ludmelia could see him breathe. Simas spoke and Zabrev shook his head.

When Vadi slashed Zabrev's back, the rope darkened with blood. Vadi moved to the front, and started all over again. The lashing continued with sharp smacks against Zabrev's flesh. Blood dripped from his nose, the corner of his mouth, and the welts on his back.

Zabrev fell to the ground. Vadi threw some water on him, pulled Zabrev to his feet, and they continued.

He deserved this, thought Ludmelia. He's a Russian. Russians had taken Papa away, and had killed the rest of her family. She was alone because of the Russians. She should be rejoicing, but even the birds had stopped singing. Every living thing in the forest seemed to have turned its attention to the gruesome ballet of the partisans and the Soviet officer.

Simas spoke. Zabrev said nothing, and the lashing went on. Minutes seemed to grow into hours. Zabrev fell to the ground and stood after the splash of water. The light faded. Zabrev collapsed again. This time, he didn't get up, despite the dousing.

Ludmelia was relieved that it was over for now. Papa wouldn't have wanted her to see this, but she had to know what the others had suffered. As Vadi dragged Zabrev past her and back into camp, she stared at the mass of bloody meat.

He deserved this. As she followed the procession, Ludmelia wondered what had happened to the girl who had complained about her boring life mere days ago. The woman who remained was willing to kill, and even wanted to kill. Her survival meant doing things that went contrary to human nature. The world was upside down.

Back at the camp, Vadi tied Zabrev to the tree again, and nodded at the guard before leaving. Simas threw the Comrade Commander's clothes over his naked body and walked away.

CHAPTER 28

A pallor hung over the camp as Vera gathered the partisans together to mourn their dead comrades. Graves had been dug outside of camp, in the forest they had defended with their lives. After the burial and prayers, the fierce warriors protecting their homeland shrank to mere men and women, who huddled in groups talking, crying, and remembering.

For Ludmelia, thoughts of Edvard pulled at her heart. She wanted to cry, but her tears would have to wait until the war was over. She had to stay strong. She needed a distraction from the death, the torture, and the memories.

"May I join you?" she asked, approaching Simas and Vera, who were already at a camp table, huddled in conversation. She glanced at Dana, who was sitting alone at the other table.

"We have some things to discuss," said Simas.

"Let her listen. She's smart," said Vera. She touched Simas' hand and smiled.

"Fine, but no talking," said Simas.

Ludmelia sat. From across the way, Dana put down his spoon and stared at her. He looked broken.

Simas spoke. "More people are joining the cause, and I don't expect to operate with this level of independence much longer. Besides, we need to continue organizing. We need a Head of Weapons, a Military Intelligence Unit, and perhaps more. We need to continue training." He glanced at Ludmelia. "We have to survive until the Allies come, but I don't think they're going to be here anytime soon. In the meanwhile, we'll have to be more disciplined, and more ruthless than the Soviets."

"The Allies may never come. Besides, we can't fight the Soviets on their terms. They outnumber us and have more weapons," said Vera. "They'll bring tanks, airplanes, hundreds of troops."

"There's no doubt the Russians will come back soon, looking for us. We have to move to another forest. This country is covered with them. We'll have to choose wisely, though."

"The people in camp say that Ludmelia knows the forests very well. Why don't you ask her which one she would choose?"

Simas frowned. Of course Ludmelia knew the forests, because her father had taken her camping so often. She could also shoot well, and had nerves of ice. Women weren't supposed to make decisions outside the family. Oh, it was all right if a woman became a doctor, like Vera, because it was in a woman's nature to help the sick. But *he* was the leader, and *he* made the decisions, not some girl.

"The forest near Didmiestis is much larger," said Ludmelia. "There's space enough to establish a permanent camp, do the proper training, and improve our chances to live and continue hurting the Russians. Papa took Matas and me there before the war. We spent weeks hiking and camping. I remember it well. There's fresh water, a canopy of trees to hide us from planes, and rough terrain we can easily defend."

Simas got to his feet. "You can't defend anything against Russian tanks."

"They won't be able to move through the forest there," said Ludmelia.

"I like the idea of going to Didmiestis. The Russians will look for us here, but we'll be gone," said Vera.

"I give the orders," said Simas.

"Relocating to Didmiestis is just a suggestion," said Vera.

"I'll think about it."

He left with Vera. Vadi went to him. They spoke for a moment before Vadi went back into the woods.

Eda sat on a stump in front of the cook tent, scrubbing a pot and trying not to look at Zabrev. But pretending he wasn't there drew her attention like a magnet. He had managed to put on his pants, but that was all. His hands were tied, and resting on his stomach. It was too dark to see his bruises. He looked like he was asleep.

Eda tried not to think about what had happened at Bablia's, but avoiding the memory only made it sharper. She hadn't resisted Zabrev. She hadn't fought with her fists, or even her voice. She had let him do what he wanted, while she screamed in silence. Afterward, when her father had smiled his approval, she knew she had become a whore.

The hellish stew of war was making her ill. She couldn't keep food down anymore, vomiting up the simplest fare, especially in the morning. For some women, the first three months were the hardest. Vera was the only one who knew. Eda didn't dare tell Simas she was pregnant. He was already becoming angrier, more sullen, and even moving with difficulty. She knew that he disappeared into the munitions tent from time to time to drink away the memories and the pain. She worried that one day the men would carry him back with bullets in his chest.

Two partisans came to one of the camp tables, glanced at Eda, and sat. The surface of the table had been scrubbed, but blood still stained the wood. One man had an arm in a sling and a bandage covering his hand. Blood showed through the wrapping. Eda put the pot down and went into the cook tent. She returned carrying sandwiches and cups of tea that she placed on the table in front of the men. As they ate, she walked away, but slipped back around the side of the tent where she could listen.

"Ludmelia did well bringing Zabrev in," said the man with the injured hand. "They say she hunted him down like a wolf."

"I don't know if Simas will be able to make him talk. I heard the interrogation was brutal, and he said nothing. Zabrev's tough," said the other man.

"Simas should let Ludmelia take a turn with him. I bet she can loosen his tongue."

"She's cunning. With that hair, she's an amber fox."

"Some of the men call her Amber Wolf."

"Nothing bothers her. That's what I admire."

"We need strong people, but I worry about Simas. The Russians deserved what they got, but he went too far killing Kazys."

"Kazys was a traitor."

"He was a friend."

"Simas spends too much time in the bottle, if you ask me."

"He goes to her tent, too." The man gestured to the pot Eda had been scrubbing.

"Why not? It's the nicest one in camp. Antanas had to give it up for her."

"The poor girl has been through a lot."

"Simas should know that love and war don't mix."

"Maybe he's getting too old for this."

Eda stormed out to where the men were sitting.

"Simas has given up everything for you. He lives for you." Her eyes glowed like hot coals.

Astonished, the men stared at her.

"After everything he's done, you call him a broken old man." Eda picked up a pot and ran at them. "Get out of here!"

The men left with their sandwiches. Eda returned to the stump, and went back to scrubbing the pots.

Ludmelia glanced at the men scrambling away as she walked by. She sat down as Eda scowled at her.

"What's wrong?" asked Ludmelia.

Eda ignored her. Eda didn't blame Simas for treating her the way he did. She was dirty. She had been with a Russian. If Simas needed to use her body to force out his demons, it was all right, for she loved him more than her own life. *If only he'd forgive her.* He didn't even have to love her anymore. She just didn't want him to hate her. She didn't want him to send her away. If Eda went home again, her father would whore her to other Russians, and she had no place else to go. She would rather be dead. She would do anything for Simas, but he was slipping away. She had to do something to save him. She had to save herself and the baby. *She had to find a way.*

"Eda, are you angry at me?" asked Ludmelia.

"Leave me alone," said Eda. She wiped a tear from her cheek with the back of a hand.

"You're going to wear a hole through that pot if you keep it up." Raminta came over, carrying some wood. She put it down, took the pot from Eda, and set it aside. "Eda, you're a lucky woman to have Simas. He's quite a man. He takes care of us. Sometimes I wish I could do something special for him. He comes to your tent at night, eh? You should count your blessings. There aren't many men like him."

"Raminta, you shouldn't gossip like that," said Ludmelia.

"I'm not gossiping. Eda's right here."

Eda got up and sat at the table. She put her hand on her stomach.

"Don't worry," said Raminta. "Marriage will come. Simas is an honorable man. If he were mine, I wouldn't wait for marriage, either. I'd make love to him as many times as I could. The men here care about others, and are willing to fight for what they believe in. These men will make good husbands, if they live."

Raminta smiled as Jurgis took off his boots and fell into one of the hammocks.

"You're very brave, too, Ludmelia," said Raminta.

Ludmelia shook her head. "I'm not brave."

"Of course you are. You fight the Russians."

"Anger isn't the same as courage."

"We're all angry, but I don't think we're all brave."

"You're a warrior. Maybe one day, you'll be our leader." Raminta smiled.

"Simas is our leader," Eda snapped. Raminta and Ludmelia looked at her.

"Who'll be our leader?" asked Vera, sitting down.

Eda scowled.

Vera smiled. "Grazyna took up a sword against the Teutonic Knights. She was a mythical hero, but you two are real heroes. Ludmelia, I heard how you fought. And not many can use a bow and arrow as well as you, Raminta."

"My father taught me when I was a girl. Knowing how to use a bow is a valuable skill for hunting animals, and other things like that rat, Petra Sukas. Soon, the Russians will also know how good I am," said Raminta.

"You killed Petra?" asked Ludmelia.

"He spied on us. People don't do that and live."

"I can't even imagine holding a gun, let alone shooting anyone," said Eda. "Killing is a job for men."

"We all have to do our part," said Vera. "Everyone has to contribute."

Eda examined her hands. "Or what? Be sent away?"

"Vera's right. Everyone has to work," said Raminta.

"Isn't scrubbing pots enough for you?" Eda's hands gripped the edge of the table. "I have no place else to go. Don't you understand that?"

"I wasn't talking about you, or anyone here."

Eda put her head down on her arms and sobbed.

"I'm sorry, Eda," said Raminta. "I didn't mean anything."

Eda's shoulders heaved as the women looked at her.

"Ladies, would you leave us alone?" asked Vera.

Ludmelia and Raminta shrugged and left.

When Eda calmed, Vera spoke. "Did the tea I gave you help?"

"A little. I'm only sick in the mornings now."

"It should pass in a few weeks."

A chill settled into Eda's belly as she considered again whether the father could possibly be Zabrev. He couldn't be, but she wondered if Simas would believe it.

"You need to think about what you're going to do. Soon, you're going to feel tired all the time. We can't have children at camp, especially babies. It's too dangerous."

"I won't leave Simas." Eda bit her lip. A tear trickled down her cheek.

"I can do an abortion. I've done it before. Unfortunately, rape and war go together. Conditions are difficult here, but I can manage, if that's what you want."

"It's a sin, Vera."

"The men carry grenades so they can blow their faces off if they're about to be captured. That way the Soviets won't be able to identify their families. Sometimes the men are captured before they can kill themselves. In Vilnius, the Soviets hung a dead partisan and his entire family from a tree in the market. They wanted everyone to see what happens when people join the cause. Children screamed, and the relatives just looked away. Parents mourned for their dead children, behind faces of marble."

Eda began to cry again.

"Is it a sin for them to die at their own hand in order to protect their families?" Vera put an arm around Eda's shoulders. "I don't like it either, but it's the way things are. I'm sorry and I know it's hard to hear, but the sooner we take care of this, the better it is for you. You'll have plenty of time to get fat and have lots of babies with Simas. Just wait until the war is over."

CHAPTER 29

When Zabrev woke up, his training kicked in, and the cloudy vestige of a soldier emerged from his battered body.

"Untie me," growled Zabrev as he turned to the guard.

The guard didn't move.

"You're one of those filthy partisan dogs," said Zabrev. "Maybe you're deaf and dumb, too."

Zabrev counted sleeping shelters, even though he couldn't see them all in the dark. They were spread out, and most were hidden under camouflage. Two hammocks hung between trees. Nine people were in camp, many with bandaged limbs, but others were probably out on patrol. Every partisan had a gun slung over his shoulder, even some of the women. Zabrev wondered if he had interrogated any of them.

He lay back on the leaves, miserable with pain. His legs shook and his face throbbed. He couldn't open his left eye. The thirst was unbearable, and he was tired beyond belief. Fatigue had become the disease of the day.

Any information he could garner about the camp seemed futile. If by some miracle he escaped, he didn't know where he was, at least not exactly. Further, the war would go on, no matter what he told the partisans. Eventually, others would come. Colonel Karmachov would assume Zabrev was dead. He would send a new leader, and more soldiers. There were always more Russian soldiers.

Zabrev knew the partisans weren't going to let him go. He was doomed, whether he talked or not. He didn't believe in heaven, so he didn't believe in hell, but if hell existed, he would burn there for eternity. His life on Earth was hell, but it would end soon.

He turned his head to something moving near the tree. "Tadnik, is that you? Why aren't you dead?" Zabrev whispered. "Tadnik, answer me!"

Yes, Comrade Commander.

"How long have we been here?"

Not long.

"Am I dead, too?"

Almost, Comrade Commander.

Ludmelia dreamed of amber eyes gazing at her. "Go away," she mumbled as she clutched the blanket. Then Mama was at her side, stroking her forehead.

Mama, I've missed you.

Mama's image faded into the fog.

Don't go, Mama.

Already aching from the feeling of loss, Ludmelia opened her eyes. She burrowed deeper into her blanket and gazed up at the stars glimmering through the leaves. Her thoughts went to the cellar, where Mama lay wrapped in a quilt. One day, Ludmelia would return to the cottage and bury Mama properly. Ludmelia would buy a coffin, and get permission from the priest in Vilkija to move Mama to holy ground. Ludmelia would buy the most beautiful carved cross she could find, and put it at the head of the grave. She would visit Mama every day, as a good daughter should.

It wasn't right that her family was gone. It wasn't right that Edvard was gone. He deserved more time. They all did.

Ludmelia flung off her blanket, pulled on her boots, and headed for the cook tent, where Raminta was coaxing the campfire to life. A pot of soup hung over the kindling. Ludmelia glanced at Zabrev lying in the dirt as she passed by. He was so still she thought he was dead, and felt disappointed when he moved.

She was almost at Raminta's side before noticing Dana sitting at a camp table with his head resting on his arms. Ludmelia turned and headed back to her bed. Before she got there, Raminta caught up with her.

"Go talk to him. All he does is suffer," said Raminta.

"We all suffer."

"We're a family."

"I have nothing to say to him."

Raminta pinched her arm. "You must."

"He's a coward."

"No he's not. Not everybody has the instincts you do, Ludmelia. He's just a man."

Ludmelia shook her head.

"You have to do this. There are too few of us left." Raminta gave Ludmelia a push in Dana's direction. He sat up as she approached. In the light of the fire, his cheeks looked gaunt. His eyes were puffy and red.

"You don't deserve to be here, and now we're stuck with you," said Ludmelia.

"I'm sorry."

"We're all sorry. We're sorry to be here, sorry to have lost the ones we love, sorry to be alive."

"I'm sorry I'm not a better man."

Her eyes narrowed.

"I can't make up for Edvard's death. I just want to feel normal again, somehow."

"How can you expect to feel normal, after what you did?"

Dana's entire body sagged.

"None of us feel normal. You can't feel normal and still fight."

"I don't know how to fight."

"So what good are you?" Ludmelia frowned.

"You may get lucky. Simas may send me away."

"So the Russians can interrogate you again?"

"I know you'll never forgive me."

She put her hands on her hips.

"Teach me to be like you," he whispered.

"What?"

"Strong, useful, brave. Everything I'm not."

Ludmelia raised her eyebrows.

"At least show me how to clean a gun," said Dana.

"You don't even know how to do that?"

"I studied law at university, not weapons. Please?"

Ludmelia took out Papa's pistol, unloaded it, and set it on the table. Handling the gun comforted her, and gave her something to think about other than Dana's vast stupidity. She slowly went through the process of field-stripping and cleaning, then loading it. Dana was slow and clumsy. His right hand seemed stiff and tender under the bandage, but he was determined. After a few tries, he seemed to get the idea. When they finished, he nodded. "Thank you."

Ludmelia walked away, and came back a few minutes later, with three more pistols. She laid them on the table. "Here, so you can practice." She went back to her bed.

As Dana disassembled another gun, he knew that here, he was less than a lowly foot soldier. The men who had once worked for him were his superiors. The girl who had cleaned his mother's kitchen was a warrior. He was nothing. He had to start at the very bottom and learn how to become a soldier. He had to learn to keep silent for the first time in his life. He had to learn how to take orders. Somehow, he had to atone for Edvard's death, if that was even possible. The war had left him no choice. He had no idea what he had gotten into, and he had to figure it out.

He hated the man he was, and didn't know the man he wanted to be, but it didn't matter. He had to define himself differently. He had to become someone else in order to survive.

He had taken the partisan oath only so they would let him stay. Now he was bound by it, even if Simas sent him away. He wanted to run until he found a safe place where he could live and forget, but that was impossible. There was no such place. Safety was an illusion.

Exhausted partisans staggered in from the forest, stopping at the cook tent for something to eat. As Raminta dished out bowls of food, one man put his hand on Dana's shoulder. "It's good you're up and about. We need men like you here."

Dana looked up at him. "No, you've got it wrong."

The man shrugged, and Dana returned to cleaning the pistols.

Eda rested in her tent with the flaps tied back, welcoming the cool night air. The canvas enclosure was a luxury she regretted, for she knew now that Antanas had given it up for her because she was Simas' woman. Antanas had to sleep under the stars, or find shelter in a cramped, leaky lean-to, because of her.

Eda's stomach churned, remembering how the men had talked about Ludmelia and her noble strength. In front of Simas, they showed their respect, but his authority was melting like snow.

Simas knew more about fighting and living in the woods than any of them. He had told her about his military training, and his knowledge of military tactics. He had told her that he had taught them how to patrol, how to watch the forest for signs of intruders, how to set explosives and traps, and how to live without leaving signs. He had kept most of them alive, yet it wasn't enough.

If Simas got Zabrev to talk, his authority would be restored. He would be redeemed. He had told her that Zabrev hadn't talked, and probably wouldn't. The Russian was stronger than Simas had ever imagined. Zabrev had already resisted one interrogation. Simas would continue torturing the man until he talked or died.

Eda had to get Zabrev to talk. What he knew could save Simas. Her future depended on it. The interrogation might start up again at any moment, even in the middle of the night. If she was going to do anything, it had to be soon.

She wasn't clever enough to use words to convince Zabrev that his silence was useless. She wasn't strong enough to hurt him physically. All she knew was how to keep house, and how to have sex.

Zabrev liked women. If she could relax him, maybe he would think she was his friend, and tell her his secrets. She could be like the women spies she had read about who slept with men. They were very effective, and she could be, too. She had to be. She had no choice.

CHAPTER 30

Zabrev didn't know what time it was, but it was still dark. He guessed the interrogation would start again at dawn.

A flaxen-haired beauty approached, carrying a cup. She stopped at the guard. "I need to speak with him alone," she said.

The guard didn't move.

"Simas ordered it."

He looked her up and down before moving away.

Eda went to Zabrev, and knelt down beside him.

"It's Eda, yes?" He knew this woman from Bablia's. She had been there with her father, although Zabrev couldn't remember his name. He just remembered her flawless legs. *She might be his chance to get away.*

She nodded.

"That's a lovely name," he said.

"What do your friends call you?" Eda put a hand on her stomach and forced a smile.

"Roman. Although I don't have any friends. Not anymore." Zabrev took a deep breath and tried to remember how to be charming.

"I don't think anyone has friends anymore." She put the cup into his bound hands.

He gulped the liquid, and licked his swollen lips when he was done. "A beautiful woman like you must have many friends and admirers."

"Beauty comes with a curse."

"What do you mean?" He lifted his hands and scratched his nose. *Be calm, Zabrev. Get her to relax.*

"People want to own beauty. You know they're going to keep hurting you until you talk. Make this stop."

"Why should I give them the satisfaction? They're going to kill me anyway."

"No they won't. I won't let them. Simas listens to me."

"I may tell you something important, if you do something for me." *This was it. All he had to do was convince this bitch to let him go.*

"What do you want?"

"Untie me."

"I can't do that."

"I know a great deal. I know plans, strategies, everything."

"Tell me something I can bring to Simas, and he'll stop beating you."

"Untie me first."

Eda looked down at the rope. If she let him go, Simas would be angry, but he'd forgive everything if Zabrev told her something important. Besides, a solitary injured man couldn't hurt them. Even if he got away, the men would find him. She had to do something. It was her duty. If she untied him, at least she wouldn't have to sleep with him.

Eda's hands shook as she fumbled with the knot. "Tell me."

"Ludmelia." The guard whispered to her.

She started awake. "What is it?"

"Eda is doing something stupid. You'd better come quickly."

Ludmelia got her gun and ran to the tree as Zabrev was stumbling to his feet, fumbling with the rope around his neck. Eda lay on the ground next to him, moaning.

"Move, and I'll kill you where you stand," said Ludmelia.

"You'd be doing me a favor," spat Zabrev.

Ludmelia struck Zabrev with the butt of her rifle. He fell to the ground. "Retie him. Tighter, this time."

The guard began retying the rope around Zabrev's hands.

Ludmelia knelt beside Eda as Simas came up.

"I've got to see Simas," mumbled Eda as she rubbed her jaw.

"Are you alright?" asked Ludmelia.

"He hit me."

Simas spoke. "You were letting him go?"

Zabrev laughed.

"For information." Eda sat up.

"You were going to leave with him, weren't you?"

Eda's face contorted in anguish. "I was trying to help you!"

"Maybe you prefer Russians."

"I did it for you."

Simas' back stiffened, and his expression faded to a look of cold distain. "Vadi will take you back to your father in the morning."

"No, Simas."

"I should kill you for what you did. You took an oath!"

"I made him talk."

"Did you fuck him again?"

"No, Simas."

"You're nothing but a dark alley whore." Simas winced, already regretting his words.

All faces turned to Zabrev, as his laughter rang through the camp.

"That bastard takes nothing more from us." Anger gripped Ludmelia as she went into the cook tent and came back holding a butcher knife. Zabrev had already stretched out on his nest of leaves, and was still chuckling.

Ludmelia straddled his legs with her knees and pulled up his hands.

He smiled at her. "Your women like me, Simas."

Ludmelia pushed his hand against the dirt and slammed the blade down below the knuckles of his right hand. She kept the knife there and pressed down as hard as she could. He yelled as she began sawing away at the fingers. She cut through the bone and blood, consumed by her task. Even his screams didn't hinder her. One by one, the fingers came free, rolling into the dirt like bits of sausage.

The partisans came out of their shelters.

Zabrev's face twisted in shouts of pain as he held up his claw of a hand. The blood flowed past his wrist, down his arm, and onto his chest.

"Shut up!" she yelled.

Zabrev continued to scream. Thoughts of Denis and Uri came to her, and Ludmelia pushed the bloody knife to his crotch.

"Talk, you filthy bastard, or I'll cut this off, too. It's sharp, and my hands are shaking." She bore down. Her desire to kill him was so intense she could barely breathe.

Zabrev's defiance deteriorated into the raw look of fear. He stopped screaming.

"Talk!" snarled Ludmelia.

He shrank away from her. Ludmelia pressed against the knife. She wanted to cut him there, too. *This is for you, Mama!* Upon hearing his voice, she eased up, almost regretting that he was speaking. In spurts, he babbled about Red Army divisions and Colonel Karmachov's orders to crush the partisans, no matter the cost. When he slowed, Ludmelia pressed the knife down harder.

"More!" she said.

He mentioned dates, numbers, the units to be deployed, and the unending supply of soldiers. Simas leaned over them, listening.

"I don't know anything else." Zabrev finally whimpered.

Ludmelia sat back. Zabrev's anguished look, and his body twisting away from her made him look like a wild animal that had been beaten down. She leaned forward and spat in his face. She stood and pushed her way through the partisans. At the cook tent, she flung the knife into the dirt.

Dizzy and sick with heartache, Eda backed through the crowd, and picked up the knife Ludmelia had thrown to the ground. She pressed it against her leg when she passed the sentry.

"Where are you going?" he asked.

"To the toilet." She smiled and he let her pass.

Eda walked as if in a dream. She went by an ancient elm, and a little sapling trying to grow next to it. As she ran her fingers over the smooth handle of the knife, she looked up at the mysterious grace of the branches in the moonlight, the moss, the stunted bushes, and the grass growing in rare patches.

She was a liability to Simas and to everyone. She couldn't do anything right. She couldn't go back to her father, and Simas didn't want her at camp. Vera had told her to get rid of the baby.

Even if she could keep it, Simas would never love her child. He'd always suspect it was Zabrev's baby. If she let Vera take it, she would mourn it for the rest of her life. Already, it felt like she and her baby were casualties of the war.

Eda walked past an outgrowth of ferns waving like black feathers. Everyone was saying the Soviet Army would be there soon. No one would survive an attack. The Soviets were just too strong, and there were too many of them for the partisans to hope for success.

She sat on the grass and smoothed her skirt. Soon, no one would even remember her. She would be a dream they had that summer, nothing more and nothing real.

Eda quickly slashed the blade across her wrist. The pain was sharp, and it throbbed, but it would be over soon. With every beat of her heart, she could feel her blood pulse out from her wrist. The night felt cold. As Eda's blood flowed onto the ground, she lay back and closed her eyes, picturing Simas sitting next to her in the rye field, sipping Krupnika liquor as they laughed together over some silly joke.

CHAPTER 31

Simas stood over Zabrev, feeling grim satisfaction, but something more. This detestable creature at Simas' feet was merely the bloody shell of a man, if he ever was a man. Zabrev was pathetic. He was nothing. As Zabrev's blood flowed into the earth, Bablia's back room began to fade. Simas' hate became a little less intense. It was still there, and it would probably be there for the rest of his life, but it had lifted enough for Simas to feel like a man again, to feel that there was hope left. He gazed around the camp. Eda wasn't there. "Vadi. Go to Eda's tent and bring her here."

Minutes later, Vadi returned. "She's not there."

"Take Jurgis and go find her." Simas sat down at the camp table, wondering what he should say to Eda. She had been willing to risk everything for him. He wouldn't make her leave after all. Maybe they didn't have a future together, but maybe, if she was willing, they could try.

Soon, the brothers came back, carrying Eda's body. Vadi placed her on the table in front of Simas as the partisans gathered round. Simas let out a cry.

Vera came up and stood next to the body. "Go back to your shelters."

Raminta handed her an old blanket, and Vera covered Eda.

Ludmelia came over in the commotion. Simas looked fragile and very old, sitting there staring down at the body. Ludmelia lifted the blanket, and started in surprise. Vera shook her head.

Ludmelia put her arm around Simas' shoulders and helped him to the rock where he usually sat. She took Simas' flask from his pocket, opened it, and handed it to him. His hands were shaking so badly, she had to help him bring it to his lips.

He drank, and handed the flask back to Ludmelia. Simas put his head in his hands, and soon his whole body shook.

Vera came over and draped her arm around Simas' shoulders. Ludmelia left to find Vadi and Jurgis.

"Take some men and dig a grave for Eda," said Ludmelia.

"There's a spot I know where there shouldn't be too many roots." Vadi pointed just beyond the sentry.

"So close to camp?"

"It won't matter soon."

As the men dug, the remaining partisans stood together watching, their faces bereft of any sign of joy or hope. Most held their caps in their hands, shifting their weight in the naked discomfort of being so close to tears.

When the grave was deep enough, Vadi carried Eda's body to it, and gently placed her on the ground, next to a small gray rock embedded in the soil. The blanket that covered Eda reminded Ludmelia of the ones that had covered Matas and Mr. Dagys.

Vera stepped forward and spoke of Eda, the war, and its toll on all of them. "There is more suffering in our future, but Eda is free. Her soul is soaring up to God and He will forgive her sins, for He knows the true nature of her heart. When she gets to heaven, the angels will greet her with arms open wide in welcome." Vera made the sign of the cross and glanced at Simas, standing off by himself.

Ludmelia stepped forward. Silence hung over the little crowd as faces turned to the woman with the amber hair. She thought of Papa, Mama, Matas, and Edvard, and found words she didn't know she had.

"The war is about many things. To Eda, it was about family. You were Eda's family, and you're my family, too. We all try to be good soldiers, and do what's needed for our cause. Eda was a good soldier.

"She decided her future in a way that we may find difficult to understand, but sometimes the battles we wage within ourselves are worse than any fight with the enemy. Rest well, dear sister. Be with those who died for country and family. Watch over us and help us be strong."

Jurgis and Vadi lowered Eda into the grave and shoveled in the dirt, covering her bit by bit, until there was nothing left but black earth. They scattered the leftover dirt, and covered Eda's grave with leaves to erase any sign that a woman and her unborn child were lying there.

Soon, the only reminder that Eda Lankus ever lived was a single gray rock in the old forest, deep within Lithuania.

By the time the group shuffled back to camp, dawn was breaking. Vadi's eyes were sunken, and his arms and face were dirty from digging.

"Come with me," said Ludmelia.

They went to the tree where Zabrev lay moaning, his face as pale as death. Dried blood covered his hand and arm.

"Get up," said Ludmelia.

He opened bloodshot eyes and closed them again. He didn't move.

"Take him," she said.

Vadi picked up Zabrev's foot, and dragged him to an oak tree at the edge of camp.

Ludmelia trained her gun on the Comrade Commander as Vadi tied a stone around the end of a long rope and threw it over a thick, low-hanging branch. He made a noose at one end and handed it to Ludmelia. It hung from her hands like a wreath. Vadi pulled Zabrev to his feet. The Russian swayed as Vadi held him up from the back. Zabrev smelled of blood and earth.

"You are like me," said Zabrev, gazing at Ludmelia as his head sagged to the side.

"I'm nothing like you," she said.

"You do what needs to be done." Zabrev bent his head down, and Ludmelia slipped the noose around his neck. "Just like me."

This was the moment she had waited for. She would avenge Mama's death and finally have satisfaction.

"Finish it," she said, nodding to Vadi.

Vadi and Ludmelia pulled the rope, lifting Zabrev until his feet pedaled frantically in the air. He bucked and gagged. His body spasmed. They watched until Zabrev became still. His lips turned blue, curled up in an odd smile. Soon, the air reeked with the stink from his bowels.

Ludmelia felt no freedom in his death. She wondered if she would eventually become immune to all that was good in the world. She wondered if one day she would become like Simas, and have nothing left to give. Zabrev's body slowly turned away from her, as if to say he didn't give a damn about her problems.

Ludmelia motioned to Vadi to lower the body. "Get rid of it," she said.

Back in camp, Ludmelia sent out a few more men to the shore to make sure no Russians had returned. She relieved the sentries guarding camp with men who were only slightly less exhausted.

Young Jonai Gabe appeared, and asked for Simas. The boy pointed to Ludmelia as he stood next to Simas and talked. Then Simas spoke to Jonai, who nodded several times. They shook hands, and Jonai left.

Simas called everyone around the cook tent. Sunken faces turned to their leader, some angry, and most still shocked from all that had happened. Simas looked withered as he stood before them. "We're going to move camp to the forest near Didmiestis. There we'll select a place where we can spend the winter."

"Why are we moving?" asked a voice.

"More Russians are coming. The forest near Didmiestis is much larger, and there, we can combine forces with other partisans when necessary for larger missions. The move has been approved by the area leader."

Ludmelia spoke up. "Besides, the Russians will be looking for us here."

The partisans nodded their approval. Some managed a chuckle at the idea of the Russians running around the old forest searching for the deserted camp. "They will think we're ghosts," said a voice. "Or wolves," said one more.

"Until you select a new leader in Didmiestis, Ludmelia will give you your orders. Do as she says."

Ludmelia turned to him, astonished.

"You're not going with us, Simas?" asked Vadi.

"Not this time."

"Why not? Where are you going?" asked others.

Simas brushed off the questions. He turned away and limped toward his hammock. Ludmelia followed him.

"What was that about?" she asked.

Simas gazed at her, his face frozen in the peculiar expression of surprise it had taken on after Eda died. He pointed at the partisans. "They look up to you."

"I can't give orders."

"You'll learn."

"Why not Vadi or any of the others?"

"They call you Amber Wolf, you know. Well, it's your code name now. Use it whenever you need to communicate with Lightning, who leads the partisan group in Didmiestis. Jurgis is already on the way there to tell him what we learned from Zabrev.

"You'll remain an independent group, at least for a while. When you get to Didmiestis, have the camp elect a group leader, but it'll probably be you. Remember to organize around military ideals. Those who were in the Lithuanian Army can help you. Lightning will help you."

"I can't lead them."

"They're planning a mission that will need your skills. Be ready."

"What mission?"

"Inspect the camp before everyone leaves, and make sure that everything important is either carried off or buried. Destroy everything else. Make sure the men still out in the woods get the word."

"I can't."

Simas touched her cheek. "You can, and you must." He bent down and began packing his things.

Vera came to them, her own knapsack slung over her shoulder.

"Are you leaving us, too?" asked Ludmelia.

"I'm taking Simas away for a while, so he can rest," said Vera. Her eyes brimmed with tears.

"But we need you."

"There's a doctor in Didmiestis. You'll be alright for a while."

Ludmelia looked at Vera, and then at Simas. She could almost see the ribbon of time and friendship that bound them together in a kind of love. She hoped that one day Simas would see it, too.

The women hugged. "I'll miss you," whispered Ludmelia.

Simas stood and slung his Mauser over his shoulder. "Victor was right, Ludmelia. You're the best among us. Take care of them. They need you."

Ludmelia went to get the things she had brought here, a mere fraction of what she had escaped with from the cottage. She opened Papa's tattered knapsack to pack. At the bottom lay the scraps of paper she had found in the garden. She'd have time to piece them together soon, and decide what to do with them. She put her paltry belongings into the pack: bullets, Matas' compass, the knife, a shirt, and the blanket. On top, she put the small wooden box containing a piece of amber jewelry that she had taken from one of the offices inside the prison.

A few people had already begun to leave in small groups, to make their departure from the forest less noticeable once they got to the roads. Everyone carried something from camp: a pot or pan, potatoes in their pockets. Women wore the clothes they had brought: a pair of trousers under a skirt, an extra shirt, a vest, a jacket. Kerchiefs framed faces that were brown from living outside. Men, hard and lean, sweated from carrying crates of supplies to hiding places. They would retrieve them later, with the help of Lightning's men. Some carried shovels. Others carried tents or folded hammocks. All worked with quiet efficiency.

Some hugged and whispered, "God bless you," as they parted.

After the camp had been broken down, and almost everyone had left, Dana found Ludmelia at Eda's grave.

"The war and the sacrifices Simas made just ate him up," Ludmelia said. "It ate them both up."

Dana nodded.

"It's hard to determine your own fate, let alone the fate of others. Sometimes, the load is just too heavy."

Dana looked down at her, his eyes soft and full of hope. "Until Didmiestis?"

Ludmelia nodded, and Dana boldly leaned in. For a split second, she thought he was going to kiss her, but instead, he whispered in her ear. "You may never forgive me, but know that I won't forgive myself either."

He left with Vadi to find a place where they could rest for a few days before making the journey to Didmiestis.

Ludmelia looked at what remained. The shelters that had been cobbled together from tree branches were gone, and the pieces scattered. The camp tables had been pulled apart. All the hammocks were gone. The black cinders of burnt wood in the cook fire were covered with dirt. Brown earth remained where the grass had been worn away. The clothing and towels hanging from tree branches were gone. The strange quiet of the forest had already crept in.

Ludmelia would go to Didmiestis right away. The forest was her home now, and it didn't matter which forest. She slung her knapsack and gun over her shoulder, and disappeared through the trees.

THE END

ABOUT THE AUTHOR

Ursula grew up working on the family dairy farm started by her grandparents, who fled Lithuania and the Bolsheviks for a better life in the U.S. After losing her father at an early age, Ursula overcame poverty and went on to college.

Armed with a degree in physics and an advanced degree in mathematics, Ursula entered the job market when mini-computers were "the new thing." She grew to become an innovator, providing solutions that address major business problems in the areas of security and messaging. While all this was going on, Ursula and her husband, Steve, had a beautiful daughter.

After decades working in the high tech field, Ursula got out of the biz and took up writing fiction. It was something she could do regardless of where she and her husband lived. She took courses and attended writers' workshops hosted at public libraries where she found the friends who continue to help and inspire her.

An adventurous traveler, scuba diver, and hiker, Ursula writes gripping stories about strong women struggling against impossible odds to achieve their dreams. Her work has appeared in *Everyday Fiction*, *Spinetingler Magazine*, and the popular *Insanity Tales* anthologies.

Her award-winning debut novel, *Purple Trees*, exposes a stark side of rural New England life in the experiences of a young woman who struggles for normalcy despite a vicious and hidden past.

Amber Wolf is Ursula's second novel.

Ursula is available for speaking events and lectures on writing and publishing. For more information, contact her at urslwng@gmail.com or through her popular Reaching Readers website at http://ursulawong.wordpress.com.

Connect Online:
Website: http://ursulawong.wordpress.com
Email: urslwng@gmail.com

Other works by Ursula Wong

Purple Trees

The Baby Who Fell From the Sky

With other Authors

Insanity Tales

Insanity Tales II: The Sense of Fear

Looking for something great to read? Get Ursula's FREE award-winning mini-tales, guaranteed to shiver, shake, and make you laugh. All you have to do is tell her where to send them. You'll get one to start, and a new one every month. Sign up at http://ursulawong.wordpress.com/mini-tales.

Read on for the explosive first chapter of Ursula Wong's next novel, *The Amber War*.

World War II ends, but the fighting continues in Eastern Europe as farmers give up their pitchforks for guns. The cunning partisans attack and vanish into the forests, inciting the mighty Soviet Army to amass its power against the tiny resistance. But sheer force is not enough to quell the will of the Freedom Fighters, and the Soviets revert to subterfuge as one of their spies enters the camp of the Amber Wolf.

Chapter 1

Dana and Ludmelia picked their way along the narrow alleyways, clinging to shadows as they passed houses with steep roofs and windows shining from the soft light of kerosene lamps. Three friends followed behind as they snaked through the back streets of Vilkija.

In the area of Bablia's grog house, a pair of drunken revelers burst through the door and tripped down the steps. The five friends slid into an alley, their backs up against the walls of a house.

With their arms locked around their shoulders, the two drunken soldiers walked in one direction, turned around, and walked back in the other direction.

Ludmelia slipped the submachine gun off her shoulder, and handed it to her friend. She motioned to Dana to do the same.

The shuffling steps of the revelers got louder, as they kicked at pebbles, one landing at Ludmelia's feet.

The drunkards passed by the house. "I have to take a piss," said one, moving toward the dark alley where the friends hid.

Ludmelia pulled Dana's head down and kissed him.

"What's this?" asked the drunkard, his voice slurred. He spoke Russian. His dung colored uniform gave him away as a soldier, a Communist, the enemy.

Ludmelia looked up and smiled at the man.

"Lovely lady, why don't you come with me instead," he said.

"Shut up, you fool," said the other. "Long live father Stalin."

They tripped, caught each other, laughed, and continued down the street.

The friends scooped up their submachine guns, and ran down the alley. A dog barked. In the dim light from a window, a curtain swayed.

They maneuvered through the maze of streets, eventually turning uphill to their destination. They stole past a broken stone column and the statue of a knight lying in the dirt next to the iron fence crushed in its fall. Flowers graced the ruin and lined the path leading to the top of the hill. An old white church stood there like a grand dame looking down on the little town.

Ludmelia motioned to her friends to wait in the graveyard next to the church, and stepped to the back door. She forced the lock with her knife, freezing at the sharp clack of the unlatching door. A moment passed in which she listened without breathing. She went inside, mindful of every creak, interpreting shades of gray to a table, chairs, glasses, crosses, doorways. She looked inside the rooms along a hallway, and opened a closet that held robes and vestments. She passed an alcove where babies were blessed. At the altar decorated with dead flowers, she waited, breathing softly, to hear others who might be breathing in the cavernous room. No one was there.

She spun around to the sound of footsteps. Dana emerged.

"We're alone," whispered Ludmelia. "Get the others."

He turned and left.

Ludmelia ran her fingers through her amber hair. Her dirty jacket and trousers weren't the dress she should be wearing to a wedding. Few people were getting married these days, for the Soviets had closed the churches, and had deported most of the priests to labor camps. The priests who were left had fled to the woods to fight.

She said a quick prayer for Papa, hoping that he was still alive. She prayed for Matas, her brother, who had already given his life in the fighting, and for Mama, who had died to save her.

Thinking about a person should bring them back, especially in a church where such miracles should be possible. Jesus' dim outline shone in the stained glass above the massive wooden door, his hands pressed together, his expression serene. It didn't feel like she was alone.

"Mama?" she whispered.

Silence.

"Matas?"

If the dead could come back, this place would be full of poor souls whose lives had been cut short by a war that just wouldn't end, at least not for them.

"Papa, are you here?"

Ludmelia fingered the cloth on the altar. Her life couldn't start until the fighting was over, but fighting *was* her life. The dead flowers quivered in agreement.

At the sound of a lonely creak, Ludmelia spun her gun around.

Behind Dana came Vadi and Jurgis, farmhands who had worked on Dana's homestead before it was destroyed by the Soviets. Raminta, a woman from camp, came in next.

Ludmelia relaxed.

Another man entered the church. Ludmelia took aim. The man stopped cold.

"Father Simkus?" asked Dana.

The stranger nodded and stepped forward. A gun hung from the strap on his shoulder. "I don't know if God still thinks of me as a man of the cloth."

"You can perform a wedding ceremony, can't you?"

"I can say the words. I just hope God is listening."

"He is."

"Where's the bride?"

Raminta stepped forward. "Here I am, Father." She took Jurgis' hand.

"We'd better do this quickly," said Ludmelia as she leaned her gun against the wall.

She opened her knapsack and pulled out a hand-woven shawl and a bouquet of wildflowers rimmed with ferns from the forest. She draped the shawl over Raminta's shoulders, covering her jacket and most of her skirt. She wrapped Raminta's fingers around the flower stems and kissed her on the cheek.

Dana slipped outside to watch for soldiers. Ludmelia stood next to Raminta.

There, in a church deserted but for a few lonely partisans, a couple bound in love stood before a priest who carried a gun.

"We are gathered together under impossible circumstances in this house of God, to witness the marriage of this man and woman. In a different time, the church would be full of flowers and people we love. Still, the bouquet in the bride's hands is as fresh as a thousand blooming buds. While the church is not full of family, the few people standing with you risk their lives to protect your joy and your future. How can a marriage starting with such love not be blessed?"

A sob burst from Raminta's throat.

"In this time of turmoil, it's more important than ever to cling to the ones we cherish, and remember the importance of love and children to carry us through to better times."

"Join hands," said Father Simkus.

After the words linking the young partisans in marriage had been said, and the blessing had been given, Jurgis leaned in to kiss his bride.

Dana rushed in from outside. "Trucks!"

They all dove to the floor.

The grumbling of the engines grew louder. The hard wood floor reminded Ludmelia of the night she had spent hiding in the attic while the soldiers had raped and killed Mama. Back then, she had wanted to kill those soldiers as much as she wanted her heart to continue beating. She felt the same way now. Ludmelia swallowed hard as she glanced at her gun leaning against the wall. If soldiers burst in, could she get to it in time? She didn't think so. It had been stupid to take it off.

A partisan is never without his gun.

Light from the headlights cast Jesus' presence in colors that grew brighter with every passing second. Ludmelia wiggled along the floor like a worm. The engines grew louder. She reached for the gun. Grasping it in her hands, she rolled onto her back. Jesus glowed. Ludmelia lifted herself from the waist. Her finger quivered on the trigger.

The light waned and the sound of the engines faded.

Ludmelia lay back in relief as the other partisans got to their feet.

"Thank you, Father," said Jurgis. "We'd better get out of here." He took Raminta's hand, and they all filed out as silently as they had come.

READING LIST

Between Shades of Gray, Ruta Sepetys, Philomel Books, NY, NY, 2011.

Bloodlands: Europe Between Hitler and Stalin, Timothy Snyder, Basic Books, NY, NY, 2012.

Forest Brothers 1945: The Culmination of the Lithuanian Partisan Movement, Vylius M. Leskys, Baltic Security & Defense Review, Volume 11, 2009.

Fugitives of the Forest, Allan Levine, the Globe Pequot Press, Guilford, Ct., 2009.

Iron Curtain, Anne Applebaum, Doubleday, New York, 2012.

Leave your Tears in Moscow, Barbara Armonas, J.B. Lippincott Company, NY, 1961.

Lithuania 700 Years, edited by Albertas Gerutis, Manyland Books, Woodhaven, NY, 1969.

Lithuania Under the Soviets, Portrait of a Nation 1940 – 65, V. Stanley Vardys Ed., Frederick A. Praeger Publishers, London, England, 1965.

Red Partisan, Nickolai I. Obryn'ba, Potomac Books, Inc., Washington, D.C., 2009.

Savage Continent, Keith Lowe, St. Martin's Press, NY, NY, 2012.

Showdown, The Lithuanian Rebellion and the Breakup of the Soviet Empire, Dr. Richard Krickus, Brassey's Inc., 1997.

Tarp Dvieju Gyvenimu, Vytautas Alantas, Lithuanian Book Club, 1960.

The Bielski Brothers, Peter Duffy, Harper-Collins Publishers, NY, NY, 2003.

The Holocaust in Lithuania, video clip, March 4, 2013, Dr. Christoph Dieckmann.

The Rise and Fall of the Third Reich, William L. Shirer, Touchstone, NY, NY, 1959.

War of the Rats, David L. Robbins, Bantam Books, NY, NY, 1999.

Made in the USA
Middletown, DE
09 May 2017